A · MASK
FOR · THE
GENERAL

A · MASK FOR · THE GENERAL

·LISA·· GOLDSTEIN

SPECTRA

BANTAM BOOKS
TORONTO · NEW YORK · LONDON · SYDNEY · AUCKLAND

A MASK FOR THE GENERAL

A Bantam Spectra Book / November 1987

Library of Congress Cataloging-in-Publication Data

Goldstein, Lisa.
A mask for the general.
I. Title.
PS3557.0397M3 1987   813'.54   86-47912
ISBN 0-553-05239-X

Published simultaneously in the United States and Canada

Bantam Books are published by Bantam Books, Inc. Its trademark, consisting of the words
"Bantam Books" and the portrayal of a rooster, is Registered in U.S. Patent and Trademark
Office and in other countries. Marca Registrada. Bantam Books, Inc., 666 Fifth Avenue, New
York, New York 10103.

PRINTED IN THE UNITED STATES OF AMERICA
FG   0 9 8 7 6 5 4 3 2 1

TO
DOUG,
WITH
LOVE

I would like to thank Mikey Roessner-Herman for conversations about masks and maskmaking.

 AST WEEK THE OLD TRAF-
fic lights nailed to the outside of the Green Dragon had popped on and
off, red, green, yellow. High above them the painted dragon had
guarded his hoard of rubies and emeralds. This week everything
looked different. Mary could have sworn the Green Dragon was on the
next block, but up ahead everything was dark. Because of electricity
rationing the bright display had only shone for an hour last week.
Could it be that late already?

The sun was setting and the Berkeley streets were almost deserted.
Mary passed a boarded-up shop, a small hardware store locked tight
for the night, another store long deserted where dust sparkled like
diamonds in the windows. A couple came around the corner in front of
her, the man dressed in government gray. The woman turned to watch
Mary as she passed and Mary tried not to smile. Then she realized her
mask concealed her expression anyway and she grinned widely. "A
tiger's mask," the woman said to the man.

"Stupidity . . ." the man said as they walked away. ". . . the
General . . ."

A few yellowing streetlights were coming on now, but most of them
were out. The slabs of pavement on this part of the street came together
awkwardly, like a jigsaw puzzle put together wrong. Mary walked

carefully, unable to see most of the sidewalk through the eyeholes of her mask. She was starting to worry now. Had she passed it? She was almost certain she was on the right street, but what if she wasn't?

Someone in a bright green and red parrot's mask walked under a streetlamp as though stepping on a stage. Mary nodded as she passed but the parrot didn't nod back. Mary walked on, feeling lonely and embarrassed. Maybe you weren't supposed to nod, she thought miserably. Maybe there was a signal. . . .

Up ahead a group of people stood in front of a dark building, moving aimlessly. In the dim light their heads looked shapeless, grotesque. Mary hurried up to them.

They stood in front of the Green Dragon, but the place was dark, deserted, changed. Mary could see now why she hadn't recognized it. The bright traffic lights were off. The only light came from the hubcaps and broken mirrors scattered across the front of the building, winking silver eyes back at the streetlamps. No one was inside; no light or sound came from beyond the windows, which had once been painted green but were now faded and peeling.

She looked around at the people on the street: a bird with a long beak, a lion, a black dog, a few others. They were clustered around a sign posted on the green double doors of the building, and she moved past them to read it. "Closed by Government Order," the sign said, and then, in smaller letters, "This building violates the law forbidding public gatherings after 10 P.M." Now she could see a steel chain wound through the door handles.

"Well, what do we do?" someone asked.

"Got a hammer?" someone else said.

"We could go to my house."

"*Your* house? I wanted *dancing*."

"I've got a harmonica."

Someone laughed derisively. "What happened?" Mary asked.

The bird mask turned to look at her but no one said anything. "Well, we knew it would happen sooner or later," the black dog said. "There is a law forbidding public gatherings after ten, though how a building can violate it someone will have to tell me."

"The Green Dragon is closed?" Mary said. "For good?" She had thought the sign meant the place was closed for that one night only.

Suddenly she felt lonelier than ever. She had only come to Berkeley from Stockton a week ago. Everyone in Stockton knew that Berkeley was filled with tribes, and everyone had been terribly envious when she'd told them she was leaving. Go to the Green Dragon, they had said. You'll meet lots of people there. But so far she had met no one outside of her job and the place where she was living.

Now all the animals were looking at her, as grave and charged with meaning as a pack of playing cards. Mary felt as though she had stumbled on an old ritual she only half understood but that she had heard about for all of her life. She envied them their easy animal grace, their jungle finery. They're only people, she thought fiercely. Don't let them intimidate you.

The bird with the long beak stepped closer to her. "Where did you get that mask?" a woman's voice said.

"What?" Mary said, startled.

"The mask," the woman said. She was medium height and very thin. She had pulled her coat, fringed with sea shells and rabbit fur, close around her, though the evening was warm. "Who told you you were a tiger?"

"No one," Mary said. "I bought it at the Blue Market."

"That's what I thought," the woman said. "I didn't think you were a tiger."

"Look, what—" Mary said. Someone else said, "Layla—" and Mary stopped. The woman was Layla, the maskmaker! She had heard of Layla even in Stockton. "Well, then, what am I?" Mary said. She was trembling with her effrontery and her desire to know. God knew what Layla charged to make a mask.

"You'd have to take off your mask for me to tell," Layla said. Then, as though realizing Mary would not take off her mask if no one else did, she lifted off the bird's mask. Mary was disappointed. Layla had lank uncombed brown hair, gray eyes, fair skin. She had expected some wild beauty.

Mary took off her mask, hoping no one would notice how young she was. Her hair was a glossy brown cap, her eyes bright blue under thick brown eyebrows, her face slightly plump. Now she was conscious of the drabness of her mask compared to everyone else's bright jungle colors. Had Layla made them all?

Layla looked at her for a long time, too long. The gray eyes were wide. Mary tried not to pull away. Finally Layla shrugged. "I don't know," she said. "I'll have to tell you—Mark, can she come Friday night?"

One of the shapes shrugged. "Sure," he said. "If you say so."

"Great," Layla said. Her eyes had never left Mary's. "I'm Layla, of the heron tribe. We meet at Mark's every Friday night at around seven-thirty—"

"Except Layla never gets there before eight-thirty—"

"Shut up, Don," someone said without rancor.

"Mark lives on Blake Street, just off Telegraph," Layla said. "It's—Mark, what's the address?"

Mark told her. "Are you going to remember that?" he asked Mary.

"Of course," Mary said. Did he think she'd forget an invitation from Layla?

"Good," Layla said. "I'll know by then. And then I can make your mask."

"My—my mask?" Mary said. "But I can't afford . . ." She felt her face grow hot and hoped Layla wouldn't realize she had just told a lie. Don't be ridiculous, she thought. How could Layla possibly know? But she watched Layla's face carefully just in case.

"Don't worry," Layla said. "What's your name?"

"Mary," Mary said. "Of—of no tribe just yet."

Layla nodded, looking satisfied. A few of the bright figures were wandering away from the group, walking off in different directions. "I'll see you Friday," Layla said, and turned to follow someone.

"Hey!" the dog—Don—said. "Where are we going?" Then they were gone, like a trick of a fantastic mechanical toy.

Mary walked home slowly, unable to believe her luck. This was something like what she had imagined would happen to her when she'd left home. A fabulous destiny, like a woman in a fairy tale. A mask by Layla. She thought of the legendary maskmakers she had heard of in Stockton, Layla and Willie and Bone Jackson, and she wondered if she would get a chance to meet the others too. If only she could tell her old friends—but she couldn't risk sending a letter home. She was not watching where she was going now, stumbling over cracked and unpaved road, trying to remember everything Layla had said. She felt her heart pounded gold, not blood, through her veins. Her loneliness was gone. Layla was going to make her a mask!

Layla let herself into her small room as the curfew sirens sounded. The lights in her building flickered and went off, and she stumbled over something and cursed loudly.

She felt for the candle she kept by the door and struck a match against the wall. The goddamn government, she thought, making her way unsteadily through the clutter of the room to the bed. The goddamn government turns the electricity off at ten o'clock, and then they go and close the Green Dragon. What the hell right do they have? She and her friends had wandered around for hours, uncertain, and had finally split up just before the curfew at ten. She thought longingly of other nights at the Green Dragon, dancing to loud music, and then the scramble at ten to get the oil lamps lit and the acoustic instruments brought out as the room was plunged into darkness. What do they expect people to do after ten anyway? she thought, sitting on the bed and holding the candle absently in her lap. It's too early to go to sleep, and they won't let us go outside. . . . You can't even watch television, not that I would ever watch any of that junk.

She stared into the candle-flame, the blue rocked within the sheltering orange like a child held by its mother. She thought of Mary, almost too young to be on her own. There was something between them, she had felt it almost the moment she had seen that sad little tiger mask. But what? She hadn't had a real friendship since Archangel died, and she wasn't ready for one now.

Her eyes never left the flame. After a while her eyes grew wide, her pupils narrowed down to points. Her face relaxed. She sat perfectly still for a long moment, long enough for the burning candle in her hand to melt unnoticed, for the wax to run over her fingers. Then she blinked and came out of her trance.

A sea-otter. That's what Mary's tribe was, that was the mask she would have to make. She probably wouldn't like that, probably wanted to be a lion or bear or something like that, but the animal-spirit had spoken. She blew out the flame. Don's right, she thought, putting down the candle and taking off her furred coat. I'm going to burn this place down one of these days. Then, fully dressed, she slipped under the covers and fell asleep immediately.

The next day Mary went to work. "Fine salads" the sign on the small building said in vaguely Japanese-style letters. The manager was trying to cater to Japanese tourists. He had even taught Mary a few phrases in Japanese when she had started to work there, but she had forgotten them all.

Mary put on her apron and got behind the counter. The sense of excitement had not left her. She could hardly wait for Friday.

"Tossed green salad," the man in the gray suit at the front of the line said. "French dressing. No onions."

Mary moved in the narrow space behind the counter to the refrigerator. It was lunch-time in downtown Berkeley, and the line of tourists and government workers stretched out the door. She took out a head of lettuce and looked at it, wondering what kind of mask Layla was going to make her. Not a tiger, because Layla had said she wasn't a tiger. But something wonderful, bright and colorful. And then she could say, whenever anyone asked her her name, "Mary, of the something tribe." Lion. She wouldn't mind being a lion, like one of the people she saw last night.

The man at the head of the line tapped his tray impatiently with his fork. Guiltily, she put the lettuce down and began to chop it, hoping he hadn't seen her. What kind of dressing had he said he wanted? Damn.

She couldn't afford to lose this job. Jobs were hard to come by, and she had been lucky to find one her second day in Berkeley. And so far the manager hadn't asked her to work the cash register. Tribes, even if she didn't have one yet, refused to handle machinery. The General had made a speech about it on television, just before she had left home. "These backward-looking segments of our society," he had said, "holding America back from achieving the greatness that was once hers."

She arranged the chopped vegetables in a bowl. No onions. French dressing, that was it. And now here she was, holding America back. She wondered what her father would say if he could see her. Probably have a stroke. And what if he saw her with her mask on? She poured French dressing over the salad and worked her way past someone getting a lettuce from the refrigerator. "There you go, sir," she said. "Five dollars." He grunted and gave her the money. The little rabbity guy at the cash register was looking away. The next person in line, a Japanese tourist, was paging through a phrase book. Smoothly she put the money in her pocket and nodded at the tourist. "Can I help you, sir?" she said.

Don had said that Layla never got to Mark's before eight-thirty, so Mary decided she wouldn't get there before then. She put on her good blouse, the green one that looked almost like silk, and the long coat that looked a little like Layla's, though without the shells and fur. And what about the mask? If she didn't wear it she'd be the only one there without one, but Layla had said she wasn't a tiger. All right, then, she wouldn't wear it. And maybe Layla would have a mask ready for her.

She walked nervously back and forth in the small room. There was no furniture, only a tangle of different colored blankets on the floor and a closet with no door half-filled with clothes. By eight she had looked at herself in the small hand mirror for the tenth time. Maybe Don had been joking. There was no reason to be afraid of these people in masks; after all, Mark himself had said she could come. She pulled her coat around her and left.

Mark's house was one of those old wooden Berkeley buildings where the second story seemed to be mostly roof. It was only a few blocks from hers. The entryway was open and she walked in and found the door with Mark's name on it. She knocked, knocked again when no one answered. Footsteps from a long way off, then a man's voice: "Who is it?" She could hear quiet conversation, a burst of loud laughter, then silence. Flustered, she said, "It's me."

"Don't know anyone named Me, go away," the voice—she was almost sure it was Don's—said.

"Mary," she said. "I'm Layla's—we met at the Green Dragon, and—"

The door opened and light spilled out. The man on the other side of the door was not wearing a mask. His straight blond hair caught the light and shone; the rest of his face was in darkness. "Right," he said. "I'm Don. Come on in."

She stepped inside, noticing as she did so Don's mask hanging loosely from his wrist. The room was dim; most of the light bulbs were out and she remembered that bulbs were still on the UC list. She saw gray peeling linoleum on which someone had long ago tried to paint some kind of animal, walls hung with posters—DOGS AGAINST MERCH; CANNERS, FIGHT FOR YOUR RIGHTS—and masks and pieces of machinery, a rickety table by the window, sagging bed in one corner, bookshelf crammed with books in another corner. On top of the bookshelf a plant had died. Newspapers and leaflets, hubcaps and sheet iron were spread over the floor. The house's ancient glamor could still be seen in the scratched redwood door and the redwood lintel over the passageway to another room.

A man came through the passageway for a moment, saw Mary and ducked back out. "I'm Mark," he called back to her. "Make yourself at home. Dump your coat." She saw what looked like a small junkyard by the door; after a moment she realized it was a pile of coats with gears and bells, shells and old ivory sewn on haphazardly. She added hers to the pile. Mark came back with a bottle of beer and handed it to her.

The beer was cold. "You—you have a refrigerator?" Mary said, astonished.

"A whole kitchen," Don said. "Why do you think we meet at Mark's place?"

Now Mary saw that Mark was wearing a gray jacket and pants. Of course. He could afford a place with a kitchen if he worked for the government. But Layla seemed to approve of him. And there, dangling from his left hand, was a mask. How could he work for the government and belong to a tribe at the same time?

Two people sat on the bed talking intently. "Ayako," Don said, "and Nicholas. This is—what? Mary?" Mary nodded.

Ayako had long black hair to her waist and bangs that nearly covered her eyes. Her legs were long and lean, a dancer's legs. From her wrist dangled the lion's mask Mary had seen at the Green Dragon. Nicholas was tall and broad-shouldered, with wavy brown hair that kept falling into his eyes. Mary looked for the mask at his wrist, but there wasn't one. They looked at her, nodded, and turned back to their conversation.

Both Nicholas and Ayako were wearing government gray. Ayako

was wearing a man's gray tunic as a dress. Who were these people? Did they all work for the government, even Layla? "Is Layla here?" Mary asked Don.

"Layla never gets here before eight-thirty," Don said, forgetting he had said that to her the last time he'd seen her. "Gotta find Mark for a second." He left her and went into the kitchen. Mary looked around for a place to sit, didn't find one, and sat awkwardly on the floor. She wished Layla would hurry up.

Someone knocked loudly at the door and Mary jumped up to answer it. "Who is it?" she said.

"Layla," the familiar voice said, "the heron tribe." Mary opened the door just as Layla was taking off her mask.

Whorled, painted designs covered her face and gave her dignity and wild grace. Why did I think she wasn't pretty? Mary thought. She's beautiful. "I like the patterns," she said as they went into the living room.

Layla put her hand to her face. "Oh, right," she said. "I forgot I did that. Got any food?"

"No," Mary said, surprised. Didn't Layla make enough from her masks to be able to afford food? "I could have brought some salad if I'd thought. Are you hungry?"

"I don't know," Layla said, sitting on the floor and drawing her coat around her. Mary sat next to her. "I can't remember if I ate today."

"Next time," Mary said. She wanted to do something for Layla, something big, even though she had seen at once that Layla hadn't brought her mask. "Listen, I wanted to ask you—I mean, do all these people work for the government? Who are they?"

She had lowered her voice but Don, coming back from the kitchen with a bottle of beer, had heard anyway. "Well, now, that's an interesting question," he said. "Who are all these people anyway? You probably think you've stumbled into a seething mass of government workers, don't you?"

Mary nodded, a little annoyed. She had wanted to talk to Layla alone, find out about her mask. "Actually, we've only got two canners among us," Don said. "There's Mark, our host, who works on the road crew. Mark's writing a novel, but so far no one's seen it. And there's Nick, who works at the TV station. You may have heard his voice on the rerun channel"—he deepened his voice and put his palm against his chest—"'You are watching *Classics from the Twentieth Century*. And now, back to our program.'"

"I don't think so," Mary said. "I just got here, and I don't have a TV set."

"Good for you," Don said. "Keep your mind free of the General's propaganda. Then we have Ayako. Don't be fooled by her outfit. She works in a supermarket. Someone gave her that shirt, and very fetching it looks on her, too. But we may lose Ayako to the canners, too—she's applied to the government-run dance center."

Now Mary saw that both Don and Layla were wearing patched and faded flannel shirts and old torn pants. The green blouse she had been so proud of a few hours ago suddenly seemed wrong, too shiny and new. I guess when these people have money they spend it on their masks and coats, she thought. And jewelry. Ayako was wearing six or seven metal bands on her arms and a few around her ankle. Her stockings were badly torn.

"What's a—a canner?" Mary said.

Don tilted his head toward her, startled, and his eyes, formerly in shadow, caught the light and shone. He's drunk, Mary thought. More than ever now she wished he'd go away. "My, you are an innocent, aren't you?" he said. "Canners are people who work for the government and belong to a tribe at the same time."

"But—can they do that?" Mary said. "I mean—"

Don laughed. "Can they do that?" he said. "Hey—I wonder if that's why they're called canners. What do you think? Some of them probably feel strange about it and some of them don't, I guess. That's human nature."

"And what do you do?" Mary asked.

Don took a sip of beer and laughed again. Beer sprayed over the top of the bottle. "Me?" he said. "I'm a writer, which during the reign of General Gleason is another way of saying I'm unemployed."

"Why?" Mary said. "I mean, there are lots of books." She gestured vaguely toward Mark's bookshelf. "Why should you be unemployed?"

"Sure," Don said. "Lots of bad books. You're not so innocent that you haven't heard of the censor, right?"

"Don't be bitter, Don," Layla said.

"Can't help it," Don said. He lifted his dog mask to his face and looked at them through the eyeholes. "A dog never forgets, kindness or cruelty. That's what you told me, Layla." He lowered the mask and looked at Mary, mouth slightly open. "And what do you do?"

"I work in a restaurant," Mary said. She had the uneasy feeling he was mocking her. "Making salad."

"Good," Don said. "Then you can bring us some food next week. You're probably too young to get ration coupons for liquor."

Mary opened her mouth to say something, but Don was no longer looking at her. "Speaking of food," he said to Layla, "Ayako couldn't get anything from the supermarket. Did you eat anything today?" Mary was surprised at the concern in his voice.

"I think I might have," Layla said. "It's hard to remember."

"And you spent the rest of the day in a trance, right?"

Layla said nothing.

"Well, I hope you've had something," Don said. "Because I've got some bad news for you, and I don't want you to have to hear it on an empty stomach. I went to the library today to do some research for this book I'm writing, and the librarian said that all the animal books are classified now."

"Classified," Layla said dully. Every attempt at an expression went out of her face. Her wide gray eyes focused past Don, on a sign in the corner of the room that said "Passengers for Tour Buses Load Here." Mary was shocked at the change; it was almost as if Layla had left the room. "Why?"

"Creeping tribalism," Don said. "You know what they say. The government doesn't like the masks. Says they're counterproductive."

"You mean," Layla said slowly, "that they think I'll stop making masks because I don't know what the animal looks like?"

Don shrugged. "It looks that way, doesn't it?" he said. "I told her I needed it for research and she suddenly got very suspicious. Wanted to know what kind of research. Wanted to take my name. I got out of there in a hurry."

Layla stared stonily at the floor. Yellow feathers hung from the coat's belt and she stroked them absently. Ayako came over and sat next to Layla, her legs stretched out in front of her. "You told her, huh?" she said to Don.

Don nodded, as if to say, "There's nothing more I can do." Layla said nothing. "Listen, Layla," Ayako said. "It shouldn't stop you—not having the books. You've got a few books at home, don't you, and you're so talented—"

"Fuck them," Layla said suddenly. She ran her hand through her uncombed hair hastily. "I'll make as many masks as I like. I'll make masks for everyone on this planet. I don't need to know what the goddamn animal looks like—I need to know the animal's inner essence, and the person's inner essence, and that's all. That librarian can rot in hell before I try to check out animal books again."

Ayako grinned. "That's right," she said. "Don't you see, they're offering you a compliment. They're afraid of you. They don't understand the masks, and it worries them."

"They goddamn better be afraid," Layla said. "They don't know what they've started. I'll make masks for *them*, that's what I'll do." The mood broke as quickly as it had started. "How was work?" she said.

Ayako shrugged. "Work was work," she said. "How've you been?"

"I met this guy yesterday," Layla said. "Just out walking. His face was painted blue, and I said, where did you get the blue, all excited, and he said, I got it before the Collapse. And I said, you mean you've been saving it for ten years? and he said, no, I travel in time and bring it back."

"A crazy," Ayako said.

"Yeah, but where did he get the blue?" Layla said. "So he said he'd meet me at the park and give me some. On Monday I think he said. Yeah, I'm pretty sure."

"Do you think he has some?"

"I don't know. Anyway, he's pretty cute. So we'll see."

Mary listened to the two women, wanting to say something, wanting them to know she was there. But the more she listened the more puzzled she became. Did Layla think the man traveled in time? Layla wasn't like everyone else, Mary knew that, but she wasn't crazy. Or was she? When she had imagined maskmakers Mary had thought of a tall woman surrounded by beautiful things, ivory, peacock feathers and ostrich plumes, working slowly and carefully, methodically. Why would Layla have to go into a trance to make her masks? And how could she actually forget to eat? Mary began to feel concerned about her, and to resent her a little for not being the way she had imagined her.

Layla and Ayako stopped talking. Everyone was watching Mark come into the room from the kitchen. He was carrying something under his arm. "A radio," Mary said, breathing the words.

"Yeah," Don said. "You've seen a radio before, haven't you?"

"Well, of course," Mary said. Why did he keep treating her like a child? There had been radios all over the place before the Collapse, and even after they'd been outlawed she had seen a few.

"Okay," Mark said. The room became suddenly quiet. He bent and plugged the radio in near the bookshelf. Nicholas stood and left the room. People seemed to hold their breath while he was gone. The redwood door opened. "All right," Nicholas said. "I didn't see anybody out there."

"Mary," Mark said. "Why don't you move closer to the window? You can see if anyone's coming."

"Okay," Mary said. She was surprised at how much her heart pounded. What if she did something wrong? She looked carefully between the homemade curtains.

Mark turned the radio on. The light behind the station band glowed briefly and then died. Everyone except Mary moved closer.

"Good evening, tribes," the announcer said, a high male voice. "Too loud," several people said immediately, and Mark turned it down a little. Mary looked out the window. "Welcome to your favorite and only evening broadcast, KVRT, your covert radio station. I hope your curtains are drawn shut and the big box with the pictures is on to explain the noise should anyone ask." Mark shrugged. There was no TV set in the room.

"And now the news.

"Lester Martin, the man who made public the government reloca-tion studies, was sentenced to indefinite imprisonment Monday. KVRT was not able to learn where Lester is being sent. Some canners and a few tribes carrying banners were present when Lester was taken away by car, and they were arrested and sentenced. We don't know where they were taken either.

"Akram Hassan, whose play *Life/Time/Subscription* was banned here, forcing him to flee to Brazil, said in an interview with a Brazilian newspaper that although he enjoys the freedom of speech in Brazil he will always miss America. His new play *Life Now* opened to rave reviews in Brasília. Good luck to you, Akram, in your new life.

"The Japanese government said Wednesday that it will not take part in a planned delegation of computer experts to the United States until it is sure—quote—that the technology supplied will be made available to the people, and not used only by the government. Unquote. General Gleason is reported to have said that the Japanese themselves can ill afford to make moral judgments. At present only Australia has responded to General Gleason's plea for informational aid.

"That's it for Friday," the announcer said, "July thirtieth, 2021. The time is now nine-thirty, and curfew starts in one-half hour. If you live far away, say your good-byes now and prepare to take that long trip back. Keep safe, all you tribes, and I hope to talk with you again next Friday."

Mark turned off the radio and took it into the kitchen. There was silence until he came back. Then Nicholas stood and said good-bye to Mark. He took out his ration book and tore out a few coupons, liquor coupons, Mary guessed, and gave them to Mark. She had registered for her ration book when she got to Berkeley but so far she hadn't gotten one. She hoped no one would ask her for coupons. The front door opened and closed. The entry-way outside was dark.

Ayako stood next. Was everyone leaving now? She hadn't had a chance to ask Layla about her mask. Maybe Layla had forgotten all about it. And was she invited back? Mark hadn't said anything one way or the other. Just as she was wondering how she could phrase the question Layla turned to her. "Do you work tomorrow?" she said.

"I—no," Mary said, surprised.

"Good," Layla said. "I've got to go to the supermarket for a few things, and then to the Blue Market. Do you want to come?"

"Sure," Mary said. "What are you going to get?"

"Paint," Layla said. "Stuff."

"Are you going to make a mask?" Mary asked. Layla nodded. "Mine?"

Layla grinned. "Not while you're around, I'm not," she said. "I'll meet you at the market on Ashby at ten, okay?"

Ayako was standing by the door, putting on her coat. "We'd better go," she said, looking pointedly at Layla.

"Is the bus still running?" Mark said. "You can stay here if you like."

"That's okay," Layla said, standing up and pulling her coat closely around her. She slipped on her heron mask and went to the door. "We're good tribespeople—we'll walk."

"Good-bye," Mark said. Ayako tore out her liquor coupons and put on her lion mask. Layla was going through her big coat pockets, her pants pockets, the small breast pocket of her flannel shirt, her coat pockets again. "Here we are," she said, taking out her ration book.

"Let's *go*," Ayako said, opening the door.

"All right, all right," Layla said, tearing out her coupons. "Good-bye." She opened the door and she and Ayako went out. Mary followed quickly.

Outside half the streetlamps were out and the streets were deserted. Light and dark came together like marbling. They went from the streetlamps to shadow and back to light again, feeling carefully in the dark for the places in the sidewalk that had not been repaired. A pair of headlights came up behind them, thrusting their shadows forward.

"Damn," Ayako said. "Cops. I knew we should have left earlier."

"It's okay," Layla said. "Don't worry."

"Don't worry?" Ayako said. "Why the hell not?"

"You three," someone yelled from the car. "Don't you know it's almost curfew?"

"God, look at them," the driver said, loudly, because they were meant to hear it. "Look at the masks."

Mary turned to look at the car as it pulled alongside her. She wished she were wearing a mask, like Layla and Ayako. "We live close by, sir," Ayako said. "We will be home before curfew." She pulled her coat closer around her and something jangled.

"We're going to have to see your identification," the man on the passenger side said. "I'm damned if I know why you do this. Why don't you just take the bus, make it easier on everyone . . ."

"The cart that moves by itself?" Layla said. "We cannot ride in it, sir, we do not understand its magic."

"Oh, *great*," Ayako said softly. She backed away a little from the car, as though disassociating herself from all of them. Mary watched Layla with amazement, a little terrified at Layla's nerve. Every few seconds she thought she might break into wild laughter.

"We are strangers in your magnificent country," Layla said.

"We've heard this before," the man on the passenger side said. "You're kids with masks on. We picked up a kid just like you a few days ago, claimed not to understand machinery, and I thought, you know, it's a damn shame. Kid was bright, could have learned how to use a typewriter or an adding machine, gotten a government job, made something of himself. Instead he had to go and spoil his chances by playing these ridiculous games."

"That is a beautiful totem," Layla said, pointing to the walkie-talkie set on the dashboard between the two men. "Does it represent your tribe?"

"Just shut up and show us your yellow," the driver said. "You'll find out what it's for."

Layla reached into her coat pocket and pulled out a button, a few plastic beads and some string. Mary and Ayako had already handed over their yellow identification cards. The two policemen watched Layla impatiently. "Here it is," she said finally, bringing out her card. String trailed from it to the ground.

The man in the passenger's seat switched on the walkie-talkie. "Layla MacKenzie," he said into it. "Ayako Nomura and Mary Owens," and spelled the names out. There was a long pause while someone at a headquarters somewhere looked through a file. The walkie-talkie squawked. A real tribeswoman would have gone on her knees and worshiped the talking box as a god, but Layla looked suddenly too tired, or too discouraged. The man on the passenger side listened a while and then said, "Which one's Layla?"

No one moved. "You've got two violations of curfew already," the man said, exactly as if someone had spoken. "One more and you could be put in a rehab center. You think that'll be fun? Why do you do this to yourselves? You," he said, motioning to Mary. "You're the one from Stockton, right?" Mary said nothing. "Well, it says so right here on your yellow," he said impatiently. "My advice to you is to go back to Stockton. Now. You don't have a mask and you should keep it that way. You're too young to get mixed up with these crazy people. You hear me?"

Mary didn't move. The man sighed and gave them back their cards. "Okay, you can go," he said.

"You hear about the law making it illegal to wear masks?" the driver said. "The General's considering it right now. We won't have to wait for you to break curfew again. Next time we see you we'll probably put you away."

"Your General would never show such discourtesy to visitors to your country," Layla said, backing away slowly from the car. Then she and Ayako began to run, and Mary followed. They reached Dana Street just as the curfew sirens sounded. "Bye," Mary said, gasping. She ran down three unpaved blocks to Carleton Street, feeling more exhilarated than she had in her life. By the time she reached her house her face was red with excitement and exertion. The policemen had not followed them. Layla should have threatened them with magic, Mary thought, letting herself in.

2

MARY WALKED UP AND down the aisles of the supermarket, staring at the half-empty shelves for what seemed like the tenth time. Without a ration booklet about the only things she could buy were bread and milk. There was a small crowd around the sugar, just arrived after a few weeks on the UC list. If she had a sugar coupon, and if Mark had an oven and some other food—flour and eggs and spices—she could bake a cake next Friday night.

She went to the front of the store and looked at the Unavailable Commodities list posted on the window, four columns of small type. Damn, chocolate was still on the list. Coffee, sewing needles, thread, eggs, cinnamon, baking powder, ham, light bulbs. What did Layla want at the supermarket? She certainly couldn't get paint here. And where was she, anyway? It had to be long after ten.

"Hi," someone said behind her, and she turned around. It was Layla. The whorls on her face had smudged and run together. In the wan light of the morning she looked tired and old.

"What time is it?" Mary said before she could stop herself. She should be grateful someone like Layla was spending time with her, not get mad at her first thing. But Layla had said ten o'clock. "It's later than ten, isn't it?"

"Yeah," Layla said. She ran her hand through her still uncombed hair and walked away from the window. There were five or six bracelets on her wrist, mostly metal but some wood. Her coat billowed out behind her as she walked.

Mary followed, still annoyed. "Well, you said ten, didn't you?" she said.

"I'm sorry," Layla said, walking down one of the aisles. Through her anger Mary couldn't help wonder what it would be like to go so lightly, to have no attachments, no responsibilities. "I lost my ration book."

"Okay," Mary said. "I'm sorry I got mad."

Layla shrugged. " 'S okay," she said, turning quickly down another aisle. "Ayako's mad at me too."

"Ayako? Why?"

"For keeping her out past curfew last night. If she's caught out even once she won't get in the dance group."

"She won't?" Mary said. What was a joke last night suddenly seemed serious in the light of day. "Why did you do it then?"

Layla slowed. "I don't know," she said. "I can't help myself sometimes, I guess. Just once, I want to get my own back from those smug little bastards."

"Yeah, I know," Mary said. She grinned. "Remember the way that guy looked when you told him we couldn't take the bus?"

"Yeah," Layla said. She was grinning too. "See? You understand."

They walked down the aisle in silence. It was true that she understood how Layla felt about policemen, but she also understood how Ayako felt about the dance group. Should she say something? But didn't Layla know what she was doing? "What are you looking for?" Mary said finally. It wasn't her place to criticize Layla.

"Eggs," Layla said.

"Eggs?" Mary said, surprised. "Eggs are on the UC list. And anyway, how were you going to get eggs without a ration book?"

Layla stopped. "Well, I found the book," she said. "Didn't I say? Are you sure about the eggs?"

"Of course I'm sure," Mary said. "I practically memorized the list before you got here."

"We'll have to go to the Blue Market, then," Layla said. "Damn.

It's going to cost about twice as much." She headed toward the front of the store.

"Hey, wait a minute," Mary said. "Do you have—can I borrow a sugar coupon? I'll pay you back when I get my ration book."

Layla stopped. "Yeah, I think . . ." She began the search through her pockets once more and finally took out her ration book. "No, sorry. I must have given it away."

"Too bad," Mary said. "They've got sugar in again. I thought maybe I could make a cake at Mark's."

"Oh, yeah?" Layla said. "Let's have a look."

The crowd around the sugar was gone. Layla looked carefully up and down the aisle, picked up a bag of sugar, and then hastily tucked it under her flannel shirt. Mary started to laugh. Layla gave her a look of immense dignity and Mary felt the laughter freeze in her throat. They walked out of the store together, Layla moving with the clumsy gait of a pregnant woman.

In the parking lot outside the supermarket recruiting officers from the General's armed forces had set up models of tanks and planes. They passed the parking lot, passed a woman who frowned at Layla disapprovingly because the hand that held up the bag of sugar had no wedding ring. Mary looked at Layla. Was she ever going to give her the sugar? The blue bag was starting to show through a frayed buttonhole. Now they were passing an older woman who smiled at them benignly. Probably remembering her youth and days of sexual freedom, Mary thought wistfully, wondering what that could have been like. The General had outlawed contraceptives for everyone except married couples.

"Can I—" Mary said tentatively.

"Where do you live?" Layla said.

"On Carleton," Mary said. "Just a couple of blocks."

"Good," said Layla. "Lead the way."

She likes playacting, Mary thought. She's really enjoying this. Like the masks, which give you a chance to be an animal, something different from what you are. It's no wonder she became a maskmaker. They went up Carleton and Mary let them into her house. The roommates—three or four of them, it varied—were all gone for the day. In the kitchen Layla took out the bag of sugar and put it in a cupboard. Mary realized she had been wrong about Layla. Layla was not just a maskmaker, a legend talked about with reverence as far as Stockton and probably beyond, but a person with quirks, eccentricities, a sense of humor. A person who might possibly become her friend. As Layla went out the front door Mary stopped, astonished by the thought. "Well?" Layla said. "Aren't you coming?"

On weekends the four blocks of Telegraph from Dwight to what used to be the campus were closed to traffic. Vendors spread blankets or erected wooden booths in the street and sold food, tobacco, alcohol, old machine parts. A lot of the sales were illegal, but the policemen who patrolled the street on horseback never seemed to interfere much. The Blue Market, people called it, since it was not secret or illegal enough to be black. The real black market exchanges, Mary knew, took place up in the hills, the locations shifting from week to week.

"I wanted to ask you," Mary said as they walked through the crowded street, elbowing past government workers in gray, tribes in fur and feathers and jingling machinery. "How come Don didn't leave with us last night? Where does he live?"

"Mark's letting him stay there," Layla said. "While he writes his novel."

"That's nice of him," Mary said.

"Yeah," Layla said. "Mark's a saint. Saved my life a few times. Him and Ayako both."

"I don't think Don likes me," Mary said.

"Don?" Layla said. "I don't think Don likes anyone," she said as though considering the thought for the first time.

The sky was high and gray, and the day grew hotter. "I have chocolate," a man whispered to Mary as he walked by. "Great stuff. Chocolate and coffee." He walked on, not stopping to see if she looked up. "Drugs, great drugs. Coffee, tea, chocolate. Chocolate cake," he said, mostly to himself. Mary stared after him.

"Who was that?" Layla asked.

"Some crazy," Mary said.

"Hey," Layla said. "We're all crazy here."

They passed a rickety wooden table covered with the insides of old machines. Layla picked up a small blue plastic square inset with gray metal and looked at it curiously. "What's that?" Mary said. "Isn't it—"

Layla shrugged. "A record?" she said.

"I don't think so," Mary said. She walked away from the booth, hoping Layla would follow her. To her relief Layla put down the square. "I think it's something to do with computers. If this were Stockton he could get arrested just for having it. The General's nuts for computer technology." She looked nervously at the policeman on the corner.

"Is that what that was?" Layla said. "Yeah, they'll probably arrest him for that. I was gonna sew it on something. Would have arrested me too, I guess." She didn't seem at all concerned at the thought.

The next booth displayed rows of steel bands set out on a blanket. Bracelets, Mary thought, or I can sew them on my coat like Ayako does. A woman called out, "Cards, palms, stars. Fortunes read." A man in torn gray pants and no shirt said to her, very reasonably, "Everything would have been all right if he hadn't killed my dog, you know what I mean?" Mary stopped and looked around. She had never seen anything like this in Stockton. When she looked up again Layla was far ahead, looking through a pile of old rags spread over the street. She shouldered past someone wearing a mask as good as any of Layla's, a cat made of silver feathers, and hurried up to her.

"Is that where you're from?" Layla said. "Stockton?"

"Yeah," Mary said. The smell of the rags was almost overpowering; Mary wished they would start moving again.

The woman selling the rags broke off a conversation with someone and hurried over. She was dressed almost entirely in her rags, layers upon layers of them, blue over pink over green. She was short and fat, with long frizzy brown hair. "Layla!" she said, sounding delighted. A gold front tooth sparkled when she talked. "It's been a long time. How've you been?"

"Fine," Layla said, fingering a red cotton shirt webbed with holes. She stood up. "Did you make any more paper?"

"Did I make more paper!" the ragwoman said. "Pounds and pounds of it. And I saved the best for you, as always." She slipped her hand under a tangled pile of clothes and immediately came up with a stack of intensely white rag paper. "Here you are."

"Great," Layla said. She put her hand in her pocket, pulled out a paintbrush, frowned and tried again.

"Now don't go trying to pay me," the ragwoman said.

"Why the hell not?" Layla said. "This is expensive stuff. What are you, Dana Cooper?"

"I still owe you for the mask you made me," the ragwoman said.

"Still?" Layla said. "It's been a long time."

"I keep everything right here," the ragwoman said, tapping her head with a short and dirty index finger. "Don't worry about that. You see Bone, tell him he owes me ten dollars."

"Okay," Layla said, taking the paper. "And thanks."

"Sure," the ragwoman said. She walked over to two men looking through a pile of used gray clothing. "What can I do for you gentlemen?" she said.

Layla tucked the paper under her arm and they walked on. "What made you decide to come to Berkeley?" Layla asked her, as though the conversation had never been interrupted.

"Oh, well," Mary said. It had seemed easy enough to explain to her friends before she left, but all the easy answers slipped away with Layla. "I—well, I'm against tyranny. You know. Against the General. I wanted to live in a place that was free, and Berkeley seemed . . . And I wanted to wear a mask."

"I don't know about tyranny," Layla said. "Sometimes I think we're freer now, after the Collapse, than we've ever been." Her eyes were wide, unfocused. "Everything's fallen apart. You can do what you want now. It's like the weeds, growing up in the cracks in the sidewalk. We're those weeds."

It had never occurred to Mary that General Gleason was anything other than evil. What Layla was saying was heresy. "Yeah, but—" she said. "But the arrests, and—and Don being censored, and the curfew, and the shortages . . ."

"Well, yeah," Layla said. She smiled a sad, resigned smile, like a new moon. "But all times have been bad lately."

"What do you mean, lately?" Mary said.

"Well, the last few thousand years," Layla said. She laughed.

Someone ran by, screaming. Mary looked up, startled, but no one else seemed to notice. "Didn't you have masks in Stockton?" Layla said.

"We had one," Mary said. "One kid wore this old plastic bear mask. They made him leave school. My father said if I ever talked to him he'd kill me."

"I see what you mean by tyranny," Layla said.

"Well, that's not . . ." Mary said. "I didn't mean my father." But as soon as she said it she realized that her father and the General were somehow mixed together for her, that she couldn't think of one without the other. She remembered being surprised whenever she saw the General on television, his tanned face and close-cropped gray hair, because in her mind he always looked something like her father. "Well, my father wasn't as bad as the General," she said. "But it was bad for me, because my brothers had left home. My mother died just before the Collapse, about ten years ago. So it was just me and him."

"Where did your brothers go?" Layla asked.

"I don't know," Mary said. "He used to take them hunting, on weekends. Then when the General outlawed guns they left. One of them joined the armed forces, and one of them joined some kind of underground group that refused to surrender their weapons. I used to imagine them killing each other in some minor battle. They're both a lot older than me."

"But then you left," Layla said.

"Yeah," Mary said. "I couldn't stand it anymore." She remembered dreaming of masks, of a place where people walked the streets as something other than what they were, dancing to the rhythm of tribal drums. "I saved up some money from working in a grocery store, but somehow he found out what I was planning. The night I was packing to go he came into my room. He said, 'I know you'll never leave me. You're not like your brothers. You're not free to go.'"

"Why did he say that?" Layla said.

"I—I don't know," Mary said, flustered. She had not meant to tell Layla so much. "And where are you from?" she said.

"Look at this, hair dye!" Layla said. "I tried painting my hair once. It all fell out. Fifty dollars, damn. I wonder where they got it." She walked gracefully past a booth selling homemade beer, another displaying old electric guitars. "Spare change?" someone asked Mary. "Spare change?" She looked at him a moment, feeling guilty, and then hurried after Layla.

"Here we go," Layla said. "Eggs. How much?"

"Fifty cents each," the man at the booth said.

"Damn," Layla said. "They were twenty a week ago at the market. I knew I should have picked some up then. Oh well." She handed the paper to Mary, took a dollar from one pants pocket, checked the other pocket and finally plunged her hand into her large coat pocket. She might have been the only person on the street wearing a coat. "Here it is," she said. She glanced ritually at the mounted policeman on the corner and handed over two dollars to the man behind the booth.

The man gave her four eggs. "Is it for paint?" he asked.

Layla stood and looked at him a moment. He moved a little, clearly embarrassed to have asked the question. Finally she said, "What kind of stupid question is that?"

"Well, you know . . ." the man said. "Well, I thought you were . . . You're Layla, aren't you? I've seen your masks around. I just wondered—well, I was wondering how much they were. How much you charge. I could bring my own eggs." He laughed a little. No one joined in.

"Usually they're fifty dollars," Layla said. "But if I disapprove of someone—say he charges fifty cents apiece for eggs—I don't make him a mask. Here, carry these two, will you, Mary?" She put the other two eggs in her coat pocket and they walked away.

"I guess we're done," Layla said, looking around.

"You really charge fifty dollars for a mask?" Mary said.

"It's free for my friends," Layla said. "I told you—don't worry about it."

"Thanks," Mary said. "But well, what I was thinking—Well, they told me in school I was pretty good at drawing, and I could use the extra money, and I thought . . ."

Layla had fallen to the ground. Mary sank down next to her, ignoring the bustle of the crowd around them. Layla was shaking a little. What was wrong?

"You . . ." Layla said. To her intense embarrassment Mary saw that Layla was laughing. She could barely get the words out. "You want—some extra money—and so you want to—want to be a mask-maker?"

"Well, I thought . . ." Mary said. "I don't see what's so funny."

Layla took a deep breath. "It's just—well, you don't know what you're asking," she said. "It's a path. It's difficult, and uneven, and scary, and beautiful, and sometimes all of those at once. And once you set foot on the path you will not be able to leave it. It's not something you do for a little extra money. And most of the time there's no money in it anyway." She rose unsteadily. "Do you still want to do it?"

"Do I still . . ." Mary said, standing up. She felt a little confused. She had asked the wrong question, but Layla was going to teach her anyway. "Yeah. Yeah, sure I do," she said.

"You're absolutely sure?" Layla said. "Remember what I told you."

"Yes, I am," Mary said. It couldn't be as hard as Layla made it out to be. What was there to making masks, after all? And it might be fun.

"All right," Layla said. She brushed dirt from her coat and reached out for Mary's hand. Mary was still holding the eggs, and she shook the hand awkwardly. "I have an apprentice," Layla said, sounding pleased. Her hand was icy cold. "Well, then. Are you busy this afternoon or do you want your first lesson?"

Mary hesitated only a moment. She had planned to go into San Francisco, but it could wait. She was already thinking about the marvelous things she would learn from Layla. "Sure," she said. "I'll take a lesson. Lemme just get some of those steel bands for my coat, and then we can go."

They had to take a bus to Layla's house, which was on Telegraph about a mile and a half from the Blue Market. "Go on in," Layla said when they got there. "It's not locked." Mary opened the door and looked curiously at the small room.

Mark's apartment, she thought, could be called neat by comparison. "Have a seat," Layla said, taking the paper from her and setting it on top of the blades of an old electric fan. Mary looked around for a chair. Finally she shrugged, pushed aside fur, feathers, bone, broken china and a rusted light switch, and sat on the floor.

Layla sat on the bed and took the eggs from her pocket. Miraculously, they were not broken. "Now your first lesson," she said, "is how to make egg tempera. First you take the egg—"

"What's that?" Mary said.

"What?"

"What you said. Egg something."

"Egg tempera," Layla said slowly. She didn't appear to be impatient at all. "It's a kind of paint. I use it because eggs are pretty easy to get, and because the colors are so bright. But other people use different things. Bone uses leather, for instance, and Rose uses feathers. Okay?"

Mary nodded. For a moment she wondered what kind of materials she would use to make her masks. Metal, she thought. Fur. Glass. Old plastic. Anything was possible. Then she realized that Layla was still speaking, that she had asked her a question. "Could you hand me that bowl over there?" Layla said again.

Mary got up and brought her the bowl. "Okay," Layla said. "Now you crack the egg"—she hit the egg against the bowl—"and then you pass the yolk from hand to hand, like this." Her fingernails, Mary noticed, were bitten to the skin.

"And then what?" Mary said.

"And then you do it for about five minutes," Layla said. "To get all the white off."

Mary yawned. Was this important? Maybe Layla didn't realize that not everyone was interested in how she made her paints. She forced herself to pay attention. When was Layla going to get to the real stuff, like how she chose what animal the mask would be?

"Now the pigments," Layla said, "are over there." She pointed with her chin to a row of small covered jars lined against the wall. Mary looked where she was pointing, her eyes still teary from the yawn. "I keep them under the window so the sun can't get them. There are different ways of getting pigments—berries, moss, flowers. You can dig them out of the earth, too. I usually go to Mount Diablo for that."

"Mount Diablo?" Mary said, interested now. "How do you get there?"

"Hitch a ride with a truck driver," Layla said. She still passed the yolk from hand to hand, carefully and methodically. "I'll take you some time."

"Hitch a ride—" Mary said, astonished. "That's illegal, isn't it? And dangerous."

"Well, the other alternative is to walk," Layla said. "I've done that too." Mary said nothing. She wondered if she could get Layla to bring back pigments for her, or if there were some other way to get paint. "And anyway, how did you get here from Stockton?" Layla said.

"Well, I hitched a ride," Mary said. "But I was terrified the whole time. I swore I'd never do it again. You don't know what happens to people—especially women—women get—" She stopped. She had been raised to think "rape" was an indecent word, something that should never be mentioned.

"Well, sure I know," Layla said. "I've done it at least ten times. Nothing's ever happened to me."

"Well, I'm not doing it," Mary said. "Not again." If Layla had asked her at that moment if she still wanted to be an apprentice she would have said no. But Layla was continuing her lesson as though she hadn't heard her.

"The hardest pigment to get is blue," Layla said. "You can get it from certain kinds of beetles, but I've never been able to find them. That's why I was so excited when I saw that guy with his face painted blue. If I can buy some from him I'll be all set."

"Was that the guy . . ." Mary said, hoping to get Layla off the subject of pigments. "Do you really think he traveled in time?"

"I don't know," Layla said. She grinned. "But wouldn't it be exciting if he did?" She cupped the yolk in one hand and felt around the side of the bed for something. At last she found what she was looking for—a long thin needle—and punctured the yolk carefully, letting it drain into a jar. "Now you mix the pigments in," she said. "Could you hand me that jar over there, the third from the left—that's it."

Mary brought her the jar. So far being an apprentice isn't much fun, she thought. It's mostly fetching and carrying. I wonder if Layla just wants free labor. "When do I get to do something?" she said.

"When you've learned the basics," Layla said. "Now when the pigments are mixed you can start to paint. Could you get me—no, never mind, I'm not really sure where it is." She stood and looked under paper and old machinery until she found an unpainted mask. Mary tried to see what kind of animal it was, hoping that it was her mask even though she knew Layla wouldn't make her mask in front of her. She thought she could see horns. "Some other day I'll teach you about papier-mâché," Layla said, going back to the bed.

Layla took two brushes out of her coat pocket, selected one and put the other one back. "You really should take better care of your brushes than I do," she said, grinning wryly. "Whatever you do, don't keep them in your coat pocket." She began to stroke paint onto the mask, slowly, laboriously. "You have to build up at least three coats with egg tempera. Your mask is going to have four."

At the mention of her mask Mary looked up. So that couldn't be her mask, then. She wondered when Layla would get around to making hers. Layla was concentrating now, carefully putting minute amounts of paint on the papier-mâché surface. How could someone be so methodical in her work and so sloppy in the rest of her life? And what did she mean about learning the basics first? Judging from what she had seen that day and at Mark's house it didn't seem like Layla had learned the basics of living from day to day. Mary began to fidget.

"How come one of the guys last night didn't have a mask?" Mary said.

"Nick?" Layla said. Mary nodded. "I just give them the mask," Layla said. "Whether or not they wear it is up to them." Mary thought Layla sounded a little hurt despite her words. "His wife wears hers all the time."

"His—wife?" Mary said. "I didn't know he was married."

"Oh, yeah," Layla said. "Jayne. She's pregnant—she's going to have a boy."

Mary looked at Layla sharply, but she didn't seem to be joking. "How do you know?" Mary said.

Layla shrugged. She dipped her paintbrush in the jar of paint and returned it to the mask, scattering drops of brown over her coat. Now Mary could see that her coat was covered with faded paint stains.

"What kind of . . . what tribe is he?" Mary said. "Nick, I mean."

"Spider," Layla said.

"Spider!" Mary said. No wonder he didn't want to wear his mask. "I didn't know you made insect masks."

"Spiders aren't insects," Layla said.

"You know what I mean," Mary said, but Layla was talking again. "I know what you're thinking," she said. "But every animal has good and bad characteristics. Spiders, you can see spiders in lots of different myths. They live in the space between earth and sky, so they have to learn how to live in two worlds. Sometimes they carry messages back and forth. In fact, spiders are a lot like maskmakers. We go between the two worlds too. Nick would probably make a good maskmaker, but he'd never ask to become an apprentice. He hasn't come to terms with the animal part of himself.''

"So is that how you do it?" Mary said, delighted that Layla was finally talking about the masks themselves. "You figure out what the person's like, and you figure out what kind of animal has those characteristics, and then you—"

"No, and I'm not going to tell you yet, either," Layla said. "You'll have to be patient. Did you have any interesting dreams last night?"

"Dreams?" Mary said. She wished she could get used to the way Layla kept changing the subject. "No. I didn't have any dreams at all last night."

"Everyone dreams," Layla said. "Every night. You should keep a piece of paper and a pencil by your bed to write them down."

"Okay," Mary said, wondering what her dreams could possibly have to do with making masks. Layla was still stroking paint on the mask without showing any sign of becoming bored. One of Mary's legs had gone to sleep.

"All right," Layla said finally. She put the mask down. "That's it for today. There's the first coat."

Mary moved closer to look. The brown paint looked faint, almost insubstantial, but she could see how it would look when it was finished, a proud antlered buck with sleek finely rendered fur. She wondered who the mask was for. For the first time she felt amazed that Layla was taking her on as an apprentice, and hoped she wouldn't disappoint her. Her own work could never be that fine. "It's beautiful," she said.

Layla didn't acknowledge the praise. Mary hadn't thought she would. After all, Layla was the best. Mary looked up, out the window, and was surprised to see that the houses across the street were darker, almost melting into the darkness around them. A few lights shone in the windows. She stood and stretched, feeling hunger for the first time that day. "Do you want to come back to my place?" Mary said, remembering that Layla went for days without eating. "I've got some food for dinner, if the roommates haven't eaten it yet."

"No, that's all right," Layla said. "I've still got some stuff to do here."

"Well, thanks for the lesson," Mary said. A part of her wondered if she would ever come back. "I'll see you."

"Next week," Layla said firmly. "We'll have another lesson next week. And keep track of your dreams," she called as Mary let herself out.

"Bye," Mary said. Maybe she'd try one more lesson. They must have covered the basics by now.

The next day Mary took the bus to the ferry landing in Emeryville and caught the ferry to San Francisco. They sailed close to the Bay Bridge and Mary could see the spot near Treasure Island where it had been blown up in the early days of the Collapse. She was surprised at how large and jagged the crack was: the few times she had seen the bridge from Berkeley the gap had looked small, easily mended.

Once, long ago, her family had driven from Stockton to San Francisco. That had been in the good days, before the Collapse, before her mother died. They had sung songs in the car on the way over, and driven all over San Francisco looking for a hotel room because they hadn't thought to make reservations. It had been late evening before they found something, near Chinatown, Mary remembered, though that memory could have been mixed up with a visit to Chinatown later.

The entire drive had taken a few hours. Now just getting into San Francisco from Berkeley took as long. Was it true that supplies of gasoline had nearly run out, or was the government hoarding gasoline?

She barely remembered the Collapse, just a tangle of events, feelings, certain colors and sounds that were somehow connected with her mother's death. One day stood out, a day she and her brothers watched television with her father. A man with short gray hair and a uniform with many medals was saying something about civil unrest. Her father leaned forward to watch the man speak. "And so I have taken control of the nuclear weapons," the man said, "to prevent them from falling into the hands of the Russians." The Russians were having their own internal problems, though Mary didn't find this out until later. The men surrounding the man on television applauded. "That's it," her father said, disgusted, sitting back in his chair. "The bastard's got the country now."

Everything had changed after that, had become duller, grayer. Even the weather seemed to be colder, or at least that was the way Mary remembered her childhood. The General wasn't responsible for the shortages, the history teacher at school had said. The General was trying to fix everything, get the economy moving again, and that took drastic measures. But no one Mary knew liked the General. And nothing in Stockton seemed to change until the kid wore his mask to school, its bright colors set like a fragile challenge against the General's gray.

At the same time she was starting to understand things the history teacher had never told them, the real causes of the Collapse. From hints and overheard conversations she learned that nine years ago a woman named Dana Cooper had broken the Bank of America's computer codes and stolen over a million dollars. She had somehow gotten around the virus program designed to destroy an intruder's software, but the virus had lodged itself inside her computer, destroying the files of the next bank she had tried to rob and spreading from there to every bank in the country. The vast interlocking financial structure of the United States, still reeling from the fall of the Bank of America, collapsed, though overseas banks managed to disconnect their computer systems in time. Uprisings started and were put down all over the country, most computerized records not attacked by the virus were destroyed by workers who had lost their jobs, large companies fled the country and small companies went under. At the end of it General Otis Gleason declared martial law. Dana Cooper was never found.

As the ship came closer to San Francisco Mary looked up at the derelict skyline, gutted by fire. It was her first time in San Francisco since the trip with her family, but she might have been visiting another country. Windows were gone, buildings were left open to the wind and rain, steel beams hung terrifyingly high, waiting to fall. She was struck by how dirty everything was, as though a fine layer of ash had descended on the city. Nothing was as she remembered it. A few other people were looking with her, but most were edging toward the exit and waiting patiently to get off. She hoped she didn't look like a tourist.

The ferry docked at the San Francisco wharf. Men on the ground caught the ropes thrown from the boat and made them secure, calling to each other in a foreign language. Mary followed the crowd of people off the boat and looked around. She wondered which way Chinatown was. People on the dock were coming forward now to meet people getting off the boat, hugging them, talking loudly. She pushed her way through.

The man on the phone had given her directions and she found the bus she had to take. The bus was full by the time she got on, and she had to stand next to a young woman who smelled of gin. A man on her other side insisted loudly that the Japanese would come around, would eventually give in and supply the United States with computers. His companion muttered something she couldn't hear.

It was nearly noon when she got off the bus and found the store the man had described. "Junk," the sign over the store said in large uneven letters. The black paint was peeling. The front window was cluttered: spools of thread, a stack of dishes, each one different, old faded magazines, dolls and china figurines with hands or ears long ago nicked off.

Inside it was cool and dark. She was the only customer there. "Hello," she said to the dim figure behind the counter. "Jeffrey sent me." She was surprised at how matter-of-fact she sounded.

The man behind the counter looked her over and then nodded to himself, as if satisfied with something. "Step this way, please." He led her through a curtained door into the back of the store.

Another man stood there, putting small boxes of something on a shelf. As her eyes grew accustomed to the dark Mary saw that the shelves stretched to the ceiling. The man turned around and faced her. His hair and eyebrows were white, and the rest of his face seemed dim, about to fade into the darkness. "Hello," he said. "What can I do for you?"

"Phenytoin," Mary said.

One of the white eyebrows raised. "For epilepsy, is it?" he said. "Yes, we have that. Fifty dollars for a box of a hundred and fifty, a hundred milligrams each."

"Fifty!" Mary said. She faced him squarely, trying not to let him see her panic. "Who do you think I am, Dana Cooper?"

"No, you're much too young for Dana Cooper," the man said. His eyebrows drew apart slightly; the effect was as if he'd smiled. "How old are you, fourteen?"

"I'm eighteen," Mary said, only adding on a year. She moved back a little, unprepared for the man's easy friendliness.

"Ummhmm," the man said. He went to the shelf and took down a box, holding it out to her as though daring her to snatch it from his hand. "Well, you see, I can't possibly sell this for less. Lots of people have taken lots of risks to get this to me, and they all have to be paid. That's the going rate for phenytoin these days. I wish I could help you, but I don't really have a choice in the matter. And unfortunately neither do you, it looks like. It's either buy the medicine or live with the fits. Or you could become a gray and get it at a government pharmacy, but you don't look the type to me."

"It's not for me," Mary said. She had never in her life told anyone about her epilepsy. Why should she? Because of the medicine she hadn't had a seizure in six years. She hated it when anyone—a teacher or a doctor—had to know. "It's for a friend."

"Ummhmm," the man said again. She couldn't tell if he believed her or not. She stood in the middle of the room, uncertain. A casual remark by a friend in Stockton who had traveled a lot had given her the name of the store as a likely place to get what she needed. The junk store was the only place she knew that sold black market medicine; the market in the hills probably wouldn't have something that specialized. If she left now she would have to go back to Stockton, where her father had a government job. She would have failed. "All right, I'll tell you what," the man said. "Since it's your first time here, I'll give you my special introductory offer. Forty dollars."

"All right," Mary said, relieved. Forty dollars was exactly the amount she had brought with her. She put her hand in her pants pocket and took out a wad of yellow bills, none larger than a five, money she had carefully stolen during her first week at the restaurant. The General's face looked up at her from the one. You made me do this, she thought, looking at the picture as she handed over the money. I don't feel guilty at all. She knew she was lying.

"Here you are," the man said, handing her the box. "Does that look like what you're after?"

"I've never seen the stuff before in my life," Mary said, taking the box and looking inside. The pills, heaped inside the box as if they were candy, looked nothing like what she had taken in Stockton. Some of them were irregularly shaped and a few were smaller than the others. She remembered hearing that phenytoin was fairly easy to make, and she realized that the man had lied to her when he'd said people had taken risks. These pills weren't from a pharmacy at all. She shrugged. There was nothing she could do about it, except hope that the pills were what he had said they were. "I told you—it's for a friend." She wondered how many times he'd heard that, wondered what he had in the other boxes. He must be a millionaire by now.

"Next time it goes back to fifty, so tell your friend to be prepared," the man said. "I can only afford to be this generous once."

"Bye," Mary said, going back out through the curtains. She was damned if she'd thank him.

She walked a few blocks and then stopped and looked inside the box again. The pills were hers now. At three pills a day she had fifty days of freedom until she had to get more.

3

F ONLY HE HADN'T GONE into the cafe, Nick would think afterward, everything would still be all right. He was wandering Telegraph Avenue, hot and waiting until three when his shift at the television station started. A man wearing layers of old clothing and no shoes, carrying a roll of blankets on his back, came up to him. He smelled as if he hadn't washed for weeks. "You must change your life," the man said. "Repent, and you will be saved. The Kingdom of America fell because the Kingdom of America was wicked, wicked like Sodom, wicked like Gomorrah. Wicked because they served the heathen idols the machines. But if you repent, if you change your life . . ."

Nick began to walk faster, hoping to shake the man off. The man followed. ". . . the Kingdom will return, but this time the Kingdom of Heaven, where all the machines serve us instead. You must not worship any graven idols, you must not wear the mask of a graven idol like the heathen tribes do. . . ."

Not much chance of that, Nick thought. He saw that the Mediterraneum, an old two-story cafe closed a few months ago by the government, was open again. He went in and ordered milk, the only drink on the menu besides orange juice. The man hadn't followed. He took the glass and went to sit at one of the round marble tables.

"Is this seat taken?" a woman's voice said.

Nick looked up, annoyed at having been jarred out of his reverie. He had been counting the months left until Jayne had the baby, wondering if they would be the same as or different from the months before them, wondering how the baby would change their lives. They were the same thoughts that had run through his mind for months, like a bad song.

The woman wore a red T-shirt and faded pants. Her face was pretty enough—blue eyes, brownish red hair—but Nick couldn't help thinking that if she had a tribe it would be the fish. Her lips seemed too big to him, for one thing, and her eyes too wide. Annoyed at himself now for taking this mask business seriously, he nodded and brushed his hair out of his eyes. He noticed that nearly every table in the cafe was empty and he wondered what the woman wanted. I can always mention that I'm married, he thought, and if she turns out to be a crazy I'll leave.

"Hot out, isn't it?" the woman said.

Nick nodded again.

"Listen," the woman said. "You probably know I'm not here to talk about the weather. I'm from the police—the Special Problems branch, to be specific."

Nick put down the glass and brushed his hair out of his eyes nervously. Everyone had heard of the SP branch of the police, but no one Nick knew had actually met someone from it. People said that among other things it was the SP branch that was responsible for mysterious disappearances. Two people at the television station had disappeared in the six months Nick had been there. He knew better than to ask about them. For the first time he felt a tendril of panic begin at his heart and work its way outward. What did she want?

"We hear you've been telling jokes at work about the General," the woman said, looking at him earnestly with her too-wide eyes.

"Who did you hear that from?" Nick said, and cursed himself immediately. He should have denied it, not tried to figure out who the snitch was.

"Here and there," the woman said. He wanted to smash that earnest expression off her face. "The point is, that sort of thing undermines morale. Especially when you consider how hard the General's been working."

37

He felt as if he'd wandered into a dream. Who at the station had informed on him? Was he going to disappear now, along with Ken and Rick? Was this morning the last time he would see Jayne? His heart was pounding frantically. He looked at the empty tables on either side of him, wondering if he could signal to someone, get a message to Jayne. Just a few short minutes ago the tables had been tables, innocent of meaning, and his only worries had been the simple ones of family.

"Well, yeah, I told a couple of jokes," Nick said. He knew she heard the nervousness in his voice. "I mean, everyone does it." Great, Nick thought. Now she'll ask you who, and you'll have to name names. You're certainly not handling this very well. "But I swear to you it won't happen again. I mean, I didn't realize how serious . . ." His voice trailed off. From somewhere he found courage. He finished the milk and said, "Well, I've got to get to work now. It's been nice talking with you."

"You don't start work until three o'clock," the woman said. Now the panic took over completely. They knew all about him. He barely heard her next words. "We want to make you a deal. All you have to do is keep your eyes and ears open. Let us know if you hear anything—anything, well, subversive. Anything the General wouldn't like to hear. Do you think you can do that?"

She was asking him to become a snitch. The snitches were the lowest form of life, everyone thought so. She wasn't telling him the other side of the deal, that if he refused he'd be put in a rehab center, but they both heard the words as clearly as if she'd spoken them aloud.

He had never thought so fast in his life. If they wanted him to snitch then they didn't know all about him. They didn't know, for example, about the Friday night meetings. He swore to himself that he would never turn in his friends, that whatever happened he would protect that sad funny little group. He was already thinking like a snitch. He couldn't have been more horrified if the woman had told him he had a terminal disease.

The silence stretched out between them. "What—what's your name?" Nick said.

The woman laughed. The laugh sounded genuine, as if Nick had told a good joke. "Now you know I can't tell you that," she said. She faced him squarely. "I don't even understand why you're hesitating," she said. "It's not as if I were asking you to do something immoral. The General's side is the right side, don't you see? It's those others, the tribes and canners and the rest of them, who are holding us back."

Nick said nothing.

"Or do you think we should stay where we are?" the woman said, taking his silence to mean he disagreed. "Stagnate, let the country go to hell? You think it's a good thing there's drought and famine in the Midwest, that half the people in this country can't afford medicine? The bubonic plague took over a hundred lives last year, did you know that?"

Nick shrugged. Why was she arguing politics with him? He had already made up his mind. He thought of Jayne, struggling through her pregnancy alone, unable to get welfare because by the time she had the baby she would be an unmarried mother. He would have ceased to exist. "All right," he said slowly, every word separating from him like an amputation. "I'll keep my eyes and ears open." There. He hadn't promised to betray anyone.

"Well, we expect results," the woman said, as if she'd read his mind. "It's not enough for you to just listen. We want you to go out there. Dig things up. You know."

He nodded miserably. Once again he looked at the tables on either side of him, this time hoping that no one was near enough to hear anything.

"Good," the woman said, nodding. "I thought you'd understand. Let's meet—why don't we meet here, every Monday at twelve. We'll have some interesting conversations, I know."

Nick said nothing. The woman stood. "It's been a pleasure meeting you, Nick," she said. "I'll see you next Monday."

He sat at the table for a long time after she'd gone, feeling soiled. He wanted to go home, take a long shower, talk for hours to Jayne. But he knew he could do none of those things: he had used up his water ration for the day, and he could never let Jayne or anyone else know what he had become. He felt cut off from the rest of humanity as if by an ax-blow. His life, which had seemed to be only beginning, had just ended in the course of a ten-minute conversation.

■ ■ ■

By Monday Mary could no longer stand it. While Nick was ordering his drink in the Cafe Mediterraneum Mary sat down to write a letter to a friend in Stockton.

Dear Jackie,

Don't worry about me, I am fine. I made it to Berkeley okay. You will never believe what's been happening to me. The first thing is that I met Layla, the famous maskmaker and she is going to make me a mask! And the second thing is that she wants me to be her apprentice!! I am learning all kinds of interesting things about masks and animals. I don't know what kind of mask she is going to make me but I am hoping for a Lion.

Do not tell my father where I am!! but if other people are worried about me you can tell them I am okay. Please write me and tell me about everything, especially about you and Rich.

Your friend,
Mary

That night she found a piece of paper and a pencil and put them by her blankets to record her dreams. In her first dream she was walking with Layla and Don and Ayako along one of Stockton's main streets. Suddenly she saw the salad bar and realized that she was late for work. She ran into the restaurant but she couldn't find her apron. She looked all over, frantic. The manager was standing over her and frowning. Just as the manager was about to say something she woke up.

When she read the dream over in the morning she was disgusted. It had seemed so meaningful when she had written it down, but now she saw it was just an ordinary boring dream. Why would Layla want something like this?

The next night she dreamed she was standing naked in her room when Layla came in without knocking. She grabbed some clothes from the floor, but Layla said, "Don't worry about that. You won't need clothes where you're going anyway."

She woke up feeling disturbed. Did the dream mean that she was attracted to Layla, or that Layla was attracted to her? She didn't think so, but she didn't write the dream down anyway. She would show Layla the other one.

Her ration booklet came in the mail on Thursday. She took it to her room and looked through it slowly and greedily, planning for the month ahead. Egg coupons for Layla, or maybe for me if she lets me paint finally. No cigarette coupons, damn. They were good for trading, but the ration board didn't give them to people under twenty-one. And look at all these sugar coupons. I wonder what it was like to eat all the sugar you wanted. I'd be as big as a house by now if it wasn't for the Collapse.

She was looking through the Unavailable Commodities list at the back of the book when someone knocked loudly on the door. "Who is it?" she said.

"Layla. The heron tribe."

How could such a light person have such a heavy knock? Mary looked around the room, confused for a moment, still tangled in the memory of the dream where Layla had come into her room without knocking. Finally she put down the ration book and opened the door.

"You've got to come with me," Layla said. "I just found out about this great place. You've got to come."

"What great place?" Mary said. "I've got to get to work."

"It's out in Oakland," Layla said. "It used to be a dump or something. A maskmaker told me. There's all kinds of great junk out there. Someone just uncovered it."

"I don't have time to go out to Oakland and back," Mary said.

"You can't miss this," Layla said. "Everyone knows about it now. It'll be all gone soon. Come on. You don't have to go to work today."

"Don't have to . . ." Mary said. "Layla, I've got to eat, I've got to keep my job. . . ." Layla's face went blank, a shuttered house. Mary sighed. Maybe it would be fun to go to the dump. Everyone in Berkeley seemed to have an apartment filled with junk. And she could certainly use something for her bare room. Her heart pounded faster at the thought of what she might uncover. Strange machinery, new artifacts . . . "All right, I'll go."

"I knew you would," Layla said. Mary was glad to see her in such a good mood. "Come on, we've got to go *now*."

The dump was in the center of a vacant lot surrounded by old ruined houses. A family stood in front of a house with boarded windows and peeling paint and stared impassively at the people working their way through the dump. A few chickens scratched at their lawn. The day had turned cold and windy. These people must be really poor, Mary thought. Not poor like me and Layla, but at the bottom. Probably no one in this family had a job, and welfare checks got smaller by the month. What did they think of these lunatics exclaiming over garbage? "Come *on,*" Layla said, taking no notice of the family, pulling on Mary's hand like a child. "Let's go."

Six or seven people were already at the dump, adding things to their little piles on the side. Broken television sets, a car door handle, a jointed piece of metal. Layla picked up an old rake and set it to one side. Her face was smudged where she had rubbed it.

Mary stood on the edge of the dump. Under the watchful eyes of the family she felt a little embarrassed. She wished she could find a phone and at least tell them at work she wouldn't be coming in today. Probably all the phones were out of order. That would make a great excuse, anyway: "Well, I tried to call but I just couldn't get through."

She sighed. The wind caught hold of her coat and played with the bands of metal she had sewn on. How did she let Layla talk her into these things? Layla had collected quite a pile by the side of the dump. Someone yelled, "Hey, look at this!" but her voice was snatched away by the wind and she sounded far away.

Mary's eyes followed Layla as she bent and straightened. What on earth was that? She moved closer. It was a squat statue of a god, a being with an enormous stomach, a small head and many wire-thin arms. Of course, a water meter. From back before they rationed water, when you could have as much water as you wanted. A god of rain.

Layla came over and stood next to her. "Do you want it?"

Mary looked at her. "We could never carry that thing," she said.

"Sure we can," Layla said. "Grab your end."

Mary positioned her fingers under the meter and they struggled to lift it. Layla was surprisingly strong. They set it on the sidewalk and Layla went back to look through the dump. Someone walked by wearing a shoddy jaguar's mask. "The people who were here before us worshiped strange and beautiful gods," he said, nodding at the meter.

Suddenly she felt disoriented, as if several seconds had been sliced out of time. She was a primitive tribeswoman, standing in awe before this twisted piece of metal. It was a spirit, a god, a messenger from across the abyss of the Collapse. The wind whistled around her. What a strange culture they had been.

She looked up. Across the dump, silhouetted against the sky, was a priestess in a coat of feathers and rabbit fur. No. It was Layla, looking closely at the wreckage in the dump. What was happening to her? Was she going to have a seizure? Maybe the pills hadn't worked. She looked around her quickly, feeling the old, nearly forgotten mixture of resignation and terror work through her, wondering if she had time to get to a place where she wouldn't hurt herself. Then the strange feeling passed, and she sank to the ground gratefully.

"Are you okay?" Layla's voice said above her.

"Yeah—I . . ." Mary struggled to stand up. "I just felt real weird for a minute. I'm okay now."

"Yeah?" Layla said. She looked at Mary intently. "Sometimes places from before the Collapse will do that to you. It's happened to me, and other maskmakers say the same thing. What did it feel like?"

"Just strange," Mary said. "I don't remember."

Layla said nothing for a long time. "I was right about you," she said finally. "You'll be a good maskmaker someday. Do you want to go? I think I've got everything I wanted."

"Sure," Mary said slowly. Layla's words had terrified her. Was this like one of Layla's trances? Was this what she would have to go through to be a maskmaker? She hadn't really thought much about the trances, but she certainly hadn't expected them to be so much like the beginning of a seizure.

If being a maskmaker would make her epilepsy worse then she would have to tell Layla she had changed her mind. But seven years of silence stopped her. She couldn't tell Layla. She hadn't even told her doctor what the seizures were like, not even when he had said he couldn't make a diagnosis unless she told him. For the first time she remembered Layla's words in the Blue Market—"Once you set foot on the path you will not be able to leave it"—and she felt that she had blundered into something more serious than she knew.

Layla was picking up things from her pile of machine parts and broken utensils. "How are we going to get all this stuff on the bus?" Mary asked. She still felt a little disoriented.

"Don't worry," Layla said. "We'll manage."

But when the bus finally pulled up the bus driver could barely contain her impatience. "Come on, come on, move it," she said. "Are you going to bring all that junk on board? Oh God, look at this. What on earth are you doing?"

"We found many beautiful pieces of ancient art today," Layla said. "We are privileged to be in your beautiful country."

"Yeah, well just hurry up with those things, will you?" the bus driver said. "I don't believe this. Look at these stupid kids."

Layla carried her rake and half a television set down the aisle. "Help me with this stuff, will you, Mary?" Layla said, coming past her to their pile on the sidewalk. Together they carried the water meter up the steps of the bus. Layla looked serious, impassive, the way she had when she had stolen the sugar or talked back to the cops. "I will treasure this statue always when I return to my country," Mary said, a little loudly, as they passed the driver. For one marvelous moment she was not an American, heir to a worn and crumbling culture, but a dignified visitor, a tourist from someplace else. She had escaped her life, gone elsewhere. Mary was grinning as they sat down, all her questions about being a maskmaker forgotten. Layla looked at her from across the aisle. In a moment they were both laughing wildly.

Mary stayed after work on Friday night and got together a bowlful of salad. Then she stopped at her house for the bag of sugar and went on to Mark's.

She could hear the change before she saw anything. The apartment was silent as Mark opened the door. What had happened? Layla, Don and Ayako waited by the door. Nick stood back a little, away from them. Layla was holding something, something brown. . . . It was a mask of a sea-otter.

"Welcome to the tribes," Mark said. Ayako took everything out of Mary's hands, slipped the mask over her head and held up a small hand mirror. "Look at that," Ayako said. "Perfect."

"Layla does it again," Mark said.

Mary looked out at the mirror, at the broad furry face of the otter. She felt changed, transformed, and at the same time she felt more herself than she ever had. She belonged somewhere now. She was one of them, part of the tribe. "Is that—Is that me?" she asked, delighted.

"If Layla says that's you then it's you," Mark said.

Mary looked at Layla. The eyeholes, she noticed, were larger and better-placed than the ones on her last mask. Was Layla going to say something, give her advice, initiate her further into the art of maskmaking? Layla was smiling her sad thin smile. "Well," Mary said. "Thank you. I don't know what to say."

"You don't have to say anything," Mark said.

"Congratulations," Ayako said.

"Yeah, congratulations," Don said. "Now you look just like everyone else."

"Oh, shut up, Don," Ayako said.

"What do you mean, everyone else?" Mary said, made bolder by the mask. She took it off to confront him, holding it lightly in her hands, like a cat. "How many otter masks have you seen?"

"Well, everyone has some kind of mask, anyway," Don said. "I mean, it's all fashion."

Mary looked over at Layla. Wasn't she going to say anything? Layla was smiling a little, unperturbed. "It's all merch," Don said. "If we'd lived fifteen years ago masks would be advertised on television along with all the other merchandise. How would you have liked that, Layla? Designer masks. Masks by Layla. Keep the economy moving. You'd be famous."

"I'm famous already," Layla said. "You should hear the offers I get."

"Yeah, but are any of them for masks?" Don said, grinning.

"Very funny, Donald," Layla said. She sat on the floor and absentmindedly reached into the salad bowl. That's right, Mary thought, eat. She sat next to her, glad that she was able to bring Layla food.

"It's all a fad, that's all it is," Don said, sitting on the bed as he spoke. "The first fad since the Collapse. Just shows you how much the economy's improved, that's all, that people can spend money on luxury items like masks. And then this fad will run its course, and we'll all be wearing lace curtains or something. Anything so that one person can sell something to someone else."

Mary was running her fingers over her mask. "Ask Mary if she thinks it's a fad," Layla said.

"Sure," Don said, looking at Mary. "Ask a fifteen-year-old. What does she know?"

The mask had given Mary rights as one of them, but as usual around Don she could not think of anything to say. Ayako filled the silence for her. "You're the most unpleasant, cynical person I ever met," she said. "Why do we let you come back week after week?"

"You have nothing to do with it," Don said. "Mark lets me come back because he has a kinder heart than you do." Mark looked away, embarrassed. "And because if he didn't let me in I'd sit on his doorstep and howl." He lifted his dog mask to his face.

Only Layla laughed. "Look at him!" she said. "Just following a fad. Has to have a mask like everyone else."

"Of course I am," Don said, lowering the mask. "But I know I'm following a fad, and the rest of you think you're—you're expressing your inner essences, or something like that."

There was a howl of outrage from nearly everyone. "You know you're a dog, Donald, that's what you know!" Layla said.

"Quiet," Mark said. "Quiet, everyone. Let's not attract any more attention than we have to." He moved toward the kitchen.

"Is it that time already?" Ayako said as Mark came back with the radio. "You must have a kind heart, Mark," she said. "I think that's the first pleasant thing Don ever said about another human being." Mark turned his head away from her and plugged in the radio. Nick opened the door and went outside. Mary moved closer to the curtains.

Mark turned the radio on and twisted the dial back and forth a few times. The door opened suddenly and Nick came in, breathing heavily. "Someone slapped me!" Nick said. His hair had fallen in front of his eyes but he made no move to brush it away. His face was an unnatural red. "Just now. Outside."

Mark turned off the radio. "Quiet," he said. No one moved.

"Let's go home," Nick said. "Give it up and go home." His hands were trembling.

"Wait a minute," Mark said. "Wait. Mary, do you see anyone out there?"

"No."

"All right," Mark said. "Here's what we'll do. We'll turn the radio down real low and sit around it. Mary, you'll have to get away from the window. Come on, guys."

Everyone except Nick went closer to the radio. Nick stood in the middle of the room. Then after a long moment he moved and sat near Mary. His face was pale now, and Mary could see the red lines like tribal paint where someone had hit him.

Mark turned the dial a fraction. There was a loud burst of static, and then, ". . . evening, tribes," the familiar voice said. The voice was low and muffled, as if it came from a room next door.

"The government relocation program is apparently continuing as planned, despite the publicity the program received last year from Lester Martin," the high voice said. "Relocation has started in New York, which the program calls the area with the highest population density problem. The first people to be relocated will do roadwork in the Midwest in an attempt to alleviate the problem of food delivery from other parts of the country. The drought in the Midwest has caused the worst crop failures in fifteen years. Although the people to be relocated are supposed to be chosen by lot, KVRT has learned that nearly all the staff of *Penguins Go to the Sea,* a paper critical of General Gleason, are among the ones selected, including the paper's editor, Sally Tran.

"The Japanese government has decided to send a delegation of computer experts to the United States after all, but the delegates' status will be that of observers rather than teachers. The Japanese government says it is—quote—curious to see what the United States intends to do with the computer technology. Unquote. The delegation arrives next week.

"Rumors that General Gleason is thinking about outlawing masks are apparently true, unfortunately. A piece of so-called legislation to outlaw masks was placed on his desk yesterday. The General said in a television interview yesterday that he thinks masks are—quote—a look backward, not forward, and un-American. We need every available worker if we are going to get the American economy moving again, and these fake tribes are only holding us back. Unquote.

"That's it for Friday," the announcer said, "August sixth, 2021. It's nine-thirty, so if you live far away you should probably leave now or prepare to spend the night. Keep safe, all you tribes, and I hope to talk with you again next Friday."

Mark quickly turned the radio off and took it into the kitchen. Everyone breathed at once, and someone laughed nervously. Mary looked toward the door. She had been expecting a loud knock all through the broadcast, a quick arrest and a trip to the rehab center. And what would her father say then?

"That was creepy," Ayako said.

"Who do you think it was?" Don asked Nick.

"I don't know," Nick said. "It was too dark to tell."

"Tall, short? Big, small?" Don said.

"I don't know, Don," Nick said. He twisted his hands together. "I don't know. I'm going home."

"Don't go by yourself," Mark said, coming back. "It might not be safe."

"Forget it," Nick said. "I just want to get home. I'll be okay." Everyone watched as he opened the door and walked out into the hallway. The darkness came down over him like an eye closing.

"He sure was acting strange, wasn't he?" Don said.

"You'd act strange too if someone had just slapped you in the face," Ayako said.

"I bet it happens to Don all the time," Layla said.

"No, I think you're right," Mary said, and stopped. Don was looking at her as though he were surprised she could talk. She made herself go on. "He was acting strange. Secretive."

"You mean you think he knew why someone slapped him?" Don said. "Maybe he's been cheating on Jayne."

"I don't know," Mary said. "But he was quiet all evening. I remember the other time I came here he was talking all the time. And after he'd been slapped he was so scared he was shaking."

"I wonder if he's got something on his mind," Mark said. "Maybe I'll talk to him next week. I hope he comes back."

"Maybe we should meet somewhere else next week," Ayako said.

"Yeah, and how will we get the radio there?" Don said. "That's a great idea."

"Let's stay here," Mark said. "We'll see. But be careful when you come over. And if anything strange happens during the week I'll let you know."

"I don't think I heard a word he said, I was so nervous," Ayako said. "Did he really say they were going to outlaw masks?"

She was looking at Layla as she spoke, but it was Mark who answered her. "Yeah, they are," he said.

"What are you going to do now, Layla?" Ayako said.

"They didn't say they're outlawing masks," Layla said. "They said they're considering it."

"Don't be so naïve, Layla," Don said. "When the General says he's considering something that means he's going to do it. What do you think—he's going to put it to a vote?"

"Yeah, but he could consider it for days," Layla said. "Weeks. And until he does I can still make masks."

"These things never take long," Don said. "All he has to do is sign something. I bet it's law tomorrow. No—tomorrow's Saturday. Monday, then."

Layla shrugged. "Look, even if they do outlaw them I can still make masks," she said. "I just have to be careful."

"Aren't you worried?" Mary said. "What if you get arrested?"

"Oh, well," Layla said. "I'll be okay."

"You'll be *okay*?" Mary said impatiently. Didn't Layla understand the danger? Mary began to worry for her safety, just as she had worried when it looked as if they were going to be out past curfew, that first night at Mark's, and when Layla had told her about hitching to Mount Diablo. I feel like her mother, Mary thought. How did that happen? She was supposed to teach me things, not make me responsible for her. I don't even know if I can take care of myself. "They could arrest you. Put you in a rehab center."

"Mary's right," Ayako said. "You'd better be careful. Or stop making masks. This is serious, Layla."

"Well, I'm going home," Layla said. She stood, pulled her coat closer and slipped on her mask.

"Maybe you'd better not wear that, Layla," Ayako said.

"Great," Mary said. "The day I get my mask it becomes illegal. Just my luck." She dangled her mask from her wrist and picked up the salad bowl, pleased to see that it was empty.

"Don't worry," Layla said. "There'll be plenty of places you can wear it. See you tomorrow?"

Mary hesitated. Now was not the time to tell Layla her doubts, though, not unless she wanted everyone in the room to know her secret. "Yeah, sure," she said.

"Great," Layla said. "Hey, you forgot to make your cake."

"I guess I had other things on my mind," Mary said. "Keep the sugar, Mark. I'll try again next week."

"Sure," Mark said. He lifted the heron mask from Layla's head, almost tenderly, as though he were about to kiss her. Had they been lovers? Mary was glad to see she didn't feel any jealousy at the thought. "You don't have to wear this tonight, Layla," Mark said, handing her the mask. Layla took it, saying nothing. Mary and Ayako said their good-byes and the three of them headed home.

When they reached Telegraph Ayako broke the silence. "Listen," she said. "I have a television—why don't both of you come over Monday night? We can listen to the news and see if they actually pass that stupid law."

"This goddamned street looks different," Layla said. "I have to see it through a mask or it doesn't make any sense."

Nick lay awake, his eyes open, barely aware of Jayne sleeping soundly beside him. Why had someone slapped him? Did someone know? Had someone overheard his conversation with the woman from the SP branch? He didn't think so, and yet there could be no other answer. Someone had passed judgment on him.

I feel as though I'm wearing a mask, Nick thought. An invisible mask, something that comes between me and everyone I meet like a wall of glass. Only instead of making me feel closer to everyone, making me tribal, this mask cuts me off from them. And I'm doubly cut off, because I won't wear that damned spider mask Layla made me. I wonder if she knew somehow. The animal for me is definitely the spider, weaving a web around all my friends, entrapping them. . . .

The past week had been hellish. He couldn't meet a friend on the street or say hello at the TV station without wondering if this was the person he would betray, would throw to the SP branch to save himself and Jayne. He found himself nodding in the middle of conversations without the slightest idea of what was being said. He had missed his cue twice at the station. And at the Friday night broadcast he had thought for a horrible moment that the announcer was going to read a list of the names of snitches, as he had done twice before. Standing over all his actions, like the billboards the General had put all over Berkeley saying SERVE YOUR COUNTRY, JOIN THE ARMED FORCES, was the question, Who would it be? Would it be the woman in Scheduling who was always so rude to him? Or the cameraman who wanted the producer's job? But he had no right to sentence people, no matter how unpleasant they were. And then he would realize that there were only three days left until Monday, and that the woman would probably let him go for a few weeks, but finally he would have to come up with something, a name, an event. And he would be back where he started.

He hadn't slept well since he'd met the woman. At around twelve or one his thoughts would melt into fantasy and he would have ideas that would seem perfectly reasonable until the stern light of morning. He would get a gun somewhere (where?) and kill her. He would seduce her, win her over to his side and start a movement to overthrow the General. He would find out who her superior was and report her. He would escape with Jayne and they would leave the country, go to Brazil. . . .

At two in the morning he turned over and slept fitfully. In a dream that lasted only a second he was being chased by a huge spider down a long, narrow street.

4

"IT'S EASIER IF YOU LOOK into a candle-flame," Layla said, sitting cross-legged on the floor, "but after a while you can do it by yourself, anytime you want." She scratched a match against the wall and lit the candle she held in her hand. Its light shone palely in the sunny room.

"Now," Layla said. "You look into the light, and you travel to the land of animals, where the animal-spirits live. You might be afraid of some of them at first, especially of the stronger ones, but they will recognize you, and you will ask them—"

"I'm afraid of all of them," Mary said, trying to distract Layla from the lesson. She looked nervously around her at the cluttered room. Layla had spread masks in various stages of construction over the floor as though she had been about to give Mary another lesson in maskmaking and had changed her mind. There were piles of stiff paper, feathers, stones, teeth, jars of paint, a half-finished leather mask—or were you only supposed to wear it over your eyes? She played with the pieces of a broken flower-pot. What if something happened to her during the trance and she couldn't get back? Could she break seven years of silence and tell Layla about her epilepsy? "Why don't you teach me about paints or something. I don't—I just don't think I'm ready for this."

Layla looked at her coolly over the candle-flame. "Of course you're ready," she said. "First we have to think of someone in particular, someone whose animal-spirit we're trying to find. A friend of yours from Stockton, maybe. Or—I know—the General."

"The *General*?" Mary asked, astonished. "Does the General have an animal-spirit?"

"Well, of course," Layla said. "Everyone has an animal-spirit."

"But wouldn't it be—well—too strong? A bear or a wolf or something?"

"Not necessarily," Layla said. Candle-wax was starting to drip onto her fingers, but she didn't seem to notice. "I've been thinking about the General's animal-spirit for a while now. If we knew what it was— well, we'd have more power than we have now, that's for sure. It's probably not even anything very strong. You shouldn't go by outer appearances. But if the idea scares you you go ahead and pick someone else."

"All right," Mary said. "Jackie." She picked up an old heavy art book and quickly flipped through the pages. "Hey, look at this," she said. "It's that animal that's painted on Mark's floor."

"The wounded bison from the Altamira caves," Layla said. "I painted that a long time ago. Look into the flame."

Damn. Mary put the book down and moved closer to Layla. I can control this, she thought. It's not like seizures. Nothing has to happen, and then Layla will give up this stupid idea.

"Don't fight it," Layla's voice said from far away. She heard the clack of Layla's bracelets. "Relax. Look into the flame."

Flame. Flame. Flame. Layla's last word seemed to echo, to call the beat for the flame to dance to. I wonder if this is bad for my eyes, Mary thought. I should stop now, she thought, but she couldn't seem to move her head. Was Layla holding her? Look into the flame. Had someone spoken the words aloud?

She was out of her body, flying. It was fun, not like a seizure at all. Higher and higher, until she left her thoughts behind and felt only the air past her cheeks. She saw the candle-flame again, only now green suffused through the orange, sending out tendrils, growing stronger. The candle-flame became a vast green meadow high up in the mountains. She went toward it, landing effortlessly.

She saw a running stream, tall trees challenging the points of starlight (for somehow the meadow held both day and night), animals as numerous as the stars running, playing, sleeping. She felt light, without form. A sea-otter lay on the shore of the stream, and she moved forward to talk to it.

The darkness behind the trees took on weight and shape. She looked up, startled. The dark animal moved forward, treading on heavy paws. "No!" she said. The animal stopped, the meadow wavered in the flame. "Stop him . . . stop . . . no . . ."

"Who?" Layla said.

Mary looked up at her gratefully. She was back beside Layla, blinking to bring the room into focus. Everything would be all right. She was not going to have a seizure. "A big . . ." She shivered. "A bear, I think. Something big, bigger than . . . than this room."

"A bear," Layla said. It was the first time Mary had seen Layla look impressed. "The bear-spirit almost never shows himself the first time, and only to the great maskmakers. I knew I was right about you. Why don't we take a break now, and try again later?"

"No," Mary said without thinking. Layla looked at her. "Layla, I'm not going to do it. I'm afraid of—of losing control—"

"Mary," Layla said. She was still holding the lit candle; waves of shadow passed back and forth over her face from the flame. She looked wise, wise and incomparably old. "You have to give up control to gain something. Where would you be if you'd stayed in Stockton, lived a safe boring controlled life? How could you learn anything, how can you learn the ways of the animals if you don't give up control to them and let them teach you in their own way? And once you've learned their lessons and come through, then you will be very powerful. Very powerful indeed. You will have control over them. To know the bear-spirit—I know maskmakers who would kill for the chance."

"Not me," Mary said. "Forget it. I don't want to do it. It felt like—like . . ." Like he wanted to eat me, Mary thought. Like the seizures.

"Well sure, it's frightening," Layla said. "It's frightening, but it's wonderful too. When the animal-spirit comes to you it's the best feeling in the world. And the worst." Mary was shaking her head. "Once more," Layla said. "Once more today, and then we'll stop."

"All right," Mary said. Once more, and then Layla would get off her back. This time she would avoid the land of animals entirely. Find something safe to stare at and ignore the candle-flame. Layla would see she was wrong about her, and she wouldn't even have to tell Layla about the epilepsy. She lifted the art book again. An unopened envelope lay beneath it. "Hey, what's this?"

Layla blew out the candle. Mary relaxed. For a moment they were just two friends sitting on a floor and talking. "What's what?"

"This envelope here," Mary said. "From Berkeley Homes. That's my landlord."

"Yeah, mine too."

"Well, why on earth didn't you open it?"

Layla shrugged. "It's gotta be bad news, that's why," she said. "Have you ever gotten good news from your landlord?"

Mary opened the envelope and began to read the letter. "It says here you haven't paid your rent in two months," she said. "One more month and they're going to throw you out."

"Well, that's okay," Layla said. "I'll come up with something."

"Do you need money?" Mary said. "I could . . ." I could what? Give you the money for my pills? What if she says yes? I guess I'll just have to steal some more.

"No, that's all right," Layla said. "Mark gave me some money."

"Well, why didn't you send it in?"

"I was going to," Layla said. She ran her hand through her hair rapidly and her bracelets clanged against each other. "I was going to, but I needed the money. For that blue paint I told you about."

"You spent your rent money . . ." Mary said, astonished. "Not even your own money, but money Mark gave you, and you spent it on paint?" She was glad she was not going to be a maskmaker after all. Maskmakers were crazy.

"Well, yeah," Layla said, unconcerned. "I needed that blue. The guy I met didn't have any more, but a friend of his sold me a tube for only fifty dollars. I guess he didn't travel in time after all." She sounded disappointed.

"Layla, how could you . . ." Mary said. "I mean, where are you going to make your masks once they throw you out? And what do you think Mark will say when he finds out what you did with the money?"

Despite her worry for Layla she felt a little better. Layla might be able to walk in the land of animals without fear, but she still needed someone to remind her to pay the rent.

"He's used to it," Layla said. "Come on, time for the lesson." She lit the candle again.

"Where do you think this guy gets his paint?" Mary said, trying one more time. Fear of the candle-flame made her stomach cramp as though she were having her period. "It's probably stolen. From the government, or something."

"Everything's stolen," Layla said. "Look into the flame."

There was no sensation of flying this time. The huge dark shape came forward almost at once. "Mar-r-ry," the bear said in a low gravelly voice. "Let me eat you, Mar-r-ry. Let me take apart your arms, and your legs, and your head, and let me suck your bones dry. And when you are reborn from the dry bones you will be a great maskmaker, as great as Layla. You will share understanding with all the animals—"

The bear came closer. His huge mouth was open and she saw the rows of his sharp teeth. She could not move. She prayed for a seizure, for unconsciousness.

"Mary," someone's voice was saying. "Mary. Mary."

It was Layla's voice. She closed her eyes, wanting nothing more than to find Layla beside her when she opened them. "Mary, come back," Layla said. Mary opened her eyes. Layla was blowing out the candle-flame. "What went wrong?"

"He wanted to eat me," Mary said. Her voice was hoarse, as if she'd been gone for days. She looked up at Layla accusingly. "You didn't tell me that—that he'd want to eat me. And I couldn't move. I just couldn't. It was like the worst dream I'd ever had. Why didn't you warn me?"

"If I'd warned you you wouldn't have wanted to do it," Layla said.

"You mean—you mean he's supposed to . . ." Mary said. She was starting to cry. "Goddamnit, Layla, you're nuts. I can't believe it. I could have died. You sent me to that place—to the land of animals— and you didn't even bother to tell me—to tell me . . ." Her face twisted with crying. She wiped one cheek but tears ran unnoticed down the other one. "I was never so scared in my life. He wanted to tear me limb from limb. He wanted to—to kill me. I didn't think I was going to come back."

"But you would have been reborn," Layla said. "You would have been reborn as a great maskmaker. You should have let him."

"Did you—did he show himself to you?" Mary asked. She wiped the other cheek.

Almost imperceptibly, Layla nodded. "And you don't know what it's like," she said. "You can't know until you've done it. I told you—it's frightening, but it's also—"

"But I do know," Mary said, thinking of the seizures. "I know what it's like to have something take you—take control of you—until you nearly die. Don't ask me how, but I know. And I'm not doing it ever again. Forget it."

"Next week—" Layla said.

"Didn't you hear me?" Mary said. "I'm not doing it. I'm done. I know you wanted me to be a maskmaker, and I know I asked for lessons, and I'm sorry I took up your valuable time, but that's it. I don't want to be a maskmaker anymore." She looked over at Layla, but Layla's expression hadn't changed. "I'm sorry," Mary said, feeling she had to say something.

"You forgot what I told you," Layla said. "Once you step on the path you can never leave. You are a maskmaker till the end of your life. Even if I don't teach you—even if you're not my apprentice anymore. The world will rearrange itself to teach you the things you have to know. From now on, whatever you do, from the minute you step outside your front door, will teach you how to be a maskmaker."

Mary stood. Whatever the world had in store for her, it would be easier than facing that bear again. And anyway Layla was crazy—you couldn't believe half the things she said. The only thing is, Mary thought, she probably won't want to be my friend again. I've lost a friend, and she's lost—well, someone who would tell her to pay her rent on time. I guess she can handle it. She's survived this long, anyway. "Well, good-bye," Mary said. She wiped her face a final time. "See you—I guess at Mark's."

Layla relit the candle and looked into the flame, saying nothing.

* * *

Nick walked through his apartment without seeing anything, picking objects up and putting them down. A book of Jayne's. A small bonnet Mark had found for the baby. A can of soup Ayako had gotten for them from the supermarket. His meeting with the woman from the police was in another hour and he had no idea what he was going to tell her. Maybe he could turn in Ayako for stealing soup.

"Nick?" Jayne said, looking up from her book. "Is something wrong?"

Nick stopped pacing and looked at her. She was reading another one of those trashy historical romance novels, about the only kind of book passed by the censor. The dark mysterious Vietnam vet comes into the heroine's life and sweeps her off her feet, but he has a tragic secret. . . . Nick tried not to feel irritated with her. It wasn't her fault there were no other books available, not her fault that the woman from the SP branch had asked him to become a snitch. But still, if he hadn't married her, if she hadn't gotten pregnant, he could have told the woman to go to hell. Alone, he could have faced the loss of his job, gone underground. . . .

"Nick?" Jayne said again.

"Yeah," Nick said. "It's nothing. Don't worry about it." That's how the government gets you, he thought. They drive a wedge between husband and wife, father and son, brother and sister. Everyone spies on everyone else. Hell, for all I know they got to Jayne, and she's spying on me.

"Because you seem sort of nervous," Jayne said. "I was wondering if anything happened."

The problem with this apartment, Nick thought, is that it's too small. It's too small, and Jayne keeps it far too neat. When I was single I was a real slob. Now there's nothing around to take my mind off things. Maybe I should collect scrap metal, like those loonies at Mark's. Don had had an entire car in his house before his money ran out and he had to live with Mark. Most of the parts were gone, of course; still, his house had always smelled of gasoline. He'd left the car there when he moved. But Jayne had asked him something. He wished he could remember what it was. "I'm fine," he said, wondering if that answered her question. "I'm under a lot of pressure at work, that's all. I should probably get going."

She stood up and he kissed her. Her belly was getting almost too big for him to reach her. She laughed a little, as though she were thinking the same thing. "Good-bye," he said quickly, before she could remember that he only started work at three. "I'll see you tonight."

Outside the sun was shining but he barely felt it. The woman was already waiting for him inside the cafe, a drink set before her. He felt a strong tide of irritation rise within him. She was so goddamn smug. She just knew he'd be there. What if he were to walk on, miss the meeting? He brushed his hair out of his eyes. If he missed the meeting he would probably be out of a job by three. "We're so sorry, Nick," his boss would say, and for a moment the picture of his boss meeting him in front of the studio, putting one hand on his shoulder, was more vivid than the cafe. He shrugged and went in.

"Well hello, Nick," the woman said, calling to him. She sounded genuinely pleased to see him. He decided not to bother with the charade of getting a drink and went over to her table and sat down. "How've you been?"

Nick laughed hollowly, as though he had been condemned to die and she had asked him that question. "Not very good," he said. "I'm not—I'm not sleeping too well. And I have bad dreams."

"That's too bad," the woman said. "You can get sleeping pills, though, can't you? Do you have a doctor?"

Nick shrugged. "Jayne does," he said.

"And how is Jayne?" the woman asked. "She's due any day now, isn't she?"

"Next month," Nick said. At the mention of his wife Nick saw her as she was a few minutes ago, standing awkwardly to kiss him, and felt a tenderness and nostalgia so strong he could scarcely bear it. He seemed to love her most when he was away from her. He remembered proposing to her at the bus station, wondering what the hell he was doing, after she had come back from visiting her parents in Los Angeles. The tenderness disappeared and was replaced by hatred. Who was this woman who threatened their innocent happiness?

"What about the Japanese delegation?" the woman said. "Isn't it wonderful?"

"What?" Nick said, struggling to come out from behind his mask.

His whole life seemed to be lived inside his head these days. "What about it?"

"Well, we'll be getting computer technology again," the woman said. "We'll be able to do so much more."

Like keep better tabs on snitches and people who break the law, Nick thought. He hoped the Japanese delegation would go home. "I thought they were just here to observe," Nick said.

"Oh, they'll give us the technology," the woman said. "Why shouldn't they?"

I could give you a few reasons, Nick thought. Suddenly he wearied of the woman's small talk. There was no reason to pretend they were friends. "Listen," he said. She had started to say something and now closed her mouth. "Let's get this over with, okay? I don't have anything for you. I didn't hear anything all week. And I just don't—I mean, I'm not the kind of person who hears these things. Subversive things." His voice had gotten lower and lower, and by the time he got to the word "subversive" he was almost whispering. "I mean, we could meet here week after week and talk about how badly I'm sleeping, but I'm sure you have more important things to do. I'd find someone else if I were you. Really. I just don't think this is going to work out."

She was smiling when he finished. What would it take for her to stop smiling? Nick thought. I guess the General would have to die. "You underestimate yourself, Nick," she said. "We picked you for very specific reasons. For one thing, you work in television, and television reaches millions of people. Do you know how easy it would be for someone to get on the air and say something against the General? Of course he'd be arrested, sent to rehabilitation, but the damage would already have been done. And it could be a coded message, something subliminal, and it would slip right by us. So you see, we have to be very careful. That's why we need people like you." She took a sip of her orange juice. "And don't worry that you don't have anything to tell us today," she said. "These things take a while, a few weeks, a month. I'm sure you'll come up with something."

Nick said nothing. Was she telling him—warning him—that he only had a month in which to find something? He remembered the slap at

Mark's house Friday night and rubbed his cheek as though he still felt it. He didn't think he could last another month.

"Well," the woman said. "I've got to get going." She stood. "It's been nice talking to you. I'll see you next week."

Nick nodded. In one of his midnight fantasies he had followed her, seen where she went and who she talked to. Maybe she wasn't from the government after all. She had never given him any identification. Maybe she was from an underground group checking on his loyalty before she asked him to join them.

He sighed. Right now it seemed too much trouble to go out into the hot still air and follow her. And it was obvious from what she said she believed in the government. He couldn't understand that. If, like him, she had been blackmailed into becoming an informer he would have trusted her more. They could have had long talks heavy with irony about General Gleason and his network of snitches, and he might have even given her some information. At least he would have known he wasn't alone. But she actually thought the General was doing a wonderful job, actually approved of the informers and the curfew and censorship. . . . He shook his head. He couldn't understand it, not at all.

Monday night Mary and Ayako sat on Ayako's couch, eating from the bowl of salad between them and watching television. Ayako wore a long flannel shirt and torn pants. Somehow she still managed to look like the almost-forgotten models of Mary's childhood. "Is Layla coming?" Mary asked.

Ayako shrugged and reached for another piece of lettuce. "Layla shows up when she feels like it," she said. "I never expect her anywhere. Hey, I hear she's made you her apprentice. Congratulations."

"I was," Mary said. "Not anymore."

"Why not?"

Mary looked around the room before answering. Everything was so neat compared to Mark's or Layla's place. A small clean brown rug, a small gray couch, a television set and a hot plate opposite the couch. . . . There were the usual bits of machinery from before the Collapse, but they were displayed tastefully on shelves and along the walls as though they were museum pieces. A line of men from the General's armed forces marched across the small black-and-white TV screen. How could she explain her fear of the land of animals to Ayako? You'd have to be another maskmaker to understand.

"I don't know," Mary said. "It was really boring at first, for one thing. Get this. Carry that. I never lifted a paintbrush the whole time."

"Well, you know," Ayako said. "Layla went through the same thing."

"She *did*?" Mary said, surprised. Somehow she had thought Layla was born knowing everything about making masks. "How do you know?"

"I was supposed to meet her one time on the old Berkeley campus," Ayako said. "I couldn't find her, so I started looking around. You know that little graveyard they have in the garden?" Mary shook her head. "Well, anyway, I saw her there putting flowers on someone's grave. No, not flowers—I think it might have been feathers or something. So I asked her who it was, and she got a little embarrassed—if you can imagine Layla embarrassed—and she said that he had been her teacher."

"Really?" Mary said. "A crazy?" She had been warned away from the campus her first day at work. The crazies lived there, sleeping in empty swimming pools, the overgrown Botanical Gardens or the aisles of vacant classrooms. Even the policemen didn't like to go there.

"Well, all maskmakers are crazy, one way or another," Ayako said.

"I'm not," Mary said. "See, that's why I didn't want to be a maskmaker. I guess Layla thought I was something I wasn't." Or maybe Layla was right, Mary thought. Maybe Layla knew about the epilepsy, and picked me for that reason. She had hoped she would see Layla at Ayako's so that they could talk, but now she found herself wishing Layla wouldn't come. "What did he die of?" Mary asked.

"Layla's teacher?" Ayako said. Mary nodded. "I don't know. Layla didn't tell me any more about him."

The face of General Gleason appeared on the screen. He looked tanned and fit, his iron-gray hair cut close to his scalp. "Production for the month of July rose point six percent," he was saying in answer to a question. "Food production rose a whole two percent, and the famine in the Midwest is nearly under control. It's only a matter of time before the American economy is back to where it was before the Collapse, and America can take her place among the great nations of the world once again. And when that happens I can assure you that we will have free elections as soon as it can be managed."

"We'll have free elections when you're dead, you bastard," Ayako said, taking her shoes off and tucking her feet beneath her. "God, I'm tired. I was on my feet all day."

The picture changed to an anchorman sitting at a desk. "General Gleason today greeted the members of the Japanese computer delegation to the United States," the anchorman said. A picture of the General shaking hands with Japanese men in business suits appeared on the screen. "Tomorrow the delegation will visit several government offices in Washington."

"You can bet they won't visit a police station," Ayako said. "And that's the first place those computers will go if Generally Gleeful gets his hands on them. How could they not know that?"

"They said they were just observing," Mary said, trying to remember the radio broadcast at Mark's. "Didn't they?"

"They're observing what the General wants them to observe," Ayako said. "They'll never see anything real. Go home!" she said to the delegation on the screen. "Don't let him con you. Go home while you can!"

The picture changed again. The delegation sat down to eat with American government officials. "God, look at those kimonos," Ayako said as the camera focused on the wives of the members of the delegation. "Silk, I bet. And hand-painted. I want one. God, it makes me crazy just to look at them."

"Your parents never should have left Japan," Mary said.

"Actually my parents came from San Francisco," Ayako said. "My great-grandparents were from Japan."

"Oh," Mary said, feeling foolish. "I thought—because of your name—"

"I think my parents were hoping I'd make it back," Ayako said. "A lot of their friends were doing that, giving their kids Japanese names. They could see the Collapse coming, I guess. But look." She nodded at the screen. The Japanese wives were sitting down at a different table from the businessmen, talking softly. "I don't think I'd like the way women are treated in Japan. It was getting better for a while, and then everyone became traditional, old-fashioned.''

"Wore kimonos," Mary said.

"Yeah, well," Ayako said. "I wish I could see what colors they were."

The anchorman was back on the screen. "And in local news, San Francisco's police chief John Clawfy discussed the effects of the law banning masks today."

Ayako leaned forward. Mary put a piece of lettuce back in the salad bowl and sat up straighter. A balding man appeared on the screen briefly and then the screen jumped and went black. The black was replaced by a white-on-black sign saying "TECHNICAL DIFFICUL-TIES." The man's voice could still be heard.

"It'll be like the curfew laws," John Clawfy was saying. "You can have up to two violations before you're sent to a rehab center. We want to give people some time to get used to this law—we don't want to start arresting people left and right. But we're not going to be lenient either. If the General says masks are outlawed that's good enough for me. I don't want to see anyone on the street wearing a mask from now on."

"What about the maskmakers?" a reporter asked.

"Well, we'll be keeping an eye on some of the more prominent maskmakers," Clawfy said. "Willie, and Bone Jackson, and Layla MacKenzie. But we won't be taking any action just yet."

"Oh, no," Mary said quietly. Her voice sounded like a whimper. Her face felt cold, as though all the blood had been drained out of it.

"What's wrong?" Ayako said.

"Didn't you hear?" Mary said. "They're going to arrest the maskmakers. Arrest Layla."

"All they said was that they were going to keep an eye on her," Ayako said calmly. "They're not arresting anyone."

"You don't understand," Mary said. "You don't understand about Layla. She doesn't know what a law is. I bet she's still making masks. I've got to warn her."

"She's okay, will you stop worrying about her?" Ayako said. "I've known her longer than you have. She can take care of herself."

"No she can't!" Mary said. She stood. The bowl of salad tumbled off the couch. "She can't take care of herself. She can't even pay her fucking rent!"

"If you go now you'll just get a curfew violation," Ayako said. "That's certainly not going to do Layla any good."

Numbly, Mary righted the salad bowl and picked up the pieces of lettuce. The dressing had left a stain on Ayako's rug. "You don't understand," she said again. She felt defeated. If Layla made a mask while she was under surveillance she would be arrested, and there was nothing Mary could do about it. Ayako was wrong. Layla was bright and fragile, different from everyone else. And Mary had to protect her. Even if Mary wasn't going to be her apprentice a bond had been created between them, and with the bond went responsibilities.

The high whine of the curfew sirens sounded. "And how am I supposed to get home?" Mary said. "Goddamnit, I can't even get home!" The television screen went dark, and a moment later all the lights went out.

Ayako lit a candle and placed it on the floor between them. "Well, I thought you'd stay here," she said. "Didn't I say?"

"No," Mary said. "No, you didn't. I wish you had." Her house was only a few blocks away; she could run home and take her pills, three pills every night . . . and get a curfew violation, just like Ayako said. No, she'd better stay. She had gone without her pills once or twice before and nothing had happened. "What if she tries to come over to my place?"

"She's not—" Ayako said. She saw Mary's face and stopped. "I don't know. There's nothing you can do. Except not worry."

"Not worry," Mary said. She felt trapped. She wanted action, a fast walk to Layla's house and then a quick trip to hide the masks somewhere. More than anything she wanted an end to the uncertainty of not knowing where Layla was. Ayako got sheets from a small closet and started putting them on the couch. Mary looked at her dully. Somehow she was going to have to try to sleep.

Curfew ended at seven in the morning. By six Mary was fully dressed and pacing between the couch where Ayako slept and the window. Each of them had insisted that the other take the couch, and finally Mary had said she had slept on the floor so long she could never be comfortable on anything else. But she had spent a frustrating night, waking every few hours to stare into the unfamiliar darkness and feel the long night pass her like an impossibly endless train.

At a few minutes before seven she put her hand on the doorknob, hesitated a moment and then went outside. Ayako stirred a little on the couch. There were no sirens to announce the end of curfew. If the cops stopped her she could tell them she had spent the night at a friend's whose clock must be fast.

It was strange to be out before seven, though, even for a few minutes. Government employees on important business stayed out past curfew—Mark, on the road crew, had probably done it a few times—and sometimes late at night she heard the rumble and hiss of brakes of trucks on the paved roads, but it felt as though she were the only one outside, as though the morning had been made for her. If she hadn't been so tired, if the morning hadn't seemed so jagged and unreal, she might have enjoyed it. The traffic lights had not yet come on. The streets were deserted, and birds sang above her.

Then of course she had to wait for the bus, which did not come until after curfew. She had forgotten that. Impatiently she started to walk down Telegraph, trying not to think of what might have happened to Layla. Why hadn't she come to Ayako's last night? It was all very well to say that Layla showed up when she felt like it, but what if something had happened to her? Something bad? She wished she could wake up. She had never been on Telegraph this early in the morning; it might almost have been another country. The bus passed her when she was halfway to Layla's.

When she saw Layla's street her heart stopped a moment and then pounded heavily, sluggishly, as though it filled her entire body. There was no answer to her knock at Layla's apartment. She knocked again. The doorknob turned when she tried it. Was that a good sign or not? She couldn't remember if Layla kept her door locked. Open the door, stupid, she told herself. The knob slipped beneath her sweat. She opened the door.

Once inside Layla's apartment she had to fight an urge to turn and run. Pigment jars lay broken in shards across the floor, leaving bright spatters of red, yellow, brown. The sheets had been pulled from the bed and the mattress slashed. A half-finished mask had been trampled.

Torn rag paper covered everything. There was no sign of the tube of blue paint Layla had spent last month's rent money on.

"Layla?" Mary said softly, almost hoping she wouldn't answer. If she answered it would mean she was hurt. "Layla?" she said, louder.

She walked through the small room, lifting sheets, old clothing, rag paper. There was no one home. Now she was hoping that the red paint she saw out of the corner of her eye was blood, because Layla hurt was better than not finding Layla at all. "Layla!" she said, knowing it was useless.

Now what? she thought. Now you were supposed to somehow get on with your life and try not to think too much about what had happened to her. People disappeared all the time. Just last week Lesley had come to work crying because she had gone to visit her brother and found a strange family living in his apartment instead. They insisted they didn't know where her brother had gone.

It's not even that much of a surprise, Mary thought. You knew this would happen eventually. She made a last halfhearted attempt to find the tube of blue paint and then closed the door behind her and walked to the bus stop.

The first thing she saw when she opened the door to her room was the water meter she and Layla had set up with so much trouble. She quickly swallowed three pills dry and paced around her room, holding her arms tight against her. She felt cold and the room was much too small. Shopping, she thought. I need food, and shopping is mindless enough. She picked up her ration booklet and walked the seven blocks to the supermarket.

It was only in the supermarket, staring at the half-empty shelves and thinking of the time Layla had stolen the sugar, that Mary began to cry. The colors of cans and bottles ran together like streaks of paint. Several people watched her sympathetically, but no one wanted to approach her in case she was in trouble with the government. She wiped her eyes. Without thinking she picked up a can of peaches and a bar of soap and went up to the check-out counter, avoiding the sugar. She was still crying quietly when she stepped outside.

When she turned up Carleton Street she saw that someone had left a large brown bag in front of her house. Now what could that be? she thought, puzzled, coming closer. The bag unfolded and stood up. It was Layla. Mary dropped the bag of groceries and ran to her, and they embraced on the porch of Mary's house, holding each other tightly, rocking back and forth. "What happened?" Mary said, wild with relief. "Didn't I tell you . . . ? Where have you *been*?"

Layla stepped back and grinned. She looked as tired as Mary. Her hair hadn't been combed in several days. "I got home late last night," she said. She followed Mary back to the dropped bag of groceries. The can of peaches had broken and was leaking through the bag but Mary didn't care. "I'd been out with a maskmaker, talking, you know. The maskmaker told me to be careful, that there were rumors about arrests." They walked back to Mary's house and Mary let them in. "So I went home, and I looked around carefully, very carefully . . . ," Layla said as they went to Mary's room. "I don't know. I guess I was a little drunk. I damn near ran into this fat cop standing across the street from my house. I said excuse me. He said did I know Layla MacKenzie. I said, no, never heard of her, all the time trying to hide my mask behind my back. Okay, he says. Then he sees the mask. I started to run, and he ran after me, but I lost him. Well, it wasn't hard."

Layla sat on the floor and ran her hand through her hair. "But I didn't have anywhere to go," she said. "It was near curfew, and I couldn't get to your house. I ended up at the old subway station, and I started to go down the steps—"

"Oh, Layla," Mary said, standing in the middle of the room, trapped by Layla's story. "No."

"But then I heard a voice," Layla said. "It was your voice, actually. The voice said, 'Don't go down there, Layla.'" Mary nearly smiled. "'There are weird guys down there. Murderers, and sexual perverts, and God knows what. I can't be responsible if you go down there.'"

They were both laughing now. "So what did you do?" Mary said.

"I went back to this woman I'd baby-sat for once or twice," Layla said. "I knew she was a canner—she'd spent an hour once telling me how much she hates the government and how bad they treat single parents. I told her my problem and she said, of course I could stay the night." Layla grinned. "Her kids love me. I tell them stories. And here I am. I told you I can take care of myself."

Mary said nothing. "Listen," Layla said. "Do you have to go to work today? I thought I'd stay here for a while, till tonight. It'll probably be safe to go home then.''

Mary sat next to her on the floor. Why does she always make me feel responsible for her? she thought. Goddamnit, she's older than I am. "You can't go back there," Mary said. "They're probably still looking for you. And I went there—I was by your apartment this morning. They've broken all the bottles of pigment, and taken the blue paint, and torn the paper—" Layla looked away from her, staring at something across the room. "Layla?" Mary said.

"Where will I go?" Layla said, still not looking at her. "What'll I do?"

"I don't know," Mary said. She hadn't thought past finding her. She sighed. If I'm responsible for her I'd better start now, she thought. God knows she can't do it. "Well, you can—you can stay here."

Layla broke her stare. "I can't stay here," she said slowly. "You'd hate it. Look how small this place is. I'd—I'd burn it down in one of my trances, or spread paint and paper over everything. I'd drive you crazy."

"No you wouldn't," Mary said quickly. She had an uneasy feeling Layla was right. "We'll work things out."

"Look—why don't I stay with Ayako?" Layla said. "Her place is bigger."

"Because Ayako really would hate it," Mary said. "She'd say it was okay, but she wouldn't last a day with you. I was over at her place yesterday, watching television. I've never seen anyone so neat."

"Well, this place is neat," Layla said.

"Only because I don't have anything," Mary said. "It's hard to make a mess with a few blankets and a water meter."

"Well, what about Mark?" Layla said. "I can stay with him."

"Sure, with him and Don," Mary said. She was starting to believe her arguments now. And it would be a good thing to have Layla with her, especially if she was wanted by the police. Maybe she could teach her some responsibility. "You're staying here, Layla. That's it."

"Okay," Layla said. She was almost smiling, her sad, distracted smile. "Thank you. But I'll pay some of the rent, at least. And food."

"With what?" Mary said, exasperated. She hadn't even thought of rent. "Some of Dana Cooper's money?"

"I've got some people interested in masks," Layla said. "When they pay me—"

"You're going to make masks?" Mary said, incredulous. "You can't make masks anymore. It's against the law."

"Well, that's what the black market is for," Layla said reasonably, as though explaining something obvious to a child. "I have connections up there, and they'll sell the masks for me. Of course it'll mean less money—"

"Wait a minute," Mary said. "You're going to sell your masks to the black market?"

Layla nodded.

"I don't believe this," Mary said. "You're wanted by the police, do you know that? I bet they were lying when they said they just wanted to keep an eye on the maskmakers. I bet they wanted to make an example of you. And after last night they know what you look like. Look, even I know it's dangerous to sell anything up in the hills. And if they arrest you they'll probably arrest me too. I'd be—what do they call it?—an accessory. You'd be putting me in danger, do you understand that?"

"Don't worry," Layla said. "I'll be careful."

"Like you were careful last night?" Mary said. "If you lived here and made masks I'd be terrified. I can't let you do it. I'm sorry."

"Then I'll live somewhere else," Layla said. "You can't afford to support me, anyway."

Mary sighed. "We've just been through that," she said. "You can't live anywhere else."

"On campus—" Layla said.

"All right," Mary said. "Sell the masks. But be careful. Please."

"Look," Layla said. "I'll stay inside most of the time. And I'll only go out when it's necessary, and I'll never bring anyone here, and I won't even go up in the hills to sell the masks. I'll meet them somewhere in the flatlands."

"I said okay," Mary said. "I give up."

"And you know what?" Layla said. She looked happier, more alert, but there was something else at the edges of her expression, almost a slyness. "Remember what I said, that the world will rearrange itself to teach you how to become a maskmaker? Well, look what happened.

Now you've got your very own teacher living with you." Mary was shaking her head, but Layla held up her hand to stop her. "If you want to learn. Only if you want to."

Mary said nothing. If Layla was right then the law against masks, and Layla's near-arrest, and the destruction of Layla's apartment had all happened so that Mary could learn to become a maskmaker. "That's ridiculous," she said finally. Something had happened to her in the last ten minutes; she had become older, more certain of herself. It was her turn to teach Layla a few things. "I've never heard anything so stupid in my life."

Layla was looking through the closet when Mary came home from work that evening. "I like this," Layla said, holding the green blouse against her. "Where did you get it?"

"Stockton," Mary said. She sat heavily on the floor and took off her shoes. "I'll probably never wear it again. People out here don't wear things like that, do they?"

"I'll wear it," Layla said, unbuttoning her blouse.

"What did you do today?" Mary said, leaning against the wall. Her worst fear had been that she wouldn't find Layla there when she got home.

"Well, the first thing was that someone knocked on the door," Layla said, putting on the green blouse.

"And you opened it?" Mary said, sitting up.

"This looks good on me, don't you think?" Layla said. "Do you have a mirror?"

"Layla," Mary said, trying to sound stern. "Did you open the door?"

"Well, yeah," Layla said. "It was one of your roommates. She said her name was Miss Benson. She never told me her first name, even though I bet she's only my age. I almost told her my name was Miss MacKenzie."

"What did she want?" Mary said. She was dying to ask Layla how old she was, but she didn't want to be sidetracked. Miss Benson must be at least thirty.

"Well, I guess the water went off in the middle of her shower," Layla said.

"Oh, my God," Mary said. "The Water Board."

"Yeah, that's what she said," Layla said. "She said she didn't mind me living here, but that I'd have to register with the Water Board. And then she spent about an hour telling me how long the government takes to do anything, and how I should register *right* away, *and* the Garbage Board . . ."

Mary tried not to laugh. Layla's imitation of Miss Benson was perfect. "But you shouldn't talk to people about the government," Mary said. "I mean, they might be snitches."

"Miss Benson?" Layla said in disbelief.

"Well, yeah, I know it's not likely," Mary said. "But you've got to be careful. You never know. And you shouldn't open the door to just anybody. You're wanted by the police, remember?"

"So, are you coming tonight?" Layla asked.

"What's tonight?" Mary said. She wondered if there might be something wrong with Layla. She had never met a person so unwilling to argue. "Anyway, listen. We can't register you with the Water Board, so we're just going to have to be careful. We'll take turns with the showers. And we'll have to be careful with the garbage too."

"Yeah, sure," Layla said. "Tonight's the tribal dance. Do you want to go?"

"I don't know," Mary said. "What is it? It sounds dangerous to me. I mean, couldn't they just arrest everybody there?"

"Nah," Layla said. "The cops are paid off. It's perfectly safe."

"Are you sure?" Mary said. "They won't be after me, but if you're arrested you'd be in lots of trouble. How do you know it's safe?"

"I know these things," Layla said. Her sly look was back. "I have contacts. Stop being so cautious. You know you want to go."

Mary realized she was nodding. It sounded exactly like what she had come to Berkeley for, a room filled with people in masks, a splendor of bright jungle colors. . . . Her pulse quickened. She would never forgive herself if she missed it. "Yeah, all right," Mary said. "But if you get arrested I don't know who you are."

"Great," Layla said. "Can I wear your blouse?"

In past years, Layla explained on the bus ride over, the tribal meetings had been held at the winter solstice and the vernal equinox. But then the cops had started to show up, not arresting anyone but watching silently, leaning against the walls. Now the dates were chosen randomly, and the places changed from year to year. This time the meeting was in an abandoned warehouse by the bay.

Mary could hear drums as the bus driver let them off a block away. Her walk adjusted to the beat of the drums, and by the time she and Layla reached the warehouse they were already dancing. They took their masks out of the bag Layla held. Someone in a badger's mask by the door looked closely at their faces and motioned them through. Mary put her mask on and went inside. It was the first time she'd worn her mask since the day she got it, and she felt a strange excitement as she looked at the warehouse through the eye-holes. She was no longer Mary Owens from Stockton, but someone else. She was changed.

The warehouse was lit by dozens of oil lamps, candles and flashlights. A keg of beer and a pile of dirty cups stood by the door. Old cassette tapes looped from the walls and ceiling. The room was crowded: The new law hadn't scared many people away. Everyone wore a mask, and nearly everyone was dancing. In dark corners people with similar masks were meeting and talking—lions, mostly, and bears, and some dogs. Mary looked for another otter but didn't see any. That's the trouble with having a mask made by Layla, she thought. You're practically unique.

At the front of the room two seated men were drumming. As Mary watched, a lion with long tangled hair approached the drummers; one of them nodded and stood, swaying, and the lion sat at the drum, pulling it toward him and holding it between his legs. He ran his knuckles over the taut skin and began to play.

Then the rhythm became too powerful to watch anymore. Mary started to dance, with leopards and cockatoos, with owls and coyotes.

At ten the curfew sirens sounded, dim and unreal under the drums. Mary surfaced briefly to look around. Sweat pooled on her face, under her arms and between her shoulder blades. She felt the weight of her heavy coat and wondered if she could take it off, but she thought someone would probably steal it. About half the dancers had gone home before curfew.

She turned back to the dance. The rhythm was slower now, like swimming. Suddenly she felt strange, disoriented, as though the world had lost ten thousand years in the time it took her to blink her eyes. She fought it, concentrating on the dance, the masks turning around her like the colored patterns of a kaleidoscope, the rich web of the drumming. The feeling went away. You see, she wanted to tell Layla. I'm not a maskmaker. I'm not. She couldn't see Layla anywhere.

An hour or a few minutes later she saw Layla talking to a group of people in fiercely colored jungle masks. The heron mask looked small and fragile among them. Layla's coat was tightly fastened, and she wondered why Layla had bothered to wear the green blouse. No one could see it anyway. There was a circle of quiet around the group, and every so often a mask would turn in their direction. Maskmakers, Mary thought, awed in spite of herself. I guess I'll never meet them now.

The tempo changed again. Only one of the drums was being played now; the other drummer sat on the floor beside his drum, head between his knees. Something was flickering against the wall opposite her, a black-and-white film that had probably been censored after the Collapse. Then she was aware of the thumping of the generator powering the projector, a sound that she realized now had run through the pounding of the drums for the past few minutes.

She wondered what time it was. The door opened on nothing but blackness. It was the marrow of the night, cold, dark, still. She limped over to the wall and leaned against it. One of the bands on her coat pressed into her thigh, but she was too tired to move. The next minute she was asleep.

Layla said good-bye to the other maskmakers and turned back to the dance. "Layla?" someone said.

She looked around, hoping it wasn't someone who wanted to talk about maskmaking. Usually she could talk for hours, but this late in the night she felt tired. Nearly everyone had left the dance floor and was sitting or sleeping against the walls. Most of the candles had burned down and a few of the flashlights had died. The other drum had stopped.

"Layla?" the voice said again, a high male voice. He was wearing a black bear's mask. The ones who wear bear masks are the most pretentious of all, Layla had once said, but on this one it looked right, proper. He truly did belong to the bear tribe.

"Can I talk to you a minute?" he said. He moved closer to her and she saw that there was something wrong with one of his legs; it had been broken and set badly by a street doctor, probably.

"Sure," she said. She was curious to see who it was who had so much power. His voice sounded a little familiar. She looked around for Mary and saw her sleeping against one of the walls. A new feeling, a tenderness, welled through her. That street doctor who had told her she would never have children had been wrong. She and the man from the bear tribe walked slowly toward the wall near Mary and sat down. The generator was quieter here.

"I guess first of all I should tell you who I am," the man said, speaking softly. "I'm—"

"You're the man on the radio broadcasts," Layla said. "I recognized your voice."

The bear mask nodded toward her. "It's lucky the police aren't as observant as you are," he said. "I've been stopped a few times, but no one's ever suspected. One of these days, though—"

"Just keep up the good work," Layla said. "We listen to you all the time, every Friday night. If it wasn't for you some people would have given up hope a long time ago."

"Well, thanks," he said. "That's the trouble with radio—you never get any feedback. Thanks a lot. My name's Brian, by the way."

"I mean it," Layla said.

"Well, anyway," Brian said. He stretched his legs out in front of him slowly. "What I wanted to say—well, I collect masks. I've got a few of yours, a few by other people. The person who sold me this mask said it was by Willie."

"It is," Layla said. "Where did you get it, the black market?"

Brian nodded. A dog holding the broken bones of an umbrella over his head danced slowly in circles in front of him.

"It suits you," Layla said.

"Thanks," Brian said, lowering his head. Layla thought he was blushing under the mask. "Anyway, I showed yours to—well, I work for the Brazilian government. Or I'm funded by them, and they give me equipment and stuff. If it wasn't for them I never could have started the broadcasts, let alone do it every week. So I showed my contacts some of your masks, and they went crazy. They're big on masks in Brazil, you know. Carnaval, and all that. And they loved your stuff—"

"Sure, I'll make them masks," Layla said. "But I'd have to meet them first."

"Well, it's not just that," Brian said. "I could get you a passport. Immigration papers."

"A—passport?" Layla said slowly, savoring the idea of travel. The world open to her, continents spread like dragon's wings. To actually see the cave-paintings done thousands of years ago, in secret places beneath the bones of the earth like a beating heart. And maybe there were still tribes in Africa, though nobody seemed to know. And tribes in Brazil—there would have to be, if Brian's friends were so interested in masks.

But she couldn't come back. She looked up at Brian and said, "No."

"No?" Brian said, startled. He had obviously been expecting another answer. "But why? Why not? You could work in freedom in Brazil. Your work wouldn't be outlawed. Wouldn't you want—"

"But see, I couldn't come back. If I tried I'd be arrested. Wouldn't I?"

"Well, yeah," Brian said. "But why would you want to?"

"This is my home," Layla said slowly. "The tribes need masks and I make them masks. I wouldn't have that in Brazil. Here I'm not just an artist, I'm—well, I can't explain it."

"A priestess," Brian said.

"No. Well, a little. Not exactly."

"All right, we can't compete with that," Brian said. "But you'd have all kinds of things in Brazil you wouldn't have here. They can arrange things for you. Grants. Gallery showings."

"Galleries?" Layla said. "But the masks aren't meant to be hung in a gallery. People have to wear them."

"That was just an example," Brian said. "You don't have to have a showing. You can do whatever you want, really. Look at Akram Hassan. Well, you've heard my broadcast on him. All I'm saying is that if you go to Brazil you'll be appreciated there."

"I'm appreciated here," Layla said.

"Well, yeah, but not by the government."

"Who cares what the government wants?"

"All right," Brian said. She thought she heard him sigh behind the mask. "So I guess I should tell them you've turned down the offer."

"Yeah," Layla said. "I mean, thanks. I'm flattered. But I just don't think I'd do my best work there."

"Well, it was nice talking to you," Brian said. He got to his feet slowly. "At least I'll get to tell people I talked to Layla. Listen. Here's my address." He lived a few blocks from Mary. Layla wondered if she had run into him at the Blue Market without knowing it. "Stop by if you change your mind. Or leave me a note. Okay?"

"Sure," Layla said. She stood and pulled her coat around her. "But I don't think I will."

"I'll see you around," Brian said.

"So long," Layla said. She watched as he limped away into the thinning crowd, and then looked around for Mary. As she turned she saw, or thought she saw, a man in a spider's mask looking at her avidly and then looking away.

5

NICK HADN'T WANTED TO
go to the Friday night meeting at all. It wasn't just that someone who
lived near Mark knew who he was, someone who had slapped him last
week but who might—who knows?—do something much worse this
week. Not all the guns had been turned in to the General when he'd
done house-to-house searches nine years ago. It was mostly the
growing estrangement he felt from the rest of the group, a thickening
of his invisible mask. They wouldn't laugh and joke with him if they
knew who he really was, if they could see the mask he really wore.

But over a dinner he barely tasted Jayne asked him if he was going
to go to the meeting. It would look suspicious if he didn't go. "Sure,"
he said. He stood and kissed her and left for Mark's.

It was late when he got there but he saw only Don and Ayako in the
living room as Mark let him in. They hadn't brought their masks.
Probably frightened by the new law, Nick thought. Now I'm not the
only one without a mask. "Where is everybody?" he asked.

"Layla didn't come," Mark said. "She thought it was too
dangerous. And Mary's in the kitchen making a cake. But listen—
wait'll I tell you what I found out. Wait till Mary comes in here."

"What?" Nick said. Mark was smiling as though he were about to
tell a joke. Had someone found out who he was? He had heard of the

things that happened to snitches: torture, castration, death. Why was Mark smiling? He was probably being paranoid; nothing would happen to him here among his friends. But what if someone *had* found out? Nick looked around the room and tried not to show panic. It was four against one, but Mary was so young. . . . What had Mark found out?

Mary came into the room from the kitchen. "I set the oven for four-fifty," Mary said, "but I think that's a little high. Is your oven—"

"Oh yeah, right," Mark said. "You'd better turn it down. I'm not sure just how accurate that oven is."

Nick looked at the front door. Should he leave now, make a break for it? He might be able to outrun them, especially if he could get to a police car. But did Mark really know something? Calm down, he told himself. You're overreacting. How could Mark have found out?

Mary came back into the room. "Okay," she said. "It's all set."

"So," Ayako said. "What's this big secret?" Nick was glad someone besides him had asked the question.

"Well, you remember when Nick got slapped last week," Mark said. Mary and Don and Ayako nodded. Nick moved a little toward the front door. He felt the blood pound in his ears and at his neck; he could barely hear what Mark was saying. "I talked to my neighbor yesterday. He said to me, 'You know, you should really be more careful with that radio of yours. Last Friday I saw someone hanging around your house, listening, looking suspicious. So I went over to him and I slapped his face.'"

Everyone except Nick laughed. "How about that, Nick?" Don said. "Looking suspicious! He does, doesn't he?"

Nick smiled weakly. He went to the bed and sat, feeling that his legs wouldn't hold him another minute. "It's not all that funny," Nick said. "I was terrified."

"Well, but I thought you'd be relieved," Mark said. "Aren't you?"

"Oh, yeah," Nick said. "You bet." You'll never know how relieved, he thought. So this was what he had worried about, agonized over, for the past week. He looked around him. "Definitely looks like an agent to me," Ayako was saying. "You can see it in his face." No, he thought. A stutter of revulsion passed through him, as though the thought had been formed by his body, not his mind. I can't live like this, cut off from my friends, spending weeks worrying about nothing. I'm not going to do it anymore. I am not a snitch. I will get out of it. I don't know how, but I will.

Mary went into the kitchen and carried out a warm cake smelling of spices. "Cake's ready," she said. To his surprise, Nick found that he was hungry.

Everyone took a piece of cake. Mark went into the kitchen and came out with the radio. "I hear you have a new roommate," Ayako said to Mary, licking crumbs off her hand. "How are you getting along?"

"Fine," Mary said. "Better than I thought we would. As long as she doesn't try to turn me into a maskmaker."

"Is she trying to?" Ayako asked.

"No, not really," Mary said. "She said the world will teach me how to be one, so she doesn't have to. Or something like that. You know how she talks."

"I'm surprised you turned her down," Mark said. "It seems like hundreds of people have asked to be her apprentice."

"Good for them," Mary said shortly. She took another piece of cake.

Mark moved closer to the radio. "Do you want to go outside, Nick?" Mark said. "Or should I get someone else to do it?"

"No, that's all right," Nick said. To refuse now would look suspicious. "But if I see your neighbor I'll slap him, okay?" Mark laughed.

No one was on the street. It was very dark. The sky was like a bowl filled with stars, more stars than Nick remembered from before the Collapse. The sunsets had been more spectacular then too. Nick took a deep breath, filled his lungs. He felt better than he had in weeks. He was himself again, no longer a snitch. He had taken off the government's mask.

"All clear," Nick said when he went inside. Mark turned the radio on.

". . . published in a newspaper in Tokyo," the announcer was saying. "The author of the unsigned article disagrees with the findings of the Japanese computer delegation, especially the delegation's statement that they are—quote—satisfied that the rehabilitation centers are just that, centers where the mentally ill are treated and, if possible, returned to society. Unquote. The author of the article says he saw enough during the tour of one of the centers to convince him that these centers are being used for political prisoners. It is for this reason, he says, that he does not think Japan should give the United States informational aid in the form of computer technology. However, it is doubtful that this one dissenting voice could have that much effect on the conclusions of the delegation, and the delegation seems to have decided in the General's favor.

"Although General Gleason announced the reopening of another steel mill last week, the fifth since the beginning of martial law, KVRT has learned that the mill was shut down Wednesday due to machine failure. Management has assured the workers that they will be back on the job by next week, but the workers aren't so sure. Once again we remind you not to believe everything you hear on television, and to put your trust in the one true medium—radio.

"And—saving the best for last—Lester Martin has escaped from his so-called rehabilitation center. We at KVRT do not know where Lester is, but if we did we wouldn't tell you. We were also unable to find out how the escape was managed, due to our understandable reluctance to get too close to one of those centers.

"That's it for Friday the thirteenth, August thirteenth, 2021. We hope the day hasn't been too unlucky for you tribes out there, and good luck to you, Lester, wherever you are."

Mark turned the radio off and took it into the kitchen. Nick said good-bye to him when he came back, and started to walk home. I'm a free man, he thought. Free. The word tasted good, like the spices in Mary's cake.

The walk to the cafe seemed shorter on Monday. For the first time in weeks Nick looked around him, noticing the people walking along Telegraph, the leaves on the trees, a government car traveling slowly down the street.

The woman was sitting at her usual place, a drink in front of her. "Well hi, Nick," she said as he sat at her table. The inflection was the same as last week's. Maybe she's a robot, Nick thought. Nah. Not even the Japanese have that kind of technology.

"Hi," Nick said casually. This was going to be tricky. He had worked the conversation out in his head every night since Friday, all her possible responses, all his replies. But she could refuse. She could always refuse.

"How've you been?" the woman said.

"Okay," Nick said. "Better."

"Well, good," the woman said warmly. "That's great. How's Jayne?"

"Jayne's fine," Nick said.

"Good," the woman said. "Do you have anything for me?"

"Yes, I do," Nick said. She looked up from her drink. Her too-wide eyes were a paler shade of blue, almost transparent. Maybe this would be easier than he'd thought.

"What is it?" the woman said. She couldn't keep the excitement out of her voice.

"Well, I'll tell you what," Nick said. His hands were shaking but his voice was as strong as if he were announcing the evening's lineup of television programs. "You must have a supervisor, right?"

"Of course," she said. She nodded slowly, puzzled.

"And your supervisor wants results, doesn't he? Or she. Wants some fact or name or address, maybe one or two a week. And the more you give him the better it is for you. Right?"

She had stopped nodding. Maybe she could see where he was going.

"Now I have a pretty interesting fact I can give you," Nick said. She was frowning; it made her look as though she were concentrating very hard on something. Had he gone too far? It was too late to stop now. "Your supervisor is really going to like it. But I just can't give this fact away for free. I want something from you." He paused, but she said nothing. "I want this arrangement to stop. Okay? I tell you what I found out, and then we never see each other again."

Two spots of red appeared high on her cheeks. "Well, we can't—we can't just bargain like that," she said. Her earnest forcefulness was gone. She was speaking slowly now, picking her words with care. "It just doesn't work that way."

"Why not?" Nick said.

"Because—because you're not supposed to do it that way," she said.

82

"Why not?" Nick said. "Haven't you ever done anything you weren't supposed to?"

"Well, no," she said. She was still trying to work out what he was getting at. Hadn't anyone ever questioned her view of the world? "I mean, we could be arrested."

"Is that what keeps you in line?" Nick said. "Fear of arrest? I thought you were doing this out of idealism. Because you believed in the General." His hands were shaking so badly he wanted to sit on them. He had made a bad mistake, questioning her motives, he knew it the minute he'd done it. Now he wouldn't get anywhere with her. She would become defensive, start to threaten.

"I do," she said. "And that's why I don't want to do this. The General wouldn't like it."

"All right," Nick said. "Then I guess I don't have anything for you after all."

"But you said—" the woman said.

"I said I wanted to make a deal with you," Nick said. "If there's no deal then I'm not talking."

"Well I could—I could have you arrested," the woman said slowly, as though thinking of it for the first time.

"Yeah, you could," Nick said. The mention of arrest seemed to calm him. What they did now didn't matter. He had played his last card. "And if you have me arrested they'll probably make me tell them what I know, but you won't be the one given credit. You won't get the promotion."

"I don't care about the promotion," she said. The spots of color were brighter. He thought she was probably lying. "If you have some information it's your duty as a citizen to tell me. That's the way it works. I don't like all this bargaining."

"And I will tell you," he said. "All I'm asking is that you don't ask me to inform on anyone anymore. You have that much power, right?" He saw her hesitate. "It's good," he said. "I promise you. If you don't think so I'll stay on as an informer. But you'll like it. I promise."

"All right," the woman said suddenly. Relief coursed through him, painful as the returning sensation in a leg that has gone to sleep. It had mattered after all. "But if this turns out to be a dead end I *will* have you arrested."

"Okay," Nick said. "You know the radio broadcasts every Friday night, the underground radio?"

"Of course," she said.

"I know who does them," he said.

Her eyes widened. "Yes?" she said. "Who?"

He told her. "I overheard him talking to someone," he said, hoping she wouldn't press him for details. He had expected to feel guilt at turning someone in, at becoming a snitch, but all he felt was more relief. It was him or me, he thought. And I'm supporting Jayne, and a baby on the way. It was three against one, really.

"Well," she said. "I'll check this out. And if it's right I guess we won't be seeing each other again."

"I guess," he said. "Are you going to get a promotion?"

She was trying not to smile. "Probably," she said. The smile overwhelmed her and she gave him the same earnest wide-eyed look as she had when they first met. She stood and held out her hand. "Good-bye, Nick."

He took her hand and shook it, trying not to pull away. "Good-bye," he said.

Layla came along with Mary to the next Friday night meeting. "I can't stand it," she said. "It's just me and four white walls, all day. I'm going nuts. I'm going to start going outside again. How long can they keep looking for me?"

"A long time," Mark said. "You'd be surprised. Especially if they want to make an example of you, which is what I think they want."

"Well, forget it," Layla said. "I mean, the choice right now is between the government's jail or jail at Mary's house. After a while I'll probably prefer the government's jail. It's more honest."

"Don't do anything stupid," Mark said.

"Maybe you can change your appearance," Ayako said. "Cut your hair, or get another kind of mask."

Layla looked at her witheringly. "Another kind of *mask*?" she said.

"Yeah, well, Layla, this is an emergency," Ayako said.

"All the more reason to keep my tribal animal," Layla said. "Besides, what other kind of mask could I wear?"

Ayako sighed. "All right," she said. "It was just a suggestion."

Mark stood and started toward the kitchen. "I wonder where Nick is," Don said.

Mark stopped. "You know, you're right," he said. "Nick's usually here by this time. And I don't think he's ever missed a meeting."

"Maybe he's sick," Ayako said.

Mark came back with the radio and plugged it in. "Maybe," he said. "Anyone want to go outside and look around? Don?"

Don nodded and stood up. A moment later he came back. "All clear," he said. "I didn't see your neighbor anywhere."

Mark turned the radio on. They heard the long hiss and gabble of static, then nothing. Mark turned the dial a little, rubbing it back and forth between his thumb and forefinger. "Maybe it's broken," Don said. "Quiet," Ayako said.

Mark twisted the dial halfway across the band. "Four. Five. One. Three," a male mechanical voice said. "Nine. Five. Six. Eight."

"What—" Mary said.

"It's some military channel," Mark said. "The radio's not broken." He looked at his clock and frowned. "Maybe they're running late." He turned the dial back to the underground station. There was still nothing. He picked up the radio and turned it with great deliberation in different directions. "Damn," he said. "Damn."

He left the radio on. For a long time no one said anything. "I—" Mark said. Don jerked his head suddenly toward the radio. Everyone looked at him. "Thought I heard something," Don said, trying to laugh.

"Oh, no," Layla said suddenly. "Oh my God, no." She pressed her head against her knees.

Mark turned sharply toward her. "What?" he said. She didn't look up. "Layla?" he said. "What is it?"

"I talked to him," Layla said, looking at the radio. Her eyes were wide, dilated. "And he heard us, and he must have told—I thought I saw him."

"Layla," Don said harshly. "What on earth are you talking about? Who did you talk to? Who heard you?"

"Brian," Layla said. "The bear tribe. At the dance."

"Brian," Don said flatly. "Who the hell is Brian?"

"He's the guy on the radio," Layla said. "I talked to him. About masks. And he heard us—I saw him listening—and then he turned him in. I know it."

"Who heard you?" Mark said.

"The spider," Layla said. "Nick."

"Nick?" Mark said incredulously. "Nick turned him in? You're saying Nick's a snitch?"

"Well, look," Don said. "Nick's not here."

"He's sick," Mark said. "Ayako said so."

"I said he might be sick," Ayako said. "I don't know."

"I can't believe it," Mark said. "How can he be a snitch? He'd've turned us in if he was a snitch, wouldn't he? And Layla. He'd've told the government where she lives, wouldn't he?" He looked over at Layla. She was rocking back and forth, moaning a little.

"Maybe he likes us," Don said.

"I did it," Layla said. She was still rocking a little. "If I hadn't talked to him, if I'd been more careful . . . And now he's gone. In a rehab center, or worse. He was from the bear tribe, strong, powerful. But they got him. Nick got him. The spider, who moves between worlds."

"Come on, Layla," Mary said. "It's not your fault."

"I should have known," Layla said. "I did know, when I made him the mask. But I forgot. You were right, Mary. I'm irresponsible."

"I didn't mean you have to be responsible for things you didn't do," Mary said. "And anyway, you don't even know if Nick did it. He never looked like a snitch to me."

"He did it," Layla said. "I know."

Mary looked helplessly at Mark and Ayako. "You'd better get her home if you want to be in before curfew," Mark said. "I know what she's like when she gets like this. It might take her a few days to come out of it. You can both stay here if you want."

Layla was still staring ahead, eyes wide. Mary put her arm across Layla's shoulders and moved her forward. Layla stood. "Come on," Mary said gently. "Bye, Mark."

"Should we come back next week?" Ayako said, standing.

"Maybe not," Mark said. He looked bewildered, as if he'd lost his reason for existing. "It might not be safe. I'll listen and tell you what happens. They might just be jamming it, and then all the station has to do is move the place they broadcast from. I'll let you know." He didn't sound too hopeful.

"Poor bastard," Ayako said softly. "I wonder what they're going to do to him."

6

FOR TWO DAYS LAYLA SAT
on the floor of Mary's room, her back against the wall. She was always in the same position whenever Mary left and came back, though Miss Benson said she had once seen her wandering in the hallway while Mary was out. Mary brought her salad, talked to her, covered her with blankets at night. Her eyes were open but unmoving.

On the third day, as Mary was leaving for work, Layla suddenly stood. As Mary watched she lost her balance and fell heavily back against the wall. Mary felt a terrible mixture of love, anger and exasperation, so strong she could barely speak. "Layla?" she said softly. Careful. Don't scare her away. "Are you all right?"

Layla blinked, seemed to see her for the first time. "I'm fine," she said. A slow smile spread across her face. "I know what to do now. The heron-spirit told me what to do."

"And what did the heron-spirit tell you to do?" Mary said, hoping it wasn't something lunatic. I wonder what time it is, she thought. I have to get to work.

"I have to fast for three days," Layla said.

"Well, you've done two already," Mary said. "You've got one more to go."

"Three more days," Layla said. "So I'll be ready."

"Ready for what?" Mary said.

"Ready," Layla said. "For the trance. And then the journey."

"Journey to where?" Mary said. What do I do if she tries to leave? Should I follow her? How did I get myself into this?

"Oh, well," Layla said. She blinked. "You'll see. You're a maskmaker too, almost. You'll understand."

"Understand *what*?" Mary said. She was balanced perfectly between anger and annoyance, unable to choose between them. Her mouth hung open.

"But I need supplies," Layla said. "What's today?"

"Monday," Mary said. "What do you mean, supplies? You're not going to go back to your apartment, are you?"

"No," Layla said. "Anyway, I can't go anywhere today. But soon."

Mary sighed loudly. "I've got to get to work now," she said. What was Layla waiting for, a full moon? "I want to see you here when I get back. Don't do anything irresponsible. All right?"

"Don't worry," Layla said. "I was irresponsible before, but I'm going to make up for it now."

"Just don't do anything stupid," Mary said. "Bye."

On Thursday Layla left the apartment after Mary had gone to work. It was good to be outside after her long imprisonment, to feel the sun and wind. In the flatlands she passed houses, abandoned gas stations, the gutted white lace structure of the Claremont Hotel. Then she started to climb. Officially no one lived in Tilden Park and so no buses ran on this part of the hill, though buses still came and went in the hills to the north. She had seen them coming down from the hills, carrying a few well-dressed people in gray, and she'd wondered what the people did to rate a house up there. Nothing good, anyway.

She walked for a while on the cracked and deserted road. On one side of her were the brown California hills, and the other side fell down to the bay and to San Francisco beyond that. Small animals rustled in the brush beside her, and she remembered the time she had seen the family of raccoons crossing the road, and the day she had been stopped, struck with wonder, by a deer standing motionless in the road. She hadn't made it to the meeting at all that day, but had stood for a long time watching the deer, trying to become as motionless.

The day was clear. Small ferries plied the bay, glinting silver where the sun struck them. She could see the jagged crack in the Bay Bridge, from this distance so tiny her eye kept wanting to close the gap and make the bridge whole. The skyline of San Francisco was farther away yet and none of the fire damage was visible. It looked almost as if there had never been a Collapse at all, as if people were still taking the subway to work and riding the elevators and staring into computer screens and walking to fancy restaurants on their lunch hours. If there had been no Collapse . . . She shied away from the thought. If there had been no Collapse there would be no tribes, no masks. And what would have become of her then?

She was tiring a little now, breathing heavily. She hadn't walked in five days and her muscles ached. She had fasted so long she was beyond hunger, but she felt weak, drained. Sometimes the colors around her seemed impossibly bright, like the neon skies of her childhood. She walked on, hearing nothing but the sounds of small animals and the songs of mosquitoes. Once she bent to pick up a stone and put it in her pocket. It's around the next bend, I know it is, she thought, but she passed three bends before she saw the other maskmakers sitting around a scarred and rotted picnic table.

Everyone said hello except Bone Jackson, who nodded. Layla sat at the table next to Rose. Bone threw his knife into the table and pried it out. "All right," he said. "What are we going to do about this stupid law?"

"There's nothing we can do," Susan said. "I didn't realize this was a discussion group. I thought it was just our usual meeting."

"Sure there's something we can do," Bone said, carefully cleaning his knife. "We can kill somebody. I'd like to start with that Clawfy bastard on TV." Bone belonged to the jackal tribe and collected skulls. He was rumored to have one or two human skulls in his collection, though Layla, who had been to his apartment, had seen nothing more ominous than a monkey skull. He was very tall—nearly six and a half feet—and very thin.

"All right, Bone," Rose said. "You kill him. We'll watch." Feathers bright as paint, probably collected on the way up, lay spread out on the table in front of her. Layla thought that Rose's feathered masks were the best work being done in Berkeley, but because of the tough macho stances of most of the maskmakers she had never been able to say so. Six or seven braids, some dyed black, some white, fell down her back. Layla had always wondered where she got the dye but Rose had never said.

"I'm not going to put my life on the line just to kill this guy," Susan said. "And if you kill him they'd just get someone to replace him. We just have to lay low for a while, that's all."

"Yeah, but this is my personal grudge," Bone said. "Most of the people who've asked me for masks have decided that—guess what?— they don't really want them after all. Some of them haven't even paid me for work done so far. I'm hurting because of this law. It's taking food out of my mouth. You can't just say to lay low about something like this. We've got to do something."

"I don't see why," Willie said, a short black man who wore a purple scarf pirate-style over his hair. I wouldn't wear that scarf now, a voice said in Layla's mind, Mary's voice. Not if the police were after me. She was surprised at herself. Before she'd moved in with Mary thoughts of the police would never have occurred to her. "Think of it. Masks are only available through the black market, and you know what that means. The price will go up. This actually works to our advantage, you see?"

"Yeah, it'll get better for us, but the basic law is wrong," Bone said. "Wrong and stupid. I mean, look at Layla, having to stay in hiding all the time. They could have just as easily gone after any of us, and they might, next time. None of us are safe."

"How are you doing, anyway?" Rose asked Layla. She brushed a white braid over her shoulder. "Are you still staying with your friend?"

"Yeah," Layla said. Rose looked worried. In past meetings Layla had talked as much as anyone. Layla knew that if Rose were concerned she wouldn't say anything. None of the maskmakers ever talked about his or her personal life; it was an unwritten law. Anyway, Layla thought, I'll talk soon enough. She wondered how the maskmakers would take her news.

"I can't believe you were the one they decided to go after," Willie said. "If they thought you were the weakest they were incredibly stupid. You get in touch with us if anything else happens, okay?"

"Do you remember what this cop looked like?" Bone said. "Maybe we should go after him instead of Clawfy."

"Look, you guys," Susan said, turning to look at Bone with her right eye. She had bought her glasses from a street doctor and the left lens was far too thick for her. "I'm really nervous sitting out here. I mean, the police would just love to find the five of us together, you know what I mean? Can we get on with it?"

"You're just upset because Clawfy didn't mention you on the news," Bone said.

"Bullshit," Susan said. Layla thought Bone was probably right. Susan wore small plastic dolls and parts of dolls sewn to her coat. Each of the dolls, Susan had explained, represented a spirit overcome during a trance and now bound to her as a servant. Layla, who had always treated those she met in the land of animals with stringent respect, had been horrified. She knew Susan had many followers and had made many good masks, sharp and jagged as stylized suns. Still, she couldn't help feeling Susan had taken a wrong turn somewhere, and she disliked her for it.

"All right," Willie said. "Let's do it."

Willie, Bone and Susan slipped off their backpacks and began pulling things out. Rose opened her bag. Paint, pigment, feathers, shells, stones and fur piled up on the table. "I brought some extra paint for you, Layla," Willie said, setting down a few colored tubes and a red jar.

"Here's some paper," Rose said. "I had it lying around the house, and I'll never use it."

This was the other side of the toughness the maskmakers displayed, unseen like the inside of a mask, a feeling of togetherness, tribalism, of us against the world. "Good," Layla said. "I'm going to need it. Because I talked to the heron-spirit. I fasted for five days. And I was told to make a mask for the General."

If the others were surprised they didn't show it. Bone nodded emphatically. "Good," he said. "I think that's a great idea."

"It is?" Susan said, scowling. "Why?" Her left eye bulged behind her glasses.

"Well, it's obvious," Bone said. "If he has a tribal animal then he'll have a soul. He'll see where he's gone wrong."

"Let the prisoners free," Layla said softly.

Susan looked from Bone to Layla and back. "I don't know," she said. "I—"

"You don't think the masks have that power?" Willie said. "After all you've seen and done?"

"Of course I do," Susan said. "But he has to wear it first. How is he going to get it?"

"I will start it on its journey," Layla said. "And the pull of the mask itself will be enough to bring it to the General."

"You will," Susan said. It was halfway between a statement and a question. Was she envious? Even if Layla failed, the maskmakers would talk about and remember her deed for years to come.

"You don't think she's up to it?" Bone said.

"I don't know," Susan said, shrugging.

"I can handle it," Layla said. "I have been eaten by the bear, the master of animals. I died and my bones were sucked of life, but now I am alive. When the bear counted my bones there was one too many, and so he knew that I was to be a maskmaker."

The stories of initiation, sometimes exaggerated, sometimes not, had been told among the maskmakers more times than they could remember. No one showed any impatience at hearing Layla's story again. "Then it's settled," Bone said. "Layla will make the mask and get it to the General, and we'll be able to come out of hiding. Do you have enough materials?"

Layla nodded. Susan was still scowling. Rose and Willie showed no expression at all.

Bone moved silently, taking a piece of rabbit fur from the pile. Layla stuffed jars and paper into her coat pockets. Others took stones and shells, and in a few minutes the pile was gone. Bone stood up and began to fill his backpack.

As always they went down the hill together. "How's your collection, Willie?" Rose asked as they neared the flatlands. Willie collected large pieces of sidewalk paving.

"Real good," he said. "That part of Ashby right near the Bay Bridge is all torn up right now. I got some great pieces."

"You don't belong to the lion tribe," Bone said. "You're a jackal like me. Look how much you love destruction." Bone had once said that his biggest regret in life was that he hadn't been in San Francisco the day a mob of unemployed workers had set fire to the financial district.

"You love destruction because you've got a mean streak, Bone," Willie said. "You like to beat up on people. I love it because it's beautiful. It's a completely different thing."

"I like destruction because of what happens after," Layla said, thinking of her walk up the hill. "Everything's sort of freed up for a while."

Rose laughed. "God, listen to us," she said. "What do you suppose they'd've done with us before the Collapse?"

"Put us in a mental institute, probably," Willie said.

They were silent for a moment. Then Susan said suddenly, loudly, "Destruction—to our enemies!"

"Destruction—to our enemies!" Bone and Willie answered. It echoed among the hills.

"Good-bye," Layla said when they reached the flatlands. The maskmakers had agreed that she wouldn't tell them where she lived in case one of them was arrested. No one said anything for a long while. Were they already thinking of her as a legendary figure?

"May the heron-spirit help you on your journey," Rose said finally.

Layla turned and started walking home. Well, you've told them, she thought. Now you've got to do it.

Layla had not returned by the time Mary came back from work. Mary tried to push away her feelings of foreboding. "I told her not to leave," she said, muttering, as she walked around the room. "I told her. If something's happened to her . . . damn."

She stopped. It was five days after Layla had started her fast. She had forgotten the fast, forgotten Layla's fragmented talk about a journey. "Where's she gone now?" Mary said, pulling her coat off the hanger and putting it on. "Goddamnit."

She left the house and headed toward Telegraph. The day was going cold, and clouds were drifting in from the bay. She was starting to feel hungry. Her hands made fists inside the coat's pockets. "I hate being responsible for her like this," she said aloud. No one turned to look at her. "Goddamnit."

She passed the Green Dragon, the padlock on the door grown tarnished with dust. There were a few people in masks standing on the corner, but the masks looked shabby and none of them was of a heron. The door to Cafe Mediterraneum was open and she looked inside.

"You don't want to go in there," a voice said behind her. She turned, startled. It was Don. "I hear they opened it again to give the cops a place to meet with their snitches."

"I'm not—" Mary said. Don was standing too close and she stepped back. "I'm looking for Layla. Have you seen her?"

"She's gone, huh?" Don said. "I wondered how long she'd stick it out."

"Well, I'm worried." How could Don be so calm? "I mean, the police are after her and everything. I just hope she hasn't . . ." She couldn't finish the sentence. There were too many things she hoped Layla hadn't done, including outlandish things only Layla could think of.

"I wouldn't worry," Don said. "Layla's taken care of herself for a long time. Nothing's happened to her yet."

"That's what Ayako said just before Layla was nearly arrested," Mary said.

"Yeah, nearly arrested," Don said. "You notice she never actually gets arrested?"

"I don't know," Mary said. "I can't help worrying about her. She makes me feel like her mother." As soon as she said the words she wished she hadn't. The statement felt oddly personal, like a confession. She realized she was blushing, and wished she had been wearing her mask.

"Hey, do you want to come back to my place?" Don said. "I was just about to break into Mark's collection of canned goods."

"Do you think she might be at Mark's?" Mary said. She didn't want to admit, to herself or to Don, that she would accept an invitation to Don's house with no good reason.

Don shrugged. "Could be," he said. "She's gone there before."

"Okay," Mary said. She was getting hungrier, and the idea of eating something from a can sounded good to her. She had eaten too many salads in the past few weeks.

Mark's house looked strange in the daytime, bigger and cleaner, less

LISA GOLDSTEIN

inviting. Layla wasn't on the porch or in the hallway in front of Mark's apartment. Don let her in and turned on the lights.

"Where's Mark?" Mary said.

"Out," Don said. He went to the kitchen and came back with a can in each hand. "Now we have here what they claim is real beef"—he held up a can—"and in this hand what they claim is real chicken. Makes you long for the old days of the Food and Drug Administration. Do you remember the Food and Drug Administration?" He didn't give her time to answer. "Which one do you want?"

"The—the beef, I guess," Mary said, sitting on the bed. "Doesn't Mark mind if you eat his food?"

"Oh, no," Don said. "Mark's a saint."

"Layla said the same thing," Mary said. But Layla had sounded as if she'd meant it. Somehow Don managed to make even his compliments sound cynical.

"Then I guess it's true," Don said. "I've got to go work my magic in the kitchen. You can amuse yourself here for a few minutes, can't you?"

Mary nodded. After he'd gone she looked around the room, which seemed even more cluttered than usual. Did Mark clean up for the Friday night meetings? She saw Layla's painting on the floor—the wounded bison, Layla had said it was—and she looked at it more critically now that she knew Layla had done it. Don was probably right—Layla could take care of herself. She was starting to feel warm and safe and a little drowsy. No one had cooked dinner for her since she'd left home.

She picked a stack of paper up off the floor and started to read. The paper was soft, browning, easily torn, and the ink was purple and hard to read against the dark paper. It was a story of some kind, about people who lived on the streets. On the third page there was a murder. On page five someone started taking film and heroin.

Don came in, carrying two plates. He laughed shortly when he saw what she was reading. "That's my novel," he said, pointing with his chin.

"It is?" she said.

"Yeah," he said. He handed her a plate and a fork and sat next to her on the bed. "What'd you think?"

"I don't know," she said. She had never had an author ask for her opinion of a book. "I like it, I guess. It just—it seems a little grim."

Don laughed again. "A little grim," he said. "But you don't think things around you are grim at all, do you? I mean, according to you we're practically in another Renaissance, right?"

"Well, no," she said. Why did he always have to make fun of her? "But not everything is grim. Some things are all right."

"Like what?"

"Well, like the tribal dance," she said. "That was fun."

"That was fun," he said, imitating her, though not unkindly. "Go argue with a fifteen-year-old."

"I'm not fifteen," she said. She looked up from her plate and saw to her vast surprise that Don's smile was almost friendly. He had been joking, then. Maybe he wasn't as bad as she'd thought. She would have to ask Layla. Made bolder by his smile she asked, "Why is it on such funny paper?"

"Because it's an underground press," Don said. "You don't think the censor would pass something as grim as this, do you? You could be arrested just for looking at it. The joke is that the cops arrest anyone with purple all over their hands, because the Purple Press uses that really awful smeary ink. An interactive adventure, a chance for one to participate more fully in the experience of reading a book."

She must have looked blank because he went on. "An interactive adventure, that was a computer game," he said. "You remember—"

"Of course I remember computers," she said.

"Of course, of course," he said. "Unbeknownst to me, you are really Dana Cooper. I am sitting here having dinner with Dana Cooper. Wait'll I tell the guys at the Press."

She took a bite of the beef stew, trying not to laugh. "Are they going to publish Mark's novel too?" she asked. She liked hearing him talk. She wished she could think of something clever to say to him.

"No," he said, his mouth full.

"Why not?"

He swallowed. "Because Mark's novel isn't very good, actually."

"Really? He let you read it?"

"Well, 'let' isn't exactly the right word to use here," he said. "Let's just say that I read it."

"You mean you found it and you read it?" she said. "And he doesn't know?"

He raised his hand to forestall her, still holding his fork. "I know, I know. It's not a very nice thing to have done."

"It—it's horrible," she said. "How could you . . ."

He looked at her from under his eyebrows, amused. "You would have done it too," he said. "He was always going *on* about it, about plot, and structure, and whether this character should fall in love with that one. . . . He was so mys*ter*ious. I couldn't stand it anymore. It's amazing I held out as long as I did, actually."

"No, I wouldn't have," she said. "I mean, here you are living off him, eating his food, staying in his house. . . . He trusted you. What did you do, search the whole house?"

"Yeah," he said. "I found his damn radio before I found the manuscript. All right, all right." He raised his hand again. "It wasn't very nice. I didn't know that then. Living with a saint, you learn these things. If I had it to do over again I probably wouldn't have done it. Okay?"

She scraped the last bits of the stew together with her fork, not looking at him. "Just set the plate on the floor with the rest of the mess," Don said. "Whenever our dishes run out we have a massive cleaning party. It's lots of fun—almost as much fun as the tribal dance."

She put the plate on the floor. "So," he said. "How's Layla doing?"

"I don't know," she said, glad for the chance to change the subject, to tell her worries to someone. "She's fasted for—I think it was for five days. She said something about a trance, and a trip somewhere, and then she wouldn't say anything else. And now she's gone."

"That's Layla," he said. "And you don't know if the trip is out to the desert somewhere or all in her head."

"Exactly," she said. "That's exactly it. Only now she's gone. So what am I supposed to think?"

"I don't know," he said. He leaned back against the wall and crossed his arms behind his head. His too-large flannel shirt was missing a few buttons, and Mary could see his chest, thin and hairless, through the gaps. Embarrassed, she looked away. "Hell, sometimes she makes *me* feel like her mother," he said. "I'll tell you what, though." He leaned forward, moving closer to her. "I think you definitely did the right thing when you decided not to be her apprentice. You don't want to get mixed up with all those crazies." A little hesitantly, he put his arm around her shoulder.

Her first thought was to pull away. The medicine she took had thickened her gums, and she was embarrassed whenever anyone came close to her. But she was also excited by Don's nearness, aroused by him as she had never been by any of the boys in her high school, and her old fear of losing control returned. Before she could decide what to do he leaned over and kissed her.

He didn't say anything when they finished. Probably he had noticed how awful her gums were. She moved away, out from under his arm, and the pounding of her blood slowed to where she could begin to think. He leaned forward to kiss her again. "No . . ." she said. The sound of her voice surprised her; she hadn't known she was going to say that.

"No?" he said. His eyebrows were raised, and he looked amused. Or was he trying not to look hurt? "I guess you and Layla have something going, is that it?"

"Me and—and Layla?" Mary said, astonished. How could anyone even think of her and Layla that way? She thought of the dream she had had, standing naked in front of Layla, and she quickly put it out of her mind. "We're friends, that's all. We don't—we're not . . ."

"No, I guess not," Don said. "Layla only goes out with crazy people, anyway."

"She does?" Mary said. No one had ever told her that. She remembered the tenderness with which Mark had removed Layla's mask and her thought that they might be lovers. They probably weren't, then, not if Layla only went out with crazies. She wished she could ask Don.

But Don was definitely looking hurt now. She owed him an explanation. But how could she explain to someone else what she didn't understand herself? Once she had seen her oldest brother and his girlfriend out in the backyard, and what they were doing looked so much like what she imagined her seizures looked like that she'd vowed she would never have sex with anyone. How could people do something like that voluntarily? And aside from that one glimpse she was not really sure what it was people did, though she and Jackie had repeated rumors endlessly to each other. Once, Jackie had told her, people had had sex education in school, and they did it right there, with the teacher looking on. That had been before the Collapse, before the General and his endless laws, when anyone could have contraceptives and not just married people. There. That was what she could tell Don.

"It's just that . . ." she said. "Well, do you have contraceptives?"

"You're right again," he said. "A saint would have made sure he had contraceptives before he tried anything. No, I don't."

"A saint wouldn't have tried anything in the first place," she said.

He gave her that amused look again. She felt as though she had said something incredibly naïve. "But I can get some," he said. "If I do, would you come back?"

"Okay," she said, surprising herself again. She did want to. But not just yet, not right away.

He leaned back against the wall. His straight hair fell across his eyes but she thought he was watching her closely. What was he thinking? "Well, I should—I should get going, I guess," she said. "Maybe Layla's come home. Thanks for dinner."

"Sure," he said. He did not get up with her to show her to the door. "Bye."

Her room was dark by the time Mary got home but she knew somehow that Layla was inside. She turned on the light. Layla looked up at her, blinking. She sat in the middle of sheets of rag paper and jars of paint. Where did she get them all?

"Hi," Layla said. Her pupils were wide, black nearly covering the gray.

"Hi," Mary said. She cleared her throat. "I was worried about you."

"I told you not to worry," Layla said. "I didn't do anything dangerous."

"Oh," Mary said. She wanted to talk to Layla about Don, but Layla seemed distant, unreachable. She nodded at the paper and paints. "Are you—are you going to make a mask?"

"Yes."

"Who's it for?"

"No one you know," Layla said.

"Okay," Mary said. Layla was making her nervous. "I guess I'll—I'll go to sleep soon. Do you want the light off again?"

"It doesn't matter," Layla said.

"Okay," Mary said again. She went into the closet and carefully, making sure Layla didn't see her, put three pills in her coat pocket. Then she went to the bathroom. She wondered how long Layla was going to stay with her. Maybe Layla could move in with Ayako after all.

7

WHEN MARY RETURNED
from work on Friday the mask had taken shape: long beak, two slits for
eyes, the slightest suggestion of feathers. "Looks like a bird," Mary
said, hanging her coat in the closet. "Is it?"

"Yes," Layla said. She sat cross-legged on the floor, the mask in her
lap. Her eyes were hooded and she seemed remote, a witch woman
from a time long past. Mary wished she could talk to her, ask her about
Don. If there were no meeting tonight at Mark's house, when would
she see him next? Did he know where she lived?

"What kind?" Mary said, trying to draw her out. If I'd known this
was what it was going to be like I'd've never asked her to stay here,
she thought. Layla held the mask up and looked at it critically from
different angles. Mary watched her closely. The sallow rings around
her eyes might almost have been painted on. Her face was the color of
bone. Was it good she had something new to work on? The mask was
stealing her energy, her life.

"A crow," Layla said. Mary hadn't expected her to answer. Her
voice was quiet; Mary had to strain to hear her. "The black bird of
death. Eater of carrion."

Mary laughed a little, nervously. "Who's *that* for?" she said.

"No one you know," Layla said.

She had said the same thing last night. The answer was like a door closing, a reminder that Layla wanted to keep parts of her life private. "Fine," Mary said angrily. Whose house was it, anyway? She put her coat back on and walked out. Maybe she'd run into Don on Telegraph. Layla did not look up as she left, or when she came back two hours later, having found nothing interesting to do on the street.

She spent Saturday in front of the new TV one of the roommates had bought, switching compulsively through the three channels. The news channel repeated once every hour with no changes, as though time and events had ended. The variety channel was boring and insipid, and the channel of programs from the twentieth century brought an aching nostalgia for a time she had never experienced, an era of smooth unbroken streets and boys on bicycles, of automobiles and re-frigerators and fathers of unshakable wisdom. Once she thought she heard Nick's voice and she remembered the last Friday night meeting. Was it true that Nick was a snitch? Layla seemed to think so, and so did Don.

Sunday she went shopping, and made vegetable soup on the hot plate in the kitchen. Over the soup she rehearsed various arguments for getting Layla out of her room. "It isn't fair to keep me out of my room like this," she would say, and Layla would say, quite reasonably, "I'm not keeping you out—you can come in any time you want." She thought of not offering Layla any of the soup, but she realized that even now she was incapable of that.

Layla was stroking paint onto the mask when she went into the room. The mask was covered with a black paint so glossy it looked enameled. The black seemed to suck all the color in the room into itself, to take all the color and animation from Layla's face. "I brought you some soup," Mary said, setting the bowl down in front of Layla.

"Thanks," Layla said, not looking up from her slow brushstrokes.

Mary shifted uncomfortably. Wherever she looked her gaze was drawn to the mask, the vibrant center of the room. It seemed finished to her. "Listen, Layla," she said finally. "Are you ever going to talk to me again?"

"Yeah," Layla said. She looked up from her work and for a moment the old Layla—playful, mischievous—was back. She ran her hand through her tangled hair, streaking it with black. "Soon. Probably sooner than you think."

Something woke her in the night. She could barely make out Layla, a darker shadow, rising from her tangle of blankets. Layla bent down and picked up something—the mask, probably—and walked silently to the door. Then she was gone.

Now what? Mary thought angrily. Without thinking she pulled on a pair of pants and a T-shirt, and took her coat from the closet. Layla was not in the hallway. In the living room Mary saw the front door closing, and she ran to open it.

There was enough light from the moon and the few working streetlamps to see Layla walking lightly down the street. What time was it? Curfew couldn't have ended. At that moment she hated Layla. I should go back to bed, she thought. Let her get arrested. Instead she closed the door behind her and ran out into the street.

Layla was about a block ahead. As Mary watched she turned down Ellsworth. She was keeping to the unpaved roads, where the police cars didn't go. Even if they catch me, Mary thought, hurrying after her, they won't arrest me for one curfew violation. But Layla already has two, and they'll probably put her in a rehab center. I've got to stop her, make her come home. What on earth is she doing?

She was getting closer to Layla now. A wild thought came to her. She tried to put it out of her mind but it was too seductive. What if I follow her, she thought. Keep an eye out for the cops and warn her if things look dangerous, but otherwise just see where she goes. Maybe mention it to her later, casually. She thinks she has secrets. She thinks she can put me out of her life, when I rescued her and let her stay with me. She thinks she knows everything, just because she can make masks, but she doesn't know I'm following her now. I'll show her.

Layla walked boldly on ahead, her back straight, her coat billowing out to the sides like wings, as though it were bright daylight. Don't be stupid, Mary thought. Tell her you're here, tell her to come home. This is dangerous. But the dark secret thrill she felt kept her silent. She thinks she knows so much about me, Mary thought. Well, now I'll know something about her.

Layla turned onto a paved street, Ashby, probably, though Mary could not see a street sign. She shrank back a little. Up ahead a building shone through the darkness like an apparition from another time. A police station. Mary stayed well back, but even so she could hear the guards by the door moving forward, exclaiming, and Layla's proud calm voice over theirs. "I've brought a mask for the General," she said.

One of the men took the mask from her and another pushed her roughly against the wall and began to search her. Even now, as Mary watched, disbelieving, she wondered how Layla was going to get out of this one. The guard finished searching her. He twisted her arm across her back and shoved her forward, into the police station. She did not resist. Then from behind her Mary heard a voice— "Hey! There's another one out here!"—and she started to run. She managed to get only a few steps before someone crashed into her, and she fell to the ground.

The man who had hit her dragged her up by her arm and started searching her. She flinched away from his prying hands but he came after her, opening her coat and feeling her breasts, her stomach, between her legs. He took her identification card from her coat pocket. When he moved away she felt a sharp pain in her wrist and she held up her arm. Blood seeped into her coat sleeve. She must have scraped her skin when she fell. She felt dazed.

"Come on," the man was saying. "Didn't you hear me?" He pushed her inside, up to a brightly lit desk, and reached for her hand. Mary tried to pull away. The man pressed each of her fingers on an ink pad, then pushed her head up. A bright light shone in her eyes and something clicked.

"We're going to let you spend the night with your friend here." He marched her down a brightly lit corridor. "Crazies," he said. "Now I've heard everything." She heard the sound of a key turning in a lock and realized that they had stopped in front of a tiny cell.

The man pushed her into the cell and closed the door behind her. Layla stood in front of her. The sharp dazzling lights, the small cell, Layla's incongruous presence—everything felt like a dream. "Hello, Mary," Layla said. For some reason she was smiling.

Mary sat on the concrete floor, her back against the wall. Her body was starting to feel sharp spikes of panic. She tried to ignore the thought trapped at the back of her mind, the thought that would overwhelm her if she let it out. If they kept her here for any length of time she wouldn't be able to get to her pills, and if she couldn't get her pills . . . She put her head in her hands. After a long time of no thoughts, somehow, she slept.

She woke to the sound of the key in the lock. The bright lights were still on, and she squinted. A guard dragged her up. "Rise and shine," he said. Layla was already standing. "It's a long bus trip."

"Bus trip?" Mary said. Her mind was still blanketed with sleep. "Where?"

The guard laughed. "You didn't think we'd let you stay here, living the easy life, did you?" he said. "We're going to put you to work. We're taking you to a rehab center."

Mary's heart jumped. "Oh God," she said. "Oh my God." She sagged against the wall.

"Come on," the guard said. "Let's go."

She followed him out into the corridor, feeling numb. What would happen to her now? If only she hadn't followed Layla to the police station. What a stupid thing that seemed now, in the bright light of the corridor. If only. What would happen to her without her medicine? Would she die?

There were ten more prisoners in the corridor, and another guard. They were marched to the bathroom and then outside to stand near a bus the color of rotting moss. The walk outside woke Mary enough for her to notice that she was hungry and tired, and that her neck hurt from sleeping against the wall. Beneath everything she felt the panic, now worn to a thin whine.

"Hey, wait a minute!" one of the guards said, calling up to the bus driver. He ran into the police station and came out with the black crow mask. "She wanted to give it to the General," he said, handing it up to the driver. "So if you see the General, you be sure and give it to him, okay?" There was a sound like laughter from the driver's seat. Then the prisoners and the other guard got on the bus and the driver rolled up the window.

The bus was dimly lit and smelled of unwashed clothes and bodies.

The windows had been covered in blackish green paint. Mary stood still a moment, trying to see, and then found a seat next to Layla.

"How are you doing?" Layla said. The driver shifted into gear and pulled away from the curb. "Mary?"

"Not too good," Mary said. "I'm worried. No, I'm scared, really. I don't want to go to a rehab center."

"It's not too bad," Layla said. "You get used to it."

"Not too—" Mary said. "Layla, what the hell were you doing last night anyway?" A young woman in the seat in front of them, with hair cut to a quarter of an inch all around her head, turned to stare at them appraisingly and then looked away.

"I wanted to give the mask I made to the General," Layla said.

"You wanted to give your mask to the General," Mary said, disbelieving. The bus hit a pothole. Mary looked past Layla, at the painted windows. "For God's sake, why? Didn't you know you'd be arrested?"

"Well, yeah," Layla said. "I thought I probably would be. But I was already under arrest, in a way. I couldn't leave your house. So it didn't really make much difference."

"But it made *some* difference," Mary said. "Just what did you think would happen if you gave that mask to the General?" The guard turned to look at her and she automatically lowered her voice. "You think he'd put it on and magically become a different person? You think that once he belonged to a tribe he'd have elections and free all the prisoners?"

"Well, no, not right away," Layla said. "But after a while. Once he had a soul."

"I can't believe this," Mary said, whispering urgently. "Every time I talk to you I think I've heard the worst, and then you come along and say something even stupider. Layla, that mask is never going to get to the General. These guys are going to throw it out, or lock it up somewhere, and no one will ever see it again. Especially not the General. And even if he does get it he would never—"

"Well," Layla said. "You don't know that."

"Yes, I do," Mary said. "I do know that. Because I live in the real world, not this dream world of yours, this land of animals crap. Whoever gave you the idea you could just go up to the General and give him a mask?" The bus turned right. Mary wished she could see where they were going.

"The heron-spirit told me," Layla said. "And then—"

"Oh, great," Mary said sarcastically. "The heron-spirit told you. There's a good reason to do something."

"And then I talked to the other maskmakers," Layla said, as though Mary hadn't spoken. "Willie, and Bone, and Rose, and Susan. They gave me the materials to make the mask."

"Then they're just as crazy as you are," Mary said. Despite herself, she felt a twinge of envy when she heard the names of the maskmakers. She would never get to meet them now. But would it be worth it to meet them, to become one of them, if you had to believe the crazy things Layla did? She remembered the circle of maskmakers at the tribal dance, the masks colorful as jungle flowers, and she sighed. It didn't matter what she believed in, she had been arrested anyway. "And all because of this crazy idea of yours you get arrested, and you get me arrested too—"

"I didn't get you arrested," Layla said. "You followed me."

"How long do you think we'll stay there?" Mary said.

"It depends on when the General gets the mask."

"And since he's not going to get the mask . . ." Mary said. "Some people never get out, right?"

Layla shrugged again.

"Even if—if they haven't done anything," Mary said. "If they're innocent."

Layla said nothing.

For the first time Mary thought of her future. Never to see anyone she knew again, Don, or Ayako, or Jackie. She should have taken Don's offer; now she might never get the chance. Never to walk down Telegraph Avenue again, or ride the bus to work, or dress in a mask and jewelry and dance to the sound of the drums. What would her father say if he knew? He had been right; she couldn't leave him. "Why are you talking to me again?" she asked Layla.

"I had to get a job done, so I was sort of preoccupied," Layla said. "But now it's over, so I can talk."

"A job," Mary said. She shook her head. "Great."

After a long time Layla fell asleep. At least I know where she is,

Mary thought. It would have been a shock if I woke up and she was gone. Finally, lulled by the rhythm of the bus on the road, she slept.

The door of the bus hissed as it opened. For a moment, confused, Mary was back on the school bus in Stockton. She looked around for her school books. "Everyone out," the guard said. "Here we are."

"Layla," Mary said. "Wake up."

Layla woke all at once, no confusion in her wide gray eyes. "Well," she said, smiling. "Here we are."

"How can you be so cheerful about it?" Mary said.

"Hey," Layla said. "Free room and board."

Mary walked down the steps of the bus, and Layla followed.

Outside, a barbed wire fence stretched around a compound of old warehouses, crumbling asphalt streets, fields of brown grass and weeds. Someone watched them from a tower nearly overhead. The land was flat and the wire seemed to go on forever—Mary could not see the end of it. She had the feeling that they were still in Berkeley, that the bus driver had driven in circles for several hours to confuse them. She turned to see where they'd come from and saw two old freeway roads arched high above them, like the bleached bones of a whale.

A commotion made her turn back. The bus driver and several guards were standing together, talking and laughing. The bus driver held out something—it was Layla's mask—and a guard, still laughing, put it on. The change was instant and obvious: He was no longer a minor officer in the General's vast army but regal, deadly. The shining obsidian black denied the flat landscape around them; it stood out like a wound. The guard must have felt something because he took it off again almost immediately.

He was still holding the mask when he came over to the prisoners and began separating the men and women. Mary felt queasy from hunger. He led the women prisoners a little way along the fence and then motioned them through a door. Mary waited for the door to clang loudly behind them, for the realization that now they were imprisoned, but it was wire and barely made a sound. The guard locked it securely behind them.

"Line up!" the guard said, and after some fumbling the prisoners formed a ragged line.

"Change places with me," the woman with short hair whispered urgently to Mary.

"No—why?" Mary said. She didn't want to lose Layla. "Wait—"

The woman shoved herself between Layla and Mary. "Just do it!" she said through clenched teeth. "They're going to count off—"

The women at the beginning of the line were already starting to count. "One." "Two." "One." "Two." "One," Layla said. "Two," said the woman with short hair. "One," Mary said.

"All ones," the guard said, "follow me. Twos follow Sergeant Anderson. Let's go."

"They like to split friends up," the woman with short hair said. She's been here before, Mary thought.

"Thanks," Mary said. "Thanks a lot."

"Don't worry," the woman said. "You called her—she's Layla, right?"

"Let's go," the guard said. "You'll have plenty of time to talk later."

The guard led them down an old cracked road past what looked like houses made of corrugated tin. They stopped in front of a long two-story building. "Here's your dormitory," he said. "This is where you'll live and eat your meals." He looked at his watch. Mary hadn't seen a watch in a long time. "Looks like you just missed lunch." Everyone sighed, a low windy sound. "And if anyone complains they won't get dinner either. You're actually lucky—you missed today's work call. You're going to work five days a week, earn your keep. You get one day a week to rest, and one day to see your shrink." He stopped, amused at the puzzled looks on the women's faces. "You're actually mental patients, see? At least, that's what we tell the Japanese. Until we get those computers, anyway. And I don't doubt that at least some of you will benefit from your visits." Was he looking at Layla? Mary felt rage, a hatred so strong that if she'd had the guard's gun she would have killed him that instant.

The guard backed toward the door, never taking his eyes off the waiting line of women. "Okay, girls," he said. He opened the door. "Two to a room. You're on your own until dinner." He moved off to the side, holding the mask a little away from him as if it were a small dangerous animal.

The line surged toward the door like a wave. The women who had been there before knew exactly what they wanted, a room on the first floor out of the heat. Mary didn't care as long as she was with Layla. They managed to get a room on the first floor, but the heat as they opened the door hit them like a fist.

Breakfast the next day was some kind of porridge, toast and a glass of water. After breakfast they were given work clothes and ordered to change. All around Mary women slipped out of their clothes and piled them on a table to be taken away. Mary and a few others stood still, too embarrassed to change in front of the guard. "Let's go," the guard said. He was not as impatient as the guard they'd had yesterday.

Layla tossed her coat, paint-spattered and decorated with shells and rabbit fur, onto the pile, and took off her flannel shirt and jeans. She's too thin, Mary thought. And look—she's shivering, and it's not that cold. Quickly Layla found a pair of pants and a shirt that looked as if they might fit her and put them on. She ran her hands over her upper arms a few times, rapidly.

"You there," the guard said. Mary started, but he wasn't talking to her. She put her coat on the pile, thinking about how long it had taken her to collect all the bands and gears and sew them on. Then she changed into the work clothes. She was surprised at how warm they felt.

The guard called roll, and then they were marched to the factory. On the way over she thought she heard a train whistle and then stop somewhere nearby.

At the factory—another low building, with narrow windows that kept the heat in—they were put in front of a long slow-moving conveyor belt. Mary watched as two strange-shaped pieces of metal came down the belt and stopped in front of her. "You take this screw here," the guard said to Mary, taking a screw from a small metal trough running the length of the belt, "and screw it on, like this. Then you," he said, turning to Layla, "attach the two pieces together. All right?" He moved off to give instructions to the rest of the women.

They had warned her, after the first few seizures, to stay away from machinery. But there hadn't been that much machinery after the Collapse and she hadn't paid much attention. Now she approached the conveyor belt warily, like a mountain climber assessing her chances. It started again, taking away the piece the guard had done, bringing her two more pieces. What if she fell forward? Was it moving slowly enough not to hurt her? If she told them the problem they might let her do some other work. But they might transfer her somewhere else, and she would never see Layla again. Finally it was the habit of silence that won out. She bent to the conveyor belt and picked up the metal piece.

She was so busy with her thoughts that several minutes passed before she realized Layla wasn't doing the work. "No, you put them like this," Mary said, showing Layla how the two pieces of metal joined together. The belt moved again and Mary turned back to her work.

Layla shrugged. "I don't know," she said, holding the two pieces in her hands and bringing them together in different ways. "These would be great in a necklace, don't you think? Only they're a little too heavy."

"Layla, you've got to do this," Mary said. The belt moved again. Layla had collected a small pile of the metal pieces in the trough in front of her and she screwed two similar pieces together. "If you don't they'll probably separate us, do something terrible to you. Like this." She showed Layla again how the pieces fit together. Her own work was piling up in front of her. "Do you want to trade? Maybe this'll be easier for you."

Layla put the pieces down on the belt and raised her hands to show she gave up. "I don't understand machinery," she said. "None of the tribespeople understand machinery."

"Layla, that's a game," Mary said. "You do so understand machinery, I bet you do. This is serious. Stop playing, for once in your life."

"I'm not," Layla said. She backed away from the belt. "I don't understand it."

Down the line people were talking softly, then raising their voices for the guard. The belt stopped. After a moment the guard came over to Layla.

"Now," he said. "What's the problem here?"

"I can't do this," Layla said. She was rubbing her arms again, though the factory had gotten hotter. Mary stared straight ahead at the belt in front of her, trying not to look as though she were eaves-dropping.

"And why not?" the guard said.

"I don't understand it."

"You don't understand . . ." the guard said, his voice heavy with disbelief. He picked up the two pieces and joined them together. "Like that. See?"

"No," Layla said.

"No," the guard said. He sighed, blowing the air past his face to cool himself. "What did you do before you were sent here?"

"I was—a painter," Layla said. Mary was surprised to hear the caution in her voice.

"Oh, you're the one," the guard said. "They hung your mask in the guards' room yesterday. Supposed to remind us of the kind of people we have to guard, I guess. So that's what you think the General looks like, huh?"

"No, it's—"

"Maybe he does at that," the guard said. "I didn't say that, if anyone asks. So you can paint, right? I mean, you understand painting." Layla nodded. "Good. I've got a job for you, painting one of the new dormitories." He raised his voice. "You guys, take a break. I'll be back with a replacement." Then, to Layla, "You. Come with me."

After a while the guard came back with another woman and the belt started up again. The work was tedious and slow. Mary wished Layla was still there. She really got lucky, Mary thought. That guard was nice, not like the other one.

At twelve the belt stopped and they were taken back to the dormitory for lunch. Mary's neck hurt and she had a headache. For lunch they were given two pieces of toast and a cup of coffee. She had never had coffee; it had been on the UC list for as long as she could remember. So this is where it goes, she thought. She drank her cup quickly, wincing at the bitter taste. Layla had not come back to the dorm.

The afternoon was much like the morning. By five she was ready to go back to her room and sleep, but they were taken to dinner and she found to her surprise that she was hungry. Then they were allowed to go to their rooms. She lay on the small metal cot and fell asleep instantly, waking only once to see Layla come in, her work clothes spotted with dull green paint.

The weekdays passed like the start-and-stop motion of the conveyor belt. One blended into the next in a gray blur. On Saturday she was taken to a small rickety wooden building next to the dormitory to see the psychiatrist.

"Hello, Mary," the psychiatrist said, coming around the desk to shake her hand. He was a big soft-looking man, slightly plump, bald except for a few wisps of pale blond hair. His shirt, Mary saw as he went back to the desk, was not tucked in in back. "Have a seat," he said as he sat behind the desk, not looking at her but at a spot on the wall over her right shoulder.

Mary sat on the only chair. The room was badly lit; she wondered why it was kept so dark. What had looked like a painting on the wall behind the psychiatrist was actually a framed diploma. The only other framed diplomas she had ever seen were in the offices of the doctors who had given her countless tests seven years ago. She shifted nervously on her seat.

"Tell me something about yourself," the psychiatrist said.

She talked a little about her childhood in Stockton and her decision to come to Berkeley, omitting as much as she told. The psychiatrist asked only a few questions. Gradually she became aware that there was something lined up in neat rows behind him, small boxes and jars that reminded her of the black market in San Francisco. The memory jolted her into realizing what they were—pills and vials and small plastic-wrapped needles. Her mouth went dry. She remembered her visits to the doctors' offices, the visits to the hospital when her mother was dying, and for a moment she couldn't speak. The doctor didn't seem to notice. Was this how they interrogated people? Was this the real reason for the psychiatrist at the center? He asked her another question and she forced herself to listen, to answer.

After an hour he shook her hand and told her he looked forward to seeing her next week. He had the same distracted look he'd had at the beginning of the session. She wondered if he'd heard anything she'd said.

Layla spent Sunday in a trance. They were allowed to wander the grounds, and a few of the women had left the dorm, but Mary lay on her cot and watched Layla. I should get up, she thought, but lethargy kept her where she was. She had put on weight from the starchy diet and lack of exercise, but Layla looked trim and fit and had darkened a little from the sun.

There was a new guard on Monday, a small dark-haired man whose black eyebrows joined over his nose. His voice shook when he called Layla's name.

"Here," Layla said. He turned to her too quickly, as though he thought she was going to hit him, and dropped the list of names he was holding.

"What was that all about?" Mary whispered to Layla. Layla shrugged. She left to paint the dormitory and he watched her go with unmistakable relief.

The next day he stared hard at Layla before he looked down at his list. Who was he? Did he know her from somewhere? He seemed about to ask her a question, but started the roll call instead.

On Saturday Mary went to the psychiatrist, came back and lay on her cot. Layla left for her session but Mary hardly noticed. She dozed a little. Screams coming from outside the building woke her. She got up quickly and ran to the psychiatrist's building. Layla stood outside the building, shouting.

"What the hell do you know about souls?" Layla was saying. "You don't even have a tribe, and if you did have a tribe it would be the baboon's ass! Don't tell me about my soul, you miserable uninitiated college student! I have more wisdom in my little finger than you have in your entire body!"

"Layla—" Mary said, looking nervously at the building. The big man was not coming out. Was he cowering? Mary nearly grinned at the thought.

"I hope you rot!" Layla said. "I hope all your fingers fall off, and all your toes—"

"Layla!" Mary said. This time Layla seemed to hear her. "What happened? What did he do? Did he use the needles?"

"No," Layla said. "He said something—"

"What did he say?"

"He said it was the Collapse that made me go crazy."

"Oh, Layla," Mary said. She felt the pity Layla managed to arouse in her, and the desire to protect her against the world. "He shouldn't have said that."

"No," Layla said.

"What does he know about who's crazy and who isn't?" Mary said.

Layla looked at her. "Well, I am crazy," she said. "He was right about that."

"Then what—"

"He said it was the Collapse that did it," Layla said. "But it wasn't the Collapse. Millions of people survived the Collapse and are just fine. I did it myself. I made my madness. It's a work of art, like a mask."

"Oh," Mary said. She wished she could think of something to say, but the only thing she could think of was that the psychiatrist was probably right.

"He asked me about my childhood," Layla said thoughtfully, frowning a little. Her anger had passed. "So I told him, but he didn't understand."

"What did you tell him?" Mary asked.

Instead of answering Layla walked away. Did I offend her? Mary thought. But Layla was only going to a stunted tree by the side of the road. Layla leaned against the tree and Mary sat next to her, trying to stay in the tree's meager shade.

"I grew up in Southern California," Layla said. Mary felt a thrill of excitement. She hadn't expected to hear anything about Layla's life after she had refused to become her apprentice. Why was Layla telling her now? "We lived in a suburb. All the houses on the block looked the same. All the families looked the same too, except my family. My mother listened to a lot of music. And my father—" Layla's face relaxed. She was smiling. Mary had never seen her so happy. "My father was unpredictable. One day he brought home about ten gallons of purple paint. Said he'd gotten them on sale, and he was going to paint the den. And he did. The neighbors didn't know what to make of him."

Layla was silent for a moment. Mary wondered if she had finished. "So of course he was one of the first people taken away after the Collapse," Layla said. She looked sad now, wistful. A little of her smile remained. "One of the neighbors informed on him, probably made up something ridiculous, and they took him away. Arrested him right there in the purple den, maybe. I don't know—I wasn't there."

She ran her hand slowly through her tangled hair. "But, see, my mother didn't tell me where he'd gone. She said he had to go somewhere for his company, or something, and that he'd be back soon. But, you know, you find these things out. I guess someone told me. That was the first time I went into a trance.

"In my trance the heron-spirit came to me." Layla's voice was lower now, almost a chant. "I climbed onto its back and it bore me away. Together we flew many miles, through a day and a night and a day again, flew without stopping. And when we stopped we were at the Berkeley campus, where I met—"

"Wait—" Mary said softly. Layla didn't hear her.

"—my teacher and was initiated. My teacher's name was Archangel, and he was of the owl tribe. He was very wise. He was in a wheelchair and he needed some medicine that he wasn't able to get, and so he died. But by that time I had made my journey to the land of animals."

"Wait," Mary said, louder this time. "You flew—you and your heron-spirit flew from Southern California to Berkeley?"

"Yes," Layla said.

"But how? I mean, are you sure you didn't just hitchhike? Maybe you just remember the heron-spirit, but really you—"

"That's exactly what the psychiatrist said," Layla said. "Of course I'm sure. I remember the way the heron's wings strained at my weight, the way they thrust at the air like oars. I remember how the blue of the heron was exactly the same as the blue of the sky. That was the beginning of my initiation into maskmaking, though I didn't know it at the time. I wouldn't forget something like that."

Mary shook her head slowly. "I don't see how something— something that's only in your mind, like the land of animals—how that can take you somewhere real."

"You will," Layla said. "When you become a maskmaker. I had had signs, even before the Collapse, but there was no one to tell me what they meant. I sang in my sleep. I wandered through the house in my sleep, and when I was awake I took long walks, looking for something but unsure of what it was I was looking for. I cut myself with knives. You're lucky—when those things begin to happen to you I will be right here to initiate you."

Mary sighed. "I'm not going to be a maskmaker," she said. "I thought you'd given up on that idea."

"Even if I'd given up," Layla said, "the land of animals would still be waiting to initiate you."

"Good for it," Mary said, but Layla was calling to someone and didn't hear her.

"Brian!" Layla said.

A man with a limp looked around, then came slowly over to them. He had a short fuzzy brown beard, and brown curly hair receding from his forehead. He looked puzzled. "Who—" he said.

"This is Mary, my apprentice," Layla said. "The sea-otter tribe." Then to Mary, "Brian is from the bear tribe. He's the guy who does— who did—the radio broadcasts."

"Layla," Brian said. "I didn't recognize you without your mask." He sat down next to Mary in the tree's shade.

"I hate not having my mask here," Layla said. "That's the worst thing about this place. I'm always seeing people and wondering what tribe they are."

Mary was so surprised she forgot to correct Layla about being her apprentice. So Layla really did know the radio announcer! She had thought Layla had made that up along with all her other hallucinations.

"What did they get you for?" Brian said.

"They didn't get me," Layla said. "I'm here because I want to be."

Brian looked puzzled. "She made a mask for the General," Mary said quickly. "Then she went out in the middle of the night and brought it to a police station. I'm here because I was stupid enough to follow her."

"But—why?" Brian said. "What kind of mask?"

"A crow," Layla said. "A black crow. They put it in the guards' room."

"She thought if she gave him the mask he'd let everyone out of prison," Mary said. "She gets these weird ideas. . . . I'm not really her apprentice."

"Oh," Brian said, nodding politely.

"See, she thinks she led the police to you," Mary said. "Maybe she did. I guess she talked to you the night of the dance. She thinks Nick—this guy we know—heard her and informed on you. She got very upset. Then she thought if she made the mask everything would be all right."

"So that's how they found me," Brian said slowly. Now Mary could hear the high strong voice of the radio announcer. "She shouldn't blame herself—I should have been more careful. It was my fault, really."

Layla was looking closely at an insect crawling over the weeds and grass. We're talking about her as though she isn't here, Mary thought. She doesn't even seem to be listening.

"The real question is, how do we get out of here?" Brian said.

"How do we?" Mary said eagerly. "Do they ever let people out? They must, right?"

Brian nodded. "They do, yes," he said. "People who've been in one of these places don't usually talk about it once they get out. I think your cases will be coming up in about a year and they might let you out then. I'm probably in for longer, though." He was silent a moment. "I guess it's about time I found out what a rehab center was like. I've talked about them enough on the radio."

"So we're here for at least a year?" Mary said. The gray boredom of the days had made her almost forget about the seizures but now her fears came back. In a year she would almost certainly have at least one.

"Or," Brian said. He looked around carefully but there was no one near the three of them. "We could escape."

"Escape!" Mary said. "That's a great idea!"

"Well, it's not that easy," Brian said. "Security around here is pretty good. We're right next to the army base. And once we get out we'll have a long way to go before we can get somewhere safe. We're close to Berkeley—"

"I thought so!" Mary said, excited. "Where are we?"

"The train station in Oakland," Brian said. "The campus is the safest place we could hope for that's close by, and that's at least a couple of miles. I don't think I can walk that far, unfortunately. But you and Layla could."

"I don't think she'll want to go," Mary said, "and I can't leave her.

She can't survive here on her own. I have to watch out for her." And there was the bond between them, grown stronger now that Layla had told her her history. As far as she knew Layla had never done that for anyone. But she couldn't tell Brian that; he wouldn't understand. There weren't any words to explain what there was between her and Layla.

Brian nodded as if he understood. "We should think about it, though," he said. Somewhere the bell for dinner rang. There were only two meals a day on the weekends, and unlike the weekdays, when the guards brought them to the dorm for meals, bells announced the times of breakfast and dinner. Mary still wasn't used to the bells. Brian stood slowly. "Maybe we can come up with something."

Mary watched him walk away. There goes my chance, she thought. Now I'm stuck with her, loony stories and all. She turned to Layla, who still hadn't moved. "Dinner," Mary said.

8

MARY SLEPT LATE AND
missed breakfast on Sunday. As she stood up she felt dizzy. All sound
disappeared, as though it had been sucked into a vortex somewhere
inside her body. Adrenaline pierced her like needles. It had been seven
years but she recognized the feeling at once. She opened her mouth to
tell Layla to move the cots out of her way, to watch out for her, but it
was too late. It was always too late. Sound came back and
overwhelmed her, and she lost consciousness.

Layla watched as Mary's arms and legs jerked, as her head arched back
against the floor. As Mary rolled over, flailing outward with her arms,
she stood and moved the metal cot so Mary wouldn't hurt herself
against it. She felt a pity so great it threatened to overtake her
completely, to make her forget everything she knew including her
name and her tribe. At the same time she thought, There, I was right.
There's something different about her. The power is in her. She'll be a
great maskmaker someday.

Mary opened her eyes slowly. She remembered the time she was
eleven, when she had to stay in the hospital for tests. She had just had a
seizure and opened her eyes to see a nurse bending over her, taking her

pulse. "I bet you're glad to be alive," the nurse said, and Mary said, "I wish I was dead. I'd rather die than have to live like this."

The nurse looked appalled. She must have been very young, Mary thought, realizing it for the first time. But Mary was not going to lie to her. She felt miserable after a seizure. Her first thought was always, It's happened again.

This time was no different. She moved her arms and legs slowly, wondering what kinds of bruises would show themselves by tomorrow. At least I didn't pee in my pants, she thought. She wondered where Layla was, what she had thought. Almost embarrassed, she turned to look at her.

"How are you?" Layla said. She was on the floor sitting next to her, not where Mary expected her to be at all. "Are you feeling okay?"

"I—yeah." She remembered other people's reactions, her father's and brothers'. "Are you okay?" she said, sitting up against the cot. It was good to be able to move again. "I didn't scare you or anything?"

"No," Layla said. "I knew something was going to happen. I knew there was something like this."

"You did?" Mary said. "How?"

Layla shrugged. "I just knew," she said. "I saw you take pills for something once. But I knew even before that. You're a maskmaker, so there has to be something different, something special."

"Yeah," Mary said. She rubbed her lip and realized by the pain that she had cut it in her seizure. Her hand was bloody when she took it away. She wondered what she looked like. "My big secret. Now you know. That's why I don't want to be a maskmaker, because when I saw the bear in the land of animals I thought I was going to have a seizure. That's what it felt like to me."

"But it's not like that," Layla said. "It's not at all—"

"Oh, yeah?" Mary said. She felt tired, old. She had thought her confession would make her feel better, but it hadn't. She would never convince Layla of anything. "When was the last time you had a seizure?"

"See, with the land of animals, you control them," Layla said. "They don't control you, the way a seizure does. After your initiation—"

"Yeah, *after* the initiation," Mary said. "Forget that. I'm not going through that." She leaned back against the bed. "I wonder if I could get some pills here somewhere. Maybe there's a black market or something." She thought of the psychiatrist and his rows of pills, put the thought out of her mind. She couldn't go to him for help.

"You shouldn't take those pills," Layla said. "I think that's why your initiation is taking so long. You have to open yourself up to the seizures, to be eaten—"

"Layla," Mary said firmly, "listen to me for once. I am not going to be your apprentice. I am not going to be initiated." Layla was silent. Maybe I've convinced her, Mary thought. Finally. She relaxed a little. "In a way it's too bad you're stuck with me. If you really had an apprentice this would be ideal. Free room and board, plenty of time for trances, no distractions . . ."

"See?" Layla said. "The universe arranges itself to teach you how to be a maskmaker."

There was a strange, remote look on Layla's face. Mary's face and hands started to tingle, as though someone had neatly taken off a layer of skin. Her heart was beating loudly. "Layla," she said, "did you lead me here on purpose?"

"You followed me," Layla said. "I had nothing to do with it."

"Yeah, and right before you went to sleep that night I asked you if you'd ever talk to me, and you said you'd talk to me sooner than I'd think. And you were so goddamn mysterious—you just knew I'd be curious and follow you. And now that I think of it you made some kind of noise before you left, so that I'd wake up. Didn't you? You brought me here so I couldn't get to my medication, so that I'd have plenty of time with you, and just because you have this lunatic idea that I'm going to be a maskmaker. Didn't you?"

"I did it to give the General a mask so he'd have a soul," Layla said. "Whatever else happened happened because you didn't finish your initiation."

"You're crazy!" Mary said. She wanted to slap Layla, to wipe that complacent look off her face. How could she ever have thought Layla was her friend? "I'm trapped here, trapped without my medication, and all because of you! I could die here, I could get cut up by that conveyor belt, and you probably wouldn't even care. Just as long as I became a maskmaker."

"I told you," Layla said calmly. "Once you step on the path you can never leave it. I gave you a chance to back out. I don't see what you're so upset about. Here we've got plenty of time for your initiation, and you've got me to help you. Lots of people would give anything to be in your place."

"I'm not lots of people," Mary said. "I'm me. That's what I'll never forgive, that you did all this without even asking me. That you took it upon yourself. You think that just because some crazy people in Berkeley hang on your every word—share your delusions—you can—can take a year out of my life. Maybe more. Just because—"

"I never said it would be easy," Layla said. "You will come to your power in suffering and silence, and only after you learn to bridge the gap between the mask and the face. Between the dream and the real. And you must bridge that gap with your body, by placing your body within the bear's mouth—"

"Don't talk to me," Mary said. "I don't want to hear any more of this nonsense. I'll tell you why you wanted me here with you. It wasn't any noble motive like teaching me to be a maskmaker. It's because you were tired of being cooped up in my room, of being the only one in jail. You wanted to take me with you." She wanted to wound Layla, to silence her, but Layla looked back at her, guileless. She stood angrily and went to the door. She was shaking.

"Mary—" Layla said. Mary opened the door and slammed it loudly behind her.

After a few hours Mary came back. She was tired and wanted to go to sleep. She hoped Layla was in a trance, or that she had gone out. Voices came from behind the door.

"That's the first time I saw them," someone was saying. "About two years ago. And then about every week after that."

The hell with this, Mary thought. It's my room too. She opened the door. A man's face turned quickly toward her, a dark face with eyebrows joined over the nose . . . the guard.

"It's all right," Layla said to the guard. "Mary's okay."

The guard relaxed. They were sitting close together on Layla's cot. Mary hesitated, then walked in and lay on her cot. I'm not going to let her throw me out of my room the way she did the last time, she thought.

"You can see them the best when there's a quarter moon," the guard said. "The lights are real bright on the dark part of the moon then. Sometimes you can even see them when there's no moon, but it's hard to tell. You sure you've never seen them? The lights on the moon?"

Layla took the question seriously. "No," she said finally. "I never did." The guard looked disappointed. His single eyebrow seemed to sag in the middle as he frowned. "But you did," she said.

"Yeah," the guard said, sitting forward. "All the time."

"Maybe it's the Japanese colony," Layla said.

"That's what I thought at first," the guard said. "But see, one of the guys in my bunk says you wouldn't be able to see them from the earth. So then I didn't know what to think. I mean, what are they? And how come I'm the only one who can see them? And then they hung your mask up in the guards' room, where I can see it every day, and it suddenly occurred to me. There are aliens on the moon. And they're beaming these messages down to earth, telling some people to make masks."

"Why?" Layla said. Mary saw with disgust that Layla looked intrigued. She remembered what Don had said, that Layla was only interested in crazies. But not this guy, Mary thought. How can she be interested in him? He's an idiot.

"I don't know why," the guard said. "They haven't told anyone yet. Some plan of theirs. First I thought they wanted to take over the earth, but now I'm not so sure. They're probably more subtle than that."

"What about the Japanese?" Layla said. "Why haven't they seen these aliens?"

"Well, it's a big planet, the moon," the guard said. "Or maybe they have seen them and they're just not telling anyone. They're in league, maybe."

In league to do *what*? Mary wanted to say, but she kept silent. She was never going to talk to Layla again.

"So anyway," the guard said, "I wanted to know if you've ever heard them. The aliens. And why you think they're telling you to make masks."

"Well, that's not the way I make a mask," Layla said. She told him about the trances and the land of animals. Mary wanted to shake her. What if the guard was a snitch? He looked fascinated by what Layla was telling him, but that and his lunatic story could be a cover. She remembered the rumor about the other guard, the friendly one, that he had been turned in by a prisoner for his jokes about the General and the army, and she wondered what this one was like, what he wanted. He had his gun in his holster.

He nodded slowly when she had finished. "I guess you know what you're talking about," he said. "You're the one that makes them, and you get your power from somewhere. It's too bad—I was hoping you could help me out. It's gotten so I can't sleep at night."

"I'm sorry," Layla said. "I'd be happy to tell you anything you want to know about maskmaking, but that's it. I don't really know anything about aliens."

"Okay," he said. He sighed, got up slowly and seemed to chop at something with his hand. Probably he had started to salute her and then thought better of it. "Can I—if I've got more questions I'll just come back and talk to you, all right?"

"Sure," Layla said. "Anytime." He opened the door and went out.

"Are you okay?" Layla said to Mary after the guard had gone.

Mary said nothing. I'm behaving just as childishly as she is, she thought. But I don't care. I'll never forgive her for doing this to me, never. I'll never talk to her again.

"Mary?" Layla said. "How do you feel?"

Mary closed her eyes. She felt a small pulse of pleasure at hearing the worry in Layla's voice. Let her see how it feels. "Mary?" Layla said again, tentatively, and then said nothing else until the bell rang for dinner.

The next seizure came on Wednesday, in front of the conveyor belt. She woke under blankets in a small cot, wearing a flimsy gray tunic. Three other cots crowded the small room. Someone was coughing loudly in the cot next to her. A woman lay immobile in the cot by the window, and the cot between her and the coughing man was empty.

Mary lay silent, remembering. Now the nurses would come in and fuss over her, and the doctor would come in last, the guest of honor at the end of the parade, ask a few questions and leave. The long deception was over. Her head hurt—she thought she had hit it against the metal trough as she fell—but nothing else seemed to be wrong.

No one came. Somewhere far off a train whistled. The sun, coming in through the window, angled over the woman in the cot. The woman still had not moved. Could she be dead? Mary began to shiver, though the room and the blankets were warm. Where was everyone? Had they forgotten her? The man beside her coughed loudly and she turned away.

Finally the door opened and a woman dressed in government gray walked in. She looked at Mary, looked at the notes in her hand and said, "You're the one who had the fit?"

Mary tried to shrink beneath her blankets. She hated the word "fit," hated all the words. "Epilepsy" sounded exactly like a person writhing on the floor. She cleared her throat. "Yeah," she said. The man beside her coughed again.

The woman—nurse? doctor?—nodded and moved on to the next cot. "Usually I take phenytoin," Mary said, speaking fast. Weren't they going to help her? "But I . . . do you have any here? I'll be okay if I can get some."

"Now why do you think we'd have some of that stuff?" the woman said, her back to Mary. "How many epileptics do you think we get in here anyway?" She held the back of her hand to the coughing man's forehead and then went on to the woman by the window. "Still hasn't moved," she said. "I told Sergeant Anderson someone was smuggling film in here but he just wouldn't listen." Then she left.

Mary lay still. Nothing in her experience had prepared her for this. They were not going to help her. They knew, and they were not going to help her. She closed her eyes. They didn't care. She would rot in this place, die here in some horrible accident, and no one would ever know. No one except Layla, and it was Layla's fault she was here in the first place. She hated Layla.

A man and a woman came in about the time the light faded at the window. They carried trays of food, which they gave to Mary and the man next to her. Then they moved the still woman to the empty cot and changed her sheets, complaining in low voices to each other.

Mary ate her dinner, the same porridge as in the dorms, and watched them. She had been in enough hospitals to know that they had no authority and that it would be of no use to talk to them. She would wait for the other woman to come back. The man beside her coughed and retched softly onto his tray.

When the woman in gray came back the next day Mary was ready. "You're being discharged today," the woman said. "You're to go back to work."

"Did they say anything about—about doing some other kind of work?" Mary asked. "Something, well, not so dangerous?"

"Not to me they haven't," the woman said. She put her hand against the coughing man's forehead. "Mmm. The fever's broken, looks like."

"Listen," Mary said desperately. "The thing is, I get the seizures more often when I'm tense. That's what my doctor told me. And I'm tense all the time now, because my roommate—I don't get along with my roommate. If I could just get moved into another room, maybe another dorm . . ."

The woman glanced into the last cot and turned to look at Mary. "I can't do anything about that," she said. "I don't think anyone can change the dorm arrangements once they're set. Someone will be in with your clothes and then you can go."

On Wednesday night Layla sat cross-legged on her cot and stared at the cracked white wall. Something was wrong. Mary hadn't come back from work at the conveyor belt, hadn't been at dinner. The green land of animals flickered against the wall, the animal spirits calling her to come play with them, but she frowned and tried to concentrate on the small room, the metal rim of the cot against her thighs, the things most people called real.

Mary hadn't spoken to her since Saturday. Mary was angry with her and she couldn't understand why. After all, it had been Mary who had wanted to learn maskmaking. She had explained to Mary how difficult the path was but Mary had asked her to go ahead. So it was up to her, the teacher, to find a way for Mary to learn. It had been important to get Mary away from the pills that controlled her, from her job and all the distractions in Berkeley. She'd thought Mary would understand that.

Someone walked down the hallway outside the dorm room and Layla's heart jumped, but the footsteps went on past her. It was true

Mary had said, over and over again, that she didn't want to be a maskmaker, but most apprentices felt that way at one time or another. No one she had ever heard of had failed to complete the initiation. Not even Archangel, who had taught her and so many others, who might have been the first maskmaker, had told her what to do when an apprentice steps off the path to initiation.

She smiled wryly at the memory of Archangel, his body soft and flabby in his wheelchair, his flint-gray eyes, the same color as his flowing beard, hard and unyielding. Archangel appeared before her as he had so many other times, shining brightly against the white wall. He no longer wore the owl mask the color of cotton; his head had become an owl's head when he died. She had told Mary the story of her first meeting with him, something she had never told anyone except another maskmaker. Mary had to become a maskmaker now.

Mary would make a great maskmaker. All the signs were there. Most maskmakers had something physically wrong with them; it helped them heal others, though Layla couldn't explain why. And Mary had met the bear on her first visit to the land of animals. Someday Mary would look past her anger and the power would be there, waiting for her to take it.

The overhead bulb went out. It must be late, Layla thought. Where was she? Layla curled up under the blanket, alert to every sound. The dorm was very quiet.

They discharged Mary after she had eaten dinner but before dinner ended in the dorms. She ate the second meal gratefully. Layla came in as she sat eating and called to her, but Mary ignored her. After dinner she went to her room and lay on the cot. "Mary?" Layla asked once, but Mary kept her eyes closed.

On Saturday Mary went to see the psychiatrist. He nodded as she took her chair and said, "Tell me something about your friend Layla."

Mary shrugged, trying to hide her surprise. "I don't really know her very well," she said.

"I think she needs help," the psychiatrist said. She noticed for the first time that he had a slight British accent and she wondered why anyone who was not a citizen would choose to live in the United States. His underarms were stained with sweat. "But I can't help her unless I know more about her. I thought you as a friend of hers would want to help. Has she talked to you about these hallucinations of hers?''

"I don't talk to her much," Mary said. She remembered Layla standing and yelling at him last week and she wondered what he was getting at.

"She's told me differently," he said. "Do you know she's unable to have children?" He looked at her inquiringly, one pale eyebrow lifted. She looked at the rows of pills and needles behind him and said nothing. "Apparently she's had at least one street abortion and it was bungled very badly."

A slight envy stirred within her. Why had Layla told this idiot something so personal when she had never said anything to her? She couldn't have told him; he had said "apparently" and that meant he didn't really know. They must have examined her somehow. The idea of Layla lying on an examining table while this jerk poked around inside her made her furious.

"She tried to tattoo herself once," the psychiatrist said. "Did you ever notice that dark spot between her thumb and forefinger, right here?" He showed her the place on his own hand. "The needle was infected. She could have lost the entire hand, but she was lucky."

Despite herself Mary's envy grew. She had once asked Layla what the dark blue spot that looked like ink was, but Layla had changed the subject. It was just like Layla to answer only the questions she wanted to answer. She would never tell her anything important, anything real.

"You ever notice how cold she always is? That's a condition called poikilothermism. It's fairly rare. She can't keep her body temperature constant, she adapts to whatever the outside temperature is. She's really only happy at temperatures in the eighties or nineties. If it ever got below twenty degrees she could lose consciousness, even die."

"Did she tell you this?" Mary asked. The question was out before she could stop herself; she hadn't wanted him to see what she felt.

"What does it matter?" the psychiatrist said. The malice in his voice brought her up short and she was able to realize what he was doing. He wanted to drive a wedge between them, set them against each other. He hadn't forgotten the things Layla had screamed at him last week, how foolish she had made him look. It was one of the first times Mary recognized childish behavior in an adult, and it surprised her. She had thought adults were beyond that.

He was looking at her expectantly. But no matter how much she hated Layla she would never side with him. Her new knowledge only made her more certain of that. "I'm sorry," she said. "I never really knew her all that well."

He frowned and said, "I just wanted to help her. You know that." She said nothing. "I hear you had a seizure this week," he said. "Did you ever take medication for your epilepsy?"

She nodded.

"Do you know what the medication is called?"

She could see where he was going but she couldn't stop herself. "Phenytoin," she said.

"Ah," he said. "I think I have some contacts who could get me some. Would you like that?"

She nodded again. What a stupid question. No, I enjoy having seizures, she thought.

"Good," he said. "I'll see what I can do. And you see what you can find out from Layla, okay? Find out what she sees when she stares at a blank wall the way she does. I'll talk to you next week."

The guard with the single eyebrow came back on Sunday. Mary lay on her cot and closed her eyes but she still heard his theories on who the aliens were and why they had chosen Layla. Layla, usually so impatient, listened to him carefully, sometimes interrupting to explain something about maskmaking. The envy Mary had felt at the psychiatrist's returned. Don't be ridiculous, she thought. You stopped talking to her. But the envy stayed. After a while she left in disgust.

Brian was walking aimlessly along the dirt paths and she ran to catch up with him. It was cool outside; fall was coming. "Hey!" she called. "Brian!"

He turned to face her. "Hi," he said. "How's it going?"

"Can I talk to you?" she said. She looked around but there was no one else on the path. "Somewhere quiet?"

"Sure," he said. He led her to a small rock by the side of the path and they sat down.

"Listen," she said, speaking softly. Her head was very close to his.

"I've got to get out of here. Escape, like you said. If you hear anything, if you're ready to go—"

"What about Layla?" he said.

"Layla wants to stay here," she said. "She likes it here. But I'm ready to go." He was looking at her with the same puzzled expression she had first seen him wear. I might as well tell him, she thought. Everyone on the conveyor belt knows—they've all been avoiding me, waiting for me to fall down. "See," she said. She took a deep breath. "I'm an epileptic. I've had a couple of seizures already. If I don't get out of here, get back to my medicine . . ." She said nothing about the psychiatrist's offer. If she couldn't escape she might have to take it, and she didn't want to think about betraying Layla.

"What about getting medicine here?" Brian said, looking concerned. Mary was glad to see that look; she had begun to think that no one cared. "There's all kinds of stuff smuggled in through the black market."

"The black market?" Mary said. "With what? I could barely afford the stuff in Berkeley."

"Well, they're paying you a wage—didn't anyone tell you?" Brian said.

"A wage?" Mary said dubiously.

"Yeah, but don't get all excited," Brian said. "It comes to a whole new dollar a day, and you don't get it until you've been here for six months. I can't believe they didn't tell you. Typical, I guess."

"Well, there you are," Mary said. "It'll take at least six months for me to afford the stuff. And besides, I don't know anyone in the black market." A guard walked down the path and she stopped talking. The guard looked at the two of them sitting silently by the road as he passed. "And I'd really like to get out," she said after he had gone. "I hate it here. I shouldn't even be here. I didn't do anything."

"I thought you were Layla's apprentice," he said. "That's what she told me."

"No, I'm not," Mary said. "She just says that."

His puzzled look, a slight lifting of the eyebrows in surprise as though someone had just hit him, was back. Maybe that's why he was such a good reporter, she thought. He's curious about everything. "Okay," he said. "I'll look around. Maybe I'll find someone in the black market. Or someone who's about to escape, but it's not going to be me. Not unless we can find a car." He laughed a little and Mary wondered what had happened to his leg, which he stuck out awkwardly in front of him. You can practically tell people's histories from their medical problems, she thought, remembering what the psychiatrist said about Layla. Everyone who had to go to street doctors, anyway. She wondered if she could ever be as casual about her own problems.

"Well," she said, wanting to do something for him, to repay his kindness, "maybe we'll find a car."

He laughed again, loudly. "And people think I'm an optimist," he said.

9

O<small>N</small> M<small>ONDAY</small> <small>NIGHT</small> L<small>AYLA</small>
sat cross-legged on her cot and watched Mary through nearly closed
eyes. She's pretending to be asleep, Layla thought. She doesn't want to
talk to me. In one of Layla's hands, resting against her knee, was a
small dull metal can, a little like a canister of photographic film.

Nothing had gone right since they had come to the rehab center.
Mary was free of the drugs but she was no closer to beginning her
initiation. And it would be impossible to continue Mary's training if
Mary refused to speak to her. Even worse, in the past few days Layla
had been unable to visit the land of animals. On Sunday she had stolen
a candle from the supply warehouse and stared into the flame until it
nearly reached her fingertips, but she had seen nothing. She had failed
the bear-spirit somehow. Even Archangel no longer came to her. There
was no one she could go to for advice.

She unscrewed the top of the metal can. Inside, rolled up and packed
in saline solution, were ten small strips of what looked like transparent
plastic. "This can is free," the man who was helping her paint the
dorm had told her. "I'll start your tab on the next one."

She had tried film before, on the Berkeley campus when she was an
apprentice. She had pressed the thin strip against her eye, and within
minutes she was back in her parents' living room listening to her father

tell a neighbor that the rabbit on the lawn was a homing rabbit. "We just let it out of its cage," her father said. "And it hops off and delivers its message and then comes back. You never heard of a homing rabbit?" He had actually never seen the rabbit before the neighbor pointed it out to him.

The memory was perfect in every detail. But the colors were brighter, and every object stood out sharply, as if cut with a knife. Everything seemed charged with significance. It reminded her of her few visits to the land of animals, or of being in love.

She never knew how Archangel found out she was using film. He said nothing directly. Instead he took her to an unfamiliar part of the campus and showed her a man standing motionless in the middle of a grove of trees. She smelled the heavy spice of eucalyptus. "That's the Stone Man," Archangel said in his deep rumbling voice. "He used to be a great maskmaker, but now no one remembers his name. Some people still come and feed him and clean him up, but after a while he won't be able to eat. Do you know what happened to him?"

She shook her head. She knew, but she was too ashamed to speak.

"He used to use film," Archangel said. "But a true maskmaker doesn't need drugs to enter the land of animals. Drugs are unpredictable, but the land of animals is constant, eternal. Do you understand?"

She nodded. That evening she dropped her canister of film on the concrete steps of the building she slept in. It was gone by morning. She never found out what happened to it.

Now she looked hard at the canister in her hand. It would help her enter a memory, but which one? Her father's disappearance? Her arrest? If only she could be sure it would be a memory of the land of animals.

"A true maskmaker doesn't need drugs to enter the land of animals," Archangel had said. Damn it, where are you? Layla thought. Show yourself, talk to me, advise me! The room was silent. She sighed, screwed the lid back on the canister and set it down.

The guard came back the next evening. "They think I'm crazy," he told Layla almost as soon as she opened the door. Mary sighed and turned over on her cot. "That bastard Anderson, he says he's going to discipline me if I keep talking about the mask the way I do. 'Look at it, you asshole,' I told him, only I didn't say asshole. 'There's something there, can't you see it?' And you know what he said to me? He said there wasn't all that much difference between me and the nuts I lock up. I beg your pardon. That's what he said."

The force of his outburst had carried him into the center of the room, and now he stood between the cots, looking around as if wondering how he got there. "Sit down," Layla said from her cot. He sat next to her.

"All right, maybe there isn't that much difference," the guard said. "But does that mean Anderson's right and I'm wrong? All he has to do is look at the mask and he knows there's something going on here. Maybe aliens. Maybe those animals of yours. I don't know. If he can't see it maybe he's the crazy one. I mean, there's more of us, right?"

Layla nodded. "There is something, definitely," she said. "The land of animals is real. I've seen it."

"Hey, I was wondering," the guard said, excited. "If everybody has a tribe, then what's mine? If you were outside could you make me a mask?"

"Well, I'd have to—to go into a trance first," Layla said. "To find out your tribal animal. And then if I had the materials, sure, I could make you a mask."

"Great," the guard said. "Could you do that? Even if you can't make me a mask it would help just to know what tribe I am. It'd help me stand up to Anderson. I bet he's from the rat tribe—he looks just like a little rat. I know, I know," he said, laughing a little. "That's not the way you do it. It doesn't matter what the person looks like. But he does look like a rat, doesn't he?"

Layla nodded, her eyes wide and unfocused. Could she find out what tribe the guard was from? If only he had asked her a few days ago, when the way to the land of animals had been clear. Now she was not sure she could do it.

"Layla?" the guard said.

She forced herself to look at him. "Sure," she said. She couldn't let him know her doubts, not when he had made such progress. "I'll find out what tribe you are. Right now I'm just—I'm a little tired."

"Well, I'll go then," the guard said. "See you later."

After he had gone Layla sat on the bed, trying to will herself into a trance. What animal was the guard? Why couldn't she find the path to the land of animals? Where was Archangel? What animal? He looked a little like a ferret. She wanted to scream. Only a novice would make the mistake of confusing a person's appearance with his tribe. Even the guard knew better. Where was the path? She couldn't admit her failure, not to the guard and not to Mary either, in case Mary wanted to continue her initiation. She stared into the light bulb hoping for a sight of the cool green land, stared long enough that when she looked away dark spots danced before her eyes. The room stayed white and black, everything in light and shadow. There was no land of animals. After a long time she took the metal canister out from beneath her mattress, opened it, and pressed one of the thin clear strips to her eye.

Archangel sat in his wheelchair in front of her. She was in a group of five or six people, and Archangel was showing them how to carve a wooden mask. Rays of light shone off his knife. The darkness in the hollows of the mask spiraled inward, shadows casting other shadows. The green of the trees and grass was the green of crayons.

A part of her stood hypnotized by the deft movement of the knife, but mostly she ached for a sight of the land of animals. She would probably not see it, not this time. If only the film had carried her back to another memory.

"The mask is not a disguise," Archangel was saying as he carved. "If anything it is your face that is the disguise. The mask serves to reveal your true nature. You must learn to sear the mask to your face in your initiation, to wear it always, even when it is not physically present. Only then will you understand what it is we do here."

That was good. She would have to remember to repeat it to Mary, if Mary ever spoke to her again.

"This mania for film," Archangel said, emphasizing his words with jabs of his knife, "exists because we have not yet let go of the past. We still yearn for the old, dead days, the days before the Collapse when we had our cars and our computers and other toys. But this mourning is foolish. Those days will not return. Instead we have a chance, unique in human history, to go back thousands of years and join our ancestors, the discoverers of the land of animals. We have a chance to put right the world our obsession with technology has made."

In the memory Layla watched him impassively, but his words made her uncomfortable. Had he really said that? She didn't remember any of this at all. Maybe her mind, guilty because she had taken the film, had invented the entire thing. The memories film showed were supposed to be real memories, stored somewhere inside the brain cells. But how could anyone know that?

The bright colors were dimming and she knew the memory was about to end. Then suddenly she was back in the small room she shared with Mary. The overhead bulb had gone out and the room seemed very cold. She started to shiver.

On Saturday Mary lay on her cot and wondered if it was time to go to the psychiatrist. Layla was on her cot, not moving. Mary closed her eyes. He could just come get her if he wanted her.

She knew that if she saw him she would break down and tell him everything. She was not strong enough to resist his offer. And even if she did answer his questions, so what? What loyalty did she owe to Layla? It had been Layla who had gotten her into the center, after all.

She needed the pills to feel normal, to feel human. The women on the conveyor belt shied away from her when she came to work, as though epilepsy were contagious. No one spoke to her. All day she worked alone on the belt, attaching a screw to a piece of metal. She felt a bitter satisfaction in the thought that people were reacting to her seizures the way she always knew they would.

But she felt enough loyalty to Layla to stay on her cot and wonder what the psychiatrist was doing. Was he angry? Would he send a guard to get her? She could always say she had had a seizure.

The guard came in without knocking. "Hey, Layla!" he said. "Wake up. I've got to tell you something!"

Layla didn't move. Mary sat up. "Can't you see she's in a trance?" Mary said scornfully. She hoped the guard would go away. "You can't talk to her now."

The guard squinted at her as if trying to remember who she was, then looked back at Layla. Her fists were tightly closed and her upper lip was lifted in a gesture of pain. "I don't think that's a trance," he said. "I think she's on film."

"Film?" Mary said. Where had she heard of film before? She felt stupid, as though everyone around her knew something she didn't. But she wasn't going to ask the guard what he meant.

"Yeah," he said. "Has she been acting any different lately?"

"I don't—I don't know," Mary said. She had been so tense waiting for the next seizure that she had barely noticed Layla at all. "Maybe."

"Well, have you ever seen her put something in her eye?" the guard said. "Or have you noticed a small metal can around here?"

Mary hesitated. If she told him, would he get Layla in trouble? But Layla seemed to trust him. "A metal can," Mary said, nodding. "But I don't know where she keeps it."

"Okay," the guard said. He looked under Layla's cot. "You look on your side. We've got to take it away from her. It's not good for her."

The room was so small they finished searching in five minutes. Neither one had found the film. "She must have hidden it outside somewhere," the guard said. "Listen. What I wanted to tell her was— I think they're getting ready to sack me. For saying what I think. You tell her that—she'll know what I mean. So I'm gonna leave before they can do it. It would be horrible to be a prisoner here after I've been a guard. I'll try to take her with me. Can you tell her that?"

"Leave," Mary said. "Can you take me too?"

The guard looked at her, then shrugged. "Sure," he said. "If it's okay with her."

After he left, Mary sat on her cot and watched Layla. She was excited, willing to forgive Layla anything if she could only escape. Layla did not move for a long time; then suddenly she sat up and looked around her as if unsure where she was. "Damn," she said finally. Mary wondered if Layla saw her. She seemed to be talking to herself. "I was back in high school. Too early."

"Layla?" Mary said. Layla looked at her and blinked. "Your friend the guard was here. He said—"

Layla stood up and went to the door. Mary followed her. "Where are you going?" Mary said. "Didn't you hear what I said? The guard was here." They were walking down the corridor. Mary lowered her voice. There might be a guard around but her message was too important to wait. "He said—he said he wants to leave. They're going to fire him and he wants to leave before they do it. And he wants to take us with him. Layla!"

Layla was nearly running. She opened the door to the outside and went down a wide dirt path leading to the barbed-wire fence. The day was cold.

At the main wire gate Layla stopped and looked around. "Ah," she said softly and went to a ring of stones by the side of the gate. Mary had once seen two or three guards sitting there by a campfire at night. Layla dipped her hand into the ashes and spread the ashes over her face.

"Archangel did this, just before he died," Layla said. Her eyes were wide. The whites of her eyes looked unhealthy, yellow. "He said most people were too afraid of death. He said if you knew your death was coming you should accept it. Welcome it if you can."

"Layla," Mary said urgently, "you're not going to die. Didn't you hear me? The guard says he can get us out. We're going to escape."

"It's too late," Layla said. She had completely covered her face in the white ashes. "I've lost the land of animals. I've lost Archangel. There's nothing left, nothing except film, and that will kill me."

"So stop taking the film!" Mary said, almost shouting. A guard with a rifle walked past on the other side of the fence and Mary moved away, hoping Layla would follow. "Stop taking the film and you'll be fine. We'll get out of here. Listen to me!"

"It won't matter," Layla said. Her face was expressionless. "Whether I'm in here or out there won't matter if I can't find the land of animals."

Mary shivered. Layla looked like an apparition, like something from the world of dreams set down in the harsh reality of the prison. "You'll feel better once you get out," Mary said. "You'll see."

Layla didn't answer.

"She doesn't want to do it," Mary told the guard when he returned the next day. A train whistled off in the distance. "She thinks she's going to die here. She wants to die because she can't find the land of animals."

The guard looked at Layla's cot. Layla had taken film again, though Mary was ready to swear she hadn't let her out of her sight. Moved by an impulse she didn't understand, Mary had wiped the ashes off Layla's face with her blanket. Now she saw she had left a white smudge running from her hairline to her chin.

"Is that what she said?" the guard said. Mary nodded. "Maybe we should leave her here then. If that's what she wants. If that's what her power tells her."

"No!" Mary said. "Haven't you listened to a word I said? Her power's left her. That's why she wants to die."

"And if she escapes, the power will return?"

"Uh-huh," Mary said. How should she know? But she was willing to lie, to do almost anything, to get out.

"Okay," the guard said. "Then we'll just have to take her with us. Carry her if we have to. Do you think you can carry her to the car?"

"I—no," Mary said, thinking fast. He had a car! "But I know someone who can help us."

"I don't know," the guard said slowly. "I don't want too many people in on this."

"Well, I can't carry her," Mary said. "And even if I could it would look suspicious, don't you think? But if it's me and this other guy we can hold her up between us and you could look like you're taking us somewhere."

"I don't know," the guard said. "The way I saw it it was just going to be the two of us. How do I know I can trust this guy?"

"How did you know you could trust me?" Mary said. "When you told me you were going to escape?"

"She said you were okay," the guard said.

"Well, I'm saying this guy is okay," Mary said.

The guard sighed. "All right," he said finally. "We've got to do it soon, before they get suspicious. Can you be ready Saturday? No, wait, better make it Friday. Anderson's off duty then. Friday before breakfast. All right?"

"Sure," Mary said.

"I'll see you then," the guard said. He looked at Layla, silent in her cot. "And try to stop her from taking film, okay?"

After he had gone Mary ran out of the dorm, elated. She hurried up and down the dirt paths, breathing heavily. Finally, as the bell rang for dinner, she found Brian.

"Hey, Brian!" she said. He turned around. Her face felt red, raw in the autumn wind. "I did it!"

"What did you do?" Brian said.

She waited until he was close enough that she wouldn't have to shout. Her heart was pounding so loud she thought she wouldn't be able to get the words out. For all his connections, his knowledge about the way things were done, she had been the one to find a way out. "I found someone who will help us escape," she said.

"You did?" Brian said. His voice was cautious, but she heard the excitement in it. "Who?"

"That guard," Mary said. Now that she had stopped running she felt the wind rise on her arms. A few people passed them, heading toward the dorms for dinner. "The short one with only one eyebrow. The one who always comes by to talk to Layla."

"Oh, Greg," Brian said.

"Is that his name?" Mary said. "How do you know? He sure doesn't look like a Greg to me."

"So he's going to help you escape," Brian said, prompting her. Was he smiling?

"Not me," Mary said. "Us. He's got a car. He wants to get away before they sack him, he said. And they will, too. He's nuts. You should hear him talk. Anyway, he's taking Layla and me, and since we might need one more person to carry Layla I said you."

"And he agreed?" Brian said. As Mary nodded he said, "Why would you need to carry Layla, though?"

"She's taking film," Mary said.

Brian was silent for a while. "Have you thought," he said finally, "that once we get out we won't have anywhere to go? They took our ID cards. And they have our fingerprints, and a retinal scan. We'd have to go underground."

"ID cards can be faked," Mary said impatiently. Surely he of all people would know that.

"Not once they get those computers from the Japanese," Brian said.

"Look," Mary said, "do you want to do this or don't you? Because I can get someone else to help us. We can worry about ID cards and all that once we're out."

"Sure I want to do it," he said. "I'm just warning you about what might happen. The other thing is that if they think Greg's crazy they're probably keeping a closer eye on him. We'll have to be careful."

"The guy that thinks he's crazy is off duty that day," she said. "Don't worry. Nothing's going to happen."

"All right," Brian said. Suddenly he smiled. "Hell, it's a chance. Thanks."

"You're welcome," Mary said stiffly. She had wanted his gratitude, but now she felt awkward under the burden of it.

"So what've we got?" Brian said, still smiling. "One crazy, one woman on film, a cripple and an epileptic. Think we'll make it?"

She started to say something sharp when he said "epileptic" and then stopped. She was an epileptic, wasn't she? And he had called himself a cripple. "Sure we will," she said confidently. "It's Friday morning, before breakfast. We'll come get you. Which one is your dorm?"

Brian pointed across the yard. "And where will we go from there?" he said. "Once we're out?"

"I don't know," Mary said, still confident. "You figure it out."

Mary watched Layla closely Monday during dinner. "The guard's going to help us escape," Mary said when they were back in their small room. "On Friday, before breakfast. So we've got to be ready to leave. Okay?"

Layla stood in the middle of the room and looked at something to Mary's right. Mary resisted the urge to turn around. "That means no film, Layla," Mary said. "Do you understand?"

Layla moved toward the cot. Did she even hear me? Mary wondered. She better not do anything to mess this up. The cot made no sound as Layla sat down. There was no sound anywhere. It had all happened so slowly that seconds passed before Mary realized she was about to have another seizure. Then sound came back, but imperfectly, a wave of noise, then silence and another wave. She was surrounded by people asking questions, explaining things, bringing her maps and papers and food and drink. Everyone was gripped by urgency. For a brief moment she knew where she was and what she was doing—knew her future—and then the noise crashed over her and she forgot everything.

She woke in the infirmary again, with her right wrist bandaged. She must have hurt it when she fell. Someone was standing over her, blocking the overhead light. She moved her head to see better. It was the psychiatrist. Embarrassed, she pulled the blanket up over her shoulders.

"You had another seizure, they tell me," the psychiatrist said.

Mary nodded. Just because you're sick everyone feels they have a right to your life, she thought bitterly. She closed her eyes.

She heard the jangle of the metal cot springs and knew he had sat on the cot next to her. "And you missed my session on Saturday, too," he said. "Why was that?"

Mary said nothing.

"Were you ill?" he said. He waited for a reply and then said, "You know, if you don't answer my questions I can have you transferred. Away from Layla."

She opened her eyes and shrugged.

"Somewhere away from here," he said. "This is pretty soft, as far as these centers go. Why don't you tell me what happened Saturday?"

"I was sick," she said.

"Ah," he said. "Another seizure?" She nodded. "You're getting them more frequently, aren't you? Have you thought about my offer?"

"No," Mary said truthfully. She had thought about nothing but the escape since Saturday. Despite what Brian had said she was sure they would make it.

"You're being foolish," he said. "Why don't you tell me what I want to know, help Layla out, and then you won't have to worry about the seizures again?"

She closed her eyes. "I don't know anything," she said, trying to sound drowsy. "I told you. I don't talk to her."

The psychiatrist stood up. "All right," he said. "I'll talk to you Saturday. We'll see if we can come to some sort of agreement then." His tone was pleasant; a nurse or doctor, had one been in the room, would not have noticed the underlying threat. He would probably have her transferred if she didn't snitch on Layla.

She heard the door open and close, and the psychiatrist's steps recede down the hall. Now she would have to escape on Friday. There was no other way.

Mary woke on Friday and wondered what time it was. She wanted to go outside and look at the sky but she was determined not to leave Layla. She lay under the blanket completely dressed, feeling pleasantly warm, for what seemed like an hour. Finally Layla sat up stiffly and rubbed her upper arms.

"Hey," Mary said, sitting up. "Remember what day it is today?" Layla looked at her blankly. "It's Friday. The day we're going to escape."

There were traces of ashes on Layla's face. She wrapped the blanket around her and walked out of the room, tiptoeing to avoid contact with the cold floor. She had high, aristocratic arches.

Mary followed her. They walked to the bathroom down the hall and Mary had a moment of panic when Layla went into the stall and locked the door behind her. But when Layla came out she looked the same, no better and no worse. Mary didn't think she'd taken film.

Layla started back to the dorm room. "No," Mary said, whispering. "This way."

Layla looked at her with no emotion. Was it too late? Surely film didn't work that fast; someone on the conveyor belt said you had to take it for years before it wore down your central nervous system. Mary shivered convulsively.

"This way," Mary said again, urgently. Layla followed without giving any sign that she understood what was being asked of her. Mary tested the front door. It was locked.

Mary sat down on the worn black-and-white-checked linoleum, her back against the door. After a while Layla joined her. Mary hoped the guard—Greg—would come soon. At any moment Layla might lose interest, wander back to the dorm room or wherever she kept her film. At any moment someone from one of the other rooms might come out and wonder what they were doing there. She felt calm, her senses heightened, almost as if she were about to have a seizure. But she knew she wasn't going to have a seizure.

The door rattled against her and she stood up quickly. What if it wasn't Greg? She had been stupid to wait by the door; they should have stayed in the room. She was so eager to escape she wasn't thinking clearly.

"Hi," Greg said.

"Hi," Mary said. She realized she had been holding her breath.

"How's Layla?"

"She didn't take any film, as far as I can tell," Mary said. "But she's acting pretty weird. Disoriented."

"I wonder if they've gone away," Greg said. Mary looked at him. "The aliens, I mean."

"Come on," Mary said impatiently. He could talk about aliens once they were safely outside. "We've got to get going. Brian's dorm is over that way."

"I brought you some coats," Greg said. "It's pretty cold out there. They're going to pass these out on Monday."

Wordlessly she took the shapeless brown coat he handed her, hoping her surprise didn't show. She never would have expected him to think of a detail like that.

"And I burned your files," Greg said, whispering. "Last night. So now they don't have anything on any of you."

It was cold outside, even with the coat. They walked in single file, Mary first, then Layla, then the guard. Once they passed another guard and he and Greg nodded at each other. Mary wondered what time it was, if they were up before curfew. This might be the earliest she had been outside in nine years. The grass was wet.

Brian was waiting for them inside his dorm. They walked silently to the front gate, Brian between Mary and Layla. Greg began to open the lock.

"Hiya, Greg," a guard on the other side of the barbed wire said. He held a rifle over his shoulder.

"Hi," Greg said. Mary hoped the other guard didn't hear his voice tremble.

"Where you going?"

"I'm transferring the prisoners," Greg said, opening the wire gate.

"Yeah?" the guard said. "Isn't that what's-her-name, the one you're always talking about? The one who made the mask?"

Mary felt all her muscles tense. Greg hesitated, too long, Mary thought. "No," he said finally. "I don't think so."

They walked through the gate, toward a police car parked by an abandoned brick building. Greg and Layla got in front, Greg at the wheel, Mary and Brian in back. "So far so good," Greg said under his breath, and started the car.

"He's talking to someone," Brian said. "He's got a walkie-talkie."

"Damn!" Greg said. He shifted into drive and the car jerked forward. "Checking on us, the idiot, who does he think—"

There was a sharp slap against the side of the car. "They're shooting at us!" Brian said. "From the watchtower!"

146

Greg pushed the accelerator down as far as it would go. They sped along the deserted road. Then they were skidding wildly, turning in a wide arc across the street. Brian fell over onto Mary, and Mary held on tight to the seat. In front of her Greg was fighting with the wheel. "Shot the tire, the bastard!" Greg said over the noise of the car.

Two big police cars came out of a side gate, sirens shrieking wildly up and down the scale. Greg straightened the wheel, turned right, then left, then right again. The police cars were close behind them. Greg turned again. Ahead of them was a short street with a warehouse at the end.

"Dead end!" Brian said.

"No it's not!" Greg said, forcing the car into the warehouse parking lot. Red brick buildings surrounded the parking lot on all sides, bouncing crazily as the car drove onward. "Goddamnit," Greg said. The police cars sounded close behind them now. "All right," he said, stopping the car. "Let's run for it." He leaned across Layla and opened her door. "Get out," he said harshly. Layla looked blank. "Outside. Run, goddamnit!" Layla stepped outside. She was still wrapped in her blanket, carefully carrying the coat Greg had given her.

Mary opened the door and ran into an empty brick building. A shot sounded and she looked outside, through a gutted window. Another shot, and Layla was down, collapsed inside her blanket. Mary gasped. Greg turned back for her, lifted her and ran toward a building across the parking lot. A few shots followed him but he continued running.

None of the policemen had seen Brian, hopping on one foot away from the car. "Brian!" Mary said. "Over here!" He stopped for only a moment and then stumbled toward her. She held the door open for him and slammed it shut as he fell, gasping, inside the building.

The policemen got out of the cars and headed in the direction Greg had gone. "What happened to Layla?" Mary said, whispering. "Did you see her? Is she okay?"

Brian put his finger to his lips and Mary nodded. The policemen went down an alleyway.

"I don't know," Brian said after a few minutes. "I didn't see them."

"She's hurt," Mary said. "Maybe killed. She said she was going to die. And I didn't—I can't—"

"Stop that," Brian said. "We've got to get going."

"Going?" Mary said, feeling dazed. "Where?"

"Anywhere," Brian said. "Probably the campus. They could come back any minute."

"Can you make it?"

Brian laughed shortly. "I'll have to try, won't I?" he said.

They walked through the empty echoing warehouse, looking for an exit. The back door was locked, but there was a jagged hole in the window nearby big enough for them to climb through.

"Where to now?" Mary said, looking around them.

"I guess—over toward those big buildings there," Brian said. "Where the freeway used to be." He pointed about a mile ahead of them.

Before them stretched flat wide streets, the asphalt and concrete starting to buckle as plants forced their way through. Jagged black shadows lay in the streets. They passed empty fields, burned-out Victorian houses, parking lots, deserted office buildings and restaurants. Birds called, and once they saw a train passing in the distance, infinitely lonely, the only moving thing in the landscape.

After half an hour the shops and office buildings were closer together and in better repair. The street was still quiet, but Mary thought people lived in these buildings. She was eager to be away, out of sight of the pair of eyes she felt watching her behind each boarded-up or painted-over window. She took off her coat and began to hurry. Brian had picked up a metal rod and was leaning against it as he followed her. "Wait . . ." he said.

"Sorry," she said. "Am I going too fast?"

"Stop . . ."

Reluctantly, she stopped. They sat on the curb, their feet stretched out before them in the street. "People live here, don't they?" she said. The street was hotter now, and the silence had become oppressive.

"Yeah," Brian said. He was breathing heavily. "We don't bother them and they won't bother us."

"You think so?" Mary asked.

Brian nodded.

"How much farther?" Mary said.

Brian shook his head. "Don't know," he said. "But I think that street up ahead might be Telegraph. See, there are the big buildings we were aiming for."

Mary looked at the street doubtfully.

"It's a long street," he said. "We still have a couple miles to go."

"But we'll be okay once we get to campus, right?" Mary said. "Greg said he burned our files, so all we have to do is get fake ID cards."

Brian laughed shortly. "It's not that easy," he said. "There's still a file on each of us at the station we were booked at—Berkeley, right?" Mary nodded. "Those files are the ones with our fingerprints and descriptions and everything. And when they get those computers that'll be the first thing to get transferred, and then every police station in the country will have access to information on us if they want it."

Mary said nothing. She didn't want to think about the police, or about what had happened to Layla, or about the hunger she was starting to feel. She wanted to think that if they made it to the campus they would be safe. Everything else could wait.

"Well," Brian said, standing up and leaning on the metal rod, "let's go."

There were no street signs when they came to the big street, but they saw a few people walking along the sidewalk and even a small store selling a few fruits and vegetables. "This has got to be it," Brian said, turning left. "Put your coat back on."

Mary stared at him. "Why?"

"You don't want people to see your clothes—they're from the rehab center," he said. "And keep an eye out for cop cars. We'll have to hide if one comes by."

They passed a few blocks gutted by fire, then more small stores, looking temporary and lost inside big department stores and the marble lobbies of tall office buildings. People walked by quickly, not looking at them. A bus drove noisily past and Mary stared after it with longing.

After nearly an hour Brian stopped at an abandoned building, opened the door and motioned her in. "Rest," he said. "Sorry."

The first-floor ceiling had fallen in and they sat on a heap of boards and plaster. Almost no light came in past the boarded-up windows. There was a dirty blanket and a pile of newspapers in one corner.

"How come the cops don't go on campus?" Mary said after a while.

"They have an agreement," Brian said. "The government wanted to close down the campus nine years ago, and the students and teachers wouldn't leave. The General sent in troops, but he wasn't as well organized then as he is now, and the students started winning. But at the same time a lot of homeless people started living on campus, and a lot of the first maskmakers, and the government let them. And they just took over. Two years later the troops came back and took away everyone who was teaching or going to classes, and made the agreement with everyone else.

"But you know what the General's like," Brian said. "He kept his side of the bargain for a few years, and then he started sending police on campus. But the people there had had time to organize, and they caught the police by surprise. And then just a few years ago two of the General's snitches were found dead. The General can't get the police to go in there. So for now the General claims the agreement still holds, though I don't know how long that will last."

"Well, why doesn't everyone live on campus then?" Mary said.

"It's not that great a place to live," Brian said. "There's lots of crime, for one thing, because the police don't go there. And you have to watch out for the crazies. And there's no heat in winter, and sometimes there are food shortages." He saw her expression and grinned. "Sorry," he said, "but it's the only safe place I know."

"How come you know so much?" Mary said. "Where do you learn it all?"

Brian laughed. "Well, that particular piece of history I know because I was there," he said. "With the students against the government. Got shot in the leg, so I won't forget that in a hurry."

"Is that why—?"

"That's what happened to my leg, yeah," Brian said. "Actually I was lucky. Could have been a lot worse."

"I hope Layla's lucky," Mary said.

"Well," Brian said, "street doctors are a lot better now." He stood up. "Should we get started?"

"Okay," Mary said. "God, I'm hungry."

"We'll try to make it to campus before dinner," Brian said, opening the door.

"Do they have dinner?" Mary said.

"Oh, yeah," Brian said as they stepped outside. "Steak and mashed potatoes, lasagna, chef's salad . . ."

Mary laughed. "Any dessert?"

"Sure," Brian said. "What do you want?" He leaned heavily against the metal rod.

They went on. Once Mary saw a police car coming toward them, and they ducked into a narrow passageway between two buildings. They rested several times. The shadows were lengthening by the time Mary recognized the street Layla had lived on and then the supermarket on Ashby. "Almost there," she said.

Even Brian was trying to hurry now. Mary felt a rush of love for the buildings, the people, the cracked uneven sidewalks. A part of her had thought she would never live to see Berkeley again. They passed her street, the Green Dragon, the other cafes. Everything looked just the same.

They walked onto the campus. Four or five people sat in a large paved square, bedrolls or coats beside them, staring blankly ahead. They looked like they haven't washed for weeks, Mary thought, and then realized that she hadn't washed in all the time at the rehab center. A woman in rags danced close to them and would have bumped into Mary if she hadn't moved away. "No room," she sang. "All filled up. No room left."

Mary looked at Brian, worried, but Brian ignored the woman and walked on. They really are all crazy here, she thought, and moved closer to Brian. A man walked by, mumbling to himself. Suddenly he turned to her. "I shot the General," he said. "Did you know that? I did. No one knows it, though. No one."

"Come on," Brian said. "We've got to find a room before we do anything else. Let's get away from the center of the campus— everything here is probably taken."

He led her past open lawns and buildings, then stopped and looked up at an ugly concrete building. "How does this look?" he asked.

"Okay," Mary said.

"Our new home," he said, sounding dubious. "Let's go see if there's a vacancy."

Sergeant Anderson sat at his desk in the guards' room and stared at the blank piece of paper in front of him. Damn that idiot Greg! He should have kept a closer watch on the guy, should have discharged him the minute he'd started babbling about masks and aliens on the moon. Now he had to make a complete report on that asshole, and on the escape. It was going to look very bad, bad for the center and bad for Anderson personally. He remembered hearing about Lester Martin's escape and how relieved he'd felt that Martin had escaped from another rehab center. And now it had happened to him, not one person escaping but three. He'd be happy when those computers came, when all you had to do was press a button and complete information about a person would appear on the screen, fingerprints, retinal scan, everything. That scum Greg and his friends had better watch out then.

He sighed and leaned back in his chair. Where to begin, how to tell it so it wouldn't look so bad, who could he shift the blame to? Almost the worst thing about this whole mess was that he'd had to come in on a Friday, his day off. He picked up a pen, sighed again, put it down.

Something moved to the right and behind him and he turned angrily. Damnit, he'd given orders not to be interrupted. But there was nothing there, just the black mask on the wall. It seemed to watch him, to mock him. It was disturbing, all right. No wonder Greg had heard voices from the moon. The moon looked like a kind of mask too when you thought about it, known and understood for what seemed like only a minute and now out of reach again, mysterious. He shook his head. That was crazy, the kind of thought that had gotten Greg in trouble and would probably get him in trouble too if he didn't watch it. As soon as he finished the report he'd throw the mask in the trash. No, even better, he'd send it on with his report to Washington. After all, it was evidence. He relaxed, grinned a little as he imagined those bureaucrats in Washington opening the package and coming face to face with the dead black mask. Served them right, they meddled in his job too much as it was. Still grinning he rolled the piece of paper into his ancient typewriter and started typing.

10

THEY CHECKED ROOMS ON the first two floors and finally found a tiny deserted office on the third floor. Brian found a scrap of paper and some tape, wrote their names on the paper and taped it to the outside of the door.

"You mean the place is ours now?" Mary asked. "That's all it takes?"

Brian nodded. "Sometimes you'll get challenged," he said. "Or someone will take your name off the door. But I don't think anyone really wants this space. Come on—let's look for food."

Mary looked around at the hallway. Every square inch of the walls and most of the linoleum floor had been painted over, mostly graffiti and nicknames, a few abstract shapes and bright splashes of color. The ceiling was a concrete grid lined with ducts and thick black wires. They walked down narrow rubber-floored stairs.

"I think this used to be for architecture students," Brian said. "The building was never really finished, so the students could get examples of how a building is built."

"Weird," Mary said. The idea of a building as something other than a space to live or work seemed an extravagance to her, another example of frivolity from before the Collapse.

"So that's probably why we found a room so easily," Brian said as they went down a wide concrete staircase. "Also it's mostly concrete, so it probably gets cold in winter. Don't lose your coat."

Up ahead Mary could see a large room being used as a cafeteria, nearly empty now. Brian went inside and walked up to the counter. "I don't know you," the woman behind the counter said. "I can't serve you if you don't live here."

"We just moved in," Brian said. "Does Julie still live here? Or Dr. Cat?"

The woman looked at him. "Not for years," she said.

Another woman came out of a door leading to the kitchen. "Brian?" she said, wiping her hands on a rag. "Is that really you? I heard you were in a rehab center."

"Luisa!" Brian said. "Could we get some food? We haven't had anything all day. We'll be glad to start working after dinner."

"I don't think we need anyone today," Luisa said. "I'll show you the sign-up sheet and you can start tomorrow, though. In the meantime I can probably give you something."

They took watery soup and peas and mashed potatoes, and found a table. "What if we'd just taken the food?" Mary said, whispering. "Who would have stopped us?"

"See that woman by the door?" Brian said. Mary saw a heavy powerfully built woman with short blond hair. "She has a gun."

Mary looked away quickly and took a bite of the mashed potatoes. After the bland porridge at the rehab center it tasted delicious. Luisa came to their table and showed them the sign-up sheets. "Working in the fields, mostly," she said. "That sound okay to you?"

Mary finished the soup. "Sure," she said.

The days developed a rhythm, slower and easier than that of the rehab center. From morning to afternoon she went out to the reclaimed fields with a group of people from the architecture building and worked to bring in the harvest. In the afternoon, when she got back, she wandered the campus. She washed in the stream that ran through the trees. She learned which of the crazy people were dangerous and which were harmless. Once she saw a truck unload meat and vegetables, and she realized that the campus was getting food from the black market, that the harvest would not be enough to feed everybody.

Probably the cops didn't interfere because of the agreement. Once she passed a building and heard what sounded like a hundred people having a fight, and when she went inside she saw people shouting and screaming and running and throwing things. Later when she asked Brian he said that that was the weekly campus meeting, and not to bother going because nothing was ever decided there.

Sometimes she asked people if they'd seen Layla. Around the third week she started hearing rumors: Layla was in the hospital, Layla was dead, Layla had come and gone. She worried about Layla, and worried too about their files in the Berkeley police station, waiting to be transferred to computer. If the files were gone they could get fake ID cards and be free to travel.

But for the most part she was happy. She grew fit working in the fields. She had a seizure one morning and then stopped worrying about them. There were worse things that could happen to her. And Brian was there to give her an example of how someone could live gracefully with a disability.

After a brief hot spell the days turned cold. The room she and Brian shared was icy at night, and she was glad for the coats Greg had given them. She woke at night and wondered where Layla was, and remembered what the psychiatrist had said about Layla's reaction to cold.

One day she was sitting in the cafeteria with Brian and a few of the people from the fields. "You know," she said, "if we could get into the police station and get our files we could get out of here."

"Great idea," someone said sarcastically. An iguana mask rested on the table next to him. "Walk into a police station and say, 'Can I have my file please? Thank you very much.'"

"No, it is a good idea," Luisa said. "I bet it could be done, if you plan it carefully. And it should be done now, before they get those computers."

"Hey," someone said, "while you're at it, get my file too."

"Sure," Mary said. It still seemed amazing to her that on campus people could talk about whatever they wanted, could even wear masks if they wanted to. A discussion about raiding a police station would never have gotten started outside the campus, and if it had everything would have been said in whispers, with people looking carefully to the right and left for police.

"Well, I'm with you," Luisa said. "Count me in."

"Me too," Brian said.

There were people on campus who would deliver a letter outside in exchange for a meal. Mary went without dinner and sent a letter to Don. A week passed, long enough for her to decide he had forgotten her, and then one day when she came off work she saw him standing in front of the architecture building. A light rain was falling. She stood still a minute, watching him, and then ran to meet him.

"Well, hi," he said. He looked at her with pleasure and a little doubt, as though she had changed since the last time he saw her. "You know, this is my first time on campus in all the time I've lived in Berkeley. If you hadn't given me such explicit directions I think I would have given up and gone home. Do all these people actually live here? Those guys, for example?"

A man was walking back and forth in front of the building, talking to himself angrily. He carried a large broken mirror on his back. A smaller man near him ripped pages from a book one by one and let them flutter away.

"Yeah, they do," Mary said. As usual around Don she wished she could think of more to say.

"Well, you're braver than I am, I'll tell you that," he said. "Why don't you give me the tour?" He put his arm on her shoulder, and after a minute she put her arm around his waist.

Without letting herself think of what she was doing she led him toward the architecture building. Her heart had started to pound so loudly she could barely hear herself talk. "This is where I live," she said. "Here's the cafeteria. Downstairs there's a generator that powers the lights, but I don't know anything about that. Brian—he's a friend of mine—he works there."

Don looked at her quickly when she mentioned Brian. She wished she hadn't said anything. They went up the concrete stair, then the narrow steps to the third floor. They had to walk single file up the steps, and when they came out on the third floor she took his hand.

"This is where I live," she said, opening the door. There was nothing inside the room except a battered metal desk that had been there when they moved in.

"Quaint," Don said. "Very quaint."

They went inside. He kissed her and moved her carefully to the floor. "I got the stuff," he said, whispering. "From Nick."

"Nick?" Mary said. "Is he—"

"Shhh," Don said. He undressed her slowly, kissing first her mouth, then her breasts. As he undressed, as if to spite her, images rose up of seizures, of naked white arms and legs flailing helplessly. She tensed and tried to sit up. "Shhh," Don said again, gentling her, guiding her slowly back to the floor.

His mouth was on her breasts, her stomach, caressing her, moving down slowly between her legs. She let herself be drawn along on a current of pleasure, floating with the movements of his tongue. He raised himself up and she felt a brief stab of pain as he went inside her. Then pleasure overwhelmed her completely.

Afterward she felt a return of her old embarrassment. She sat up awkwardly and started to dress, trying to think of something to say. For once Don was silent. "So what happened to Nick?" she said finally. "Is he still around?"

"Yeah," Don said. He reached for his pants and pulled them on. "Everybody knows he's a snitch, though. People mostly avoid him. He says he doesn't snitch anymore, but I don't know how much of that you can believe."

"And Ayako? And Mark?"

"Ayako's the same," Don said. He sat against the wall and she tried not to stare at his lean naked chest. "Mark, now—Mark's jealous of you, I think."

"Of me?" she said, surprised.

"Yeah," he said. "Because you've been in a rehab center. Because you opposed the General, or did something to annoy him."

"I didn't oppose him," she said. "It was a mistake, the whole thing."

"Well, but then you got out," he said. "How the hell did you do that, anyway? I nearly died when I got your letter. And Layla—you said Layla's out too?"

She told him what happened. "Poor Layla," he said. "She sounds like she's gotten lots worse."

"I just wish I could find her," she said. "Find her and get those files out of the police station. Then I could relax."

"You want to raid a police station?" he said. For the first time she heard him sound astonished at something.

"Yeah," she said. She forced herself to look directly at him.

"Well, why not?" he said. "Why not indeed? Escaping a rehab center, robbing a police station . . . you better watch it or you'll become a legendary figure. Like Layla."

"Stop being so cynical—"

He raised his hand to stop her. "Cynical?" he said. "Hell, if you ever do it I'll join you."

"You would?"

"Sure. And I bet Mark would want to do it too. Don't think I'll ask Nick, though."

She laughed. "Well, I'd better get going," he said, putting on his shirt. "Unless you can offer me dinner."

"No," she said. "I'm sorry. You have to work here to get dinner." He stood up. "Are you—do you think you'll come back?"

"Sure," he said.

"Mark thinks we should ask Nick for help," Don said in her room a few days later.

"Nick?" Mary said.

"Yeah. Mark says Nick's feeling guilty. He'd probably want to help you out."

"You think so?"

Don shrugged. "This is Mark's theory, not mine," he said. "Maybe he's right. I don't know."

"But what can Nick do?"

"Nick can probably do all kinds of things," Don said. "He's a snitch—he might even have access to the police station. He could draw us a map, or have you thought about a map?"

"Well, not yet," Mary said. She didn't want Don to know how little planning she'd done.

"How many people have you got so far?"

"Me and you and Mark. And Luisa—she works in the kitchen—and two or three of her friends. And Brian wants to help, but I don't think he can, the way his leg is."

"That sounds like enough right there," Don said.

"What about Nick?"

Don sighed. "I don't know," he said. "This whole thing is crazy. But if it works you might start something—some kind of underground movement. We could even get the Purple Press in on it."

She stared at him. "You think so?" she said.

He laughed. "Maybe," he said. He reached for her and they began to make love, slower and more expertly than the last time.

When it was over he held her for what seemed like a long time. How does he feel about me? she thought. He never says anything. And how do I feel about him? If we do this are we supposed to be in love? How do you know if you love someone or not?

He rolled away and ran his hand over her hip. "Where did you get this bruise?" he asked.

"Falling down," she said. "I fall down a lot." He raised an eyebrow. "I'm an epileptic," she said.

"You never told me that," he said. His hand moved idly up and down her leg. "Can't you get—something? Medicine or something?"

"Sure," she said. "Fifty dollars on the black market. I don't have any money."

"I could ask Mark—"

"No," she said. "Look. I was taking pills when I first got to Berkeley, but I was always afraid. Would I have enough money for them, or would I get caught buying from the black market, or would my connection get arrested? Now all I have to be afraid of is the seizures, and I only had one since I got to campus. I'm eating better, or I'm less afraid, or something. And I'm not dependent on anyone. I feel freer this way." His hand rested lightly on her bruise. "Does that make you feel weird?" she said. "That I could have a seizure at any time?"

"A little," he said. He stood and started to dress. "But not enough to keep me away."

A few days later nearly everyone brought a mask down to dinner and Mary realized with surprise that it was Hallowe'en. She had lost all track of the days. Some people wore the mask of their tribe but most of the masks were fragile, fanciful, made of paper and ribbon and pieces of cloth. Hallowe'en was not as serious a holiday as the days of the tribal dances.

"Don't you have a mask?" someone at Mary's table asked her. "What's your tribe, anyway?"

"She doesn't have a tribe," Luisa said. There was something in her tone—menace?—that made Mary stop eating and look at her in surprise.

"What do you mean?" Mary said. "Of course I have a tribe."

"Yeah?" Luisa said. "Then where's your mask?"

"I couldn't take my mask to the rehab center," Mary said. "What do you think—they let you wear masks in one of those things? I'm from the sea-otter tribe."

"Then you should have gotten another mask when you got here," Luisa said. "But I know why you didn't. You've lost your tribal soul."

"What are you talking about?" Mary said, annoyed and worried. She had only been on campus for a month. What if they decided to throw her out of the architecture building? Did Luisa have that power? She looked at Brian for reassurance.

"You know what I'm talking about," Luisa said. "I talked to Layla—"

"Layla?" Mary said. "Where? Is she all right?"

Luisa looked surprised. Probably she had expected Mary to say something else. "She's in the anthropology building, with some other maskmakers," she said. "I heard her talk. She said that this whole idea of the police raid is wrong. That we shouldn't worry about politics, about the General. That we should concentrate on tribal things and let the General do whatever he wants." A few of the people around the table were nodding. "She said anyone who would go on this raid doesn't have a tribe or a soul. And if Layla says it it's good enough for me. You can forget about me going with you."

"Me too," said one of Luisa's friends, and the rest nodded in agreement.

Mary sat back, feeling stunned. In one move Layla had wiped out their only chance for getting off campus. Why had she done it? Did Layla hate her that much? She felt small, powerless against the kind of influence Layla had. "Are you sure that's what she said?" Mary said. "We were friends—she made my mask. She wouldn't—wouldn't say—"

"She didn't sound like any friend of yours," Luisa said. "She was pretty definite. Anyone who goes on this raid would lose their tribal soul. That's what she said.''

"How was she?" Mary said. "Was she—hurt or anything?"

"Okay," Luisa said. She looked at Mary with suspicion, as though Mary had asked for information she had no right to. "She was walking kind of funny. And there was this short guy that she leaned on. But I think she was all right."

"Where's the anthropology building?" Mary asked. "Is it close by?"

Luisa stood. "I have to do the dishes tonight," she said. "I'd better get started, if I want to get to the party on time. I shouldn't even be talking to you, if Layla says you've lost your soul, but I wanted to tell you." She picked up and stacked a few of the dishes and walked away.

There was silence after she had gone, and then all her friends started talking among themselves. Mary turned to Brian. Would he back out too? How seriously did he take this mask business? "The anthropology building is just one building over, down that way," Brian said. "There used to be a museum there with all kinds of masks and statues and art, so I guess that's why some maskmakers still live there, mostly apprentices. All that stuff is gone now, though. Every so often you'll see someone on campus wearing a pre-Columbian necklace or something."

"Just our luck," Mary said. "We picked the building next to a bunch of fanatics."

"What are you going to do now?" Brian said.

"I don't know," Mary said. "I guess I'm going to think about it. How can we do it with just a few people, though? And there's a part of me that doesn't want to go against Layla. We were friends, and—and we still might be, if I can just talk to her, find out what she really said. I can't believe she'd say that about me." But what if she had? What if after everything they had been through together Layla thought Mary had no soul? What if the friendship had been all on Mary's side? She couldn't talk to Layla after all.

"Maybe you should talk to her," Brian said. "Are you coming to the party?"

Mary shrugged. "I don't have a mask," she said. "And anyway, I don't have a soul, according to Luisa. Maybe I'd better just watch."

After dinner people put on their masks and went outside. The night was cold and clear, and the stars shone among the trees. Mary followed as the glittering crowd, most of them carrying candles, moved down the paths and converged on the meeting hall. There were too many of them to fit into the hall and they spilled out onto the main plaza. A lot of these people must be from off campus, Mary thought, and she looked for Don's black dog mask. The moon and the candlelight cast silver and gold on the masks as the people moved past her, as they inclined their faces to her, each of them trying to see who it was who wore her naked face in the midst of hundreds of masks. After a while, feeling lonely and unhappy, she went back to her room and tried to sleep. The soft noise of the revelers kept her awake for a long time.

Don was waiting for her on the concrete steps the next day when she came back from work. "I talked to Nick," he said.

"You did?" Mary said, sitting next to him. "What did he say?"

"He wants to help," Don said. "It was pathetic. He was so grateful someone wanted to trust him he practically fell all over me. Then he said that he wasn't a snitch anymore, and that even when he was he never had access to police stations."

"You sound like you don't believe him," Mary said. "Do you think he's lying?"

"Of course I think he's lying," Don said. "I never heard of anyone who was a snitch one day and not a snitch the next. I don't think he'll turn us in—he doesn't seem to turn in people he knows. But he won't go on the raid with us—it would jeopardize his precious career if he were caught in a police station. That's the trouble with canners—"

"Well, he's got a family—"

"The trouble with canners," Don said as though he hadn't heard her, "is that they just want to go along. They're terrified of doing anything that might get them into trouble. The General's rule rests entirely on the scared little canners. Nothing will ever happen to him as long as there are people like that supporting him."

"Aren't you being a little hard on him?" Mary said. People in the architecture building called everyone who lived off campus a canner. "After all, you're being supported by a canner."

"And Ayako doesn't want to do it either," Don said. "She got into the government dance group, and she's not doing anything that might get her into trouble. Another scared little canner." He shook his head. "So it's just me, you and Mark, and your friends."

"My friends don't want to do it either," she said, and repeated what Luisa had told her.

"Layla," Don said when she had finished. "You know why she's doing this, don't you?"

"Because she's nuts," Mary said. "Because she's not rational when it comes to her masks."

"I think there's more to it than that," he said. "I think on some level she still wants to control you. She wants you to do only what she tells you to. This is her way of getting back at you for doing something that wasn't her idea."

"You think so?"

"Yeah," he said. "I think you're going to have to talk to her."

"Yeah, I know," Mary said. "But I don't want to. If she really feels that way about me I don't want to know. If she really wants to control me—if she won't like me because I didn't become a maskmaker—"

"Well, she won't," Don said. "Get used to it. Why should you care if she likes you or not, anyway? After all she's done to you?"

"That doesn't matter," Mary said. "I like her—I can't help it. No matter what she's done to me. You can't choose the people you're going to like."

"Sure you can," Don said. "You'd better, if you want to survive. Some people you just don't want to be around. Nick, for instance."

"Never mind," Mary said. "You don't understand."

"Do you think she'll agree to the raid if you ask her?" he said. "Because as long as she's against it I don't think anyone will dare to oppose her. We can do it with three people though, don't you think?"

"No," she said. "Three people? And with Layla against us? I— no."

"We'll have to," he said. "The General gets the computers next month. You have to do it now."

"No I don't," she said. "I can stay on campus—"

"For the rest of your life?" he said. "You're the one who takes risks, who escaped from a rehab center, who goes without medication to feel freer. How long do you think you can stay here?"

"I don't take risks!" she said. "I'm just living my life, trying to exist. That's all. I'm not going to risk my freedom going into a police station with only two people to protect me."

"Okay, okay," he said. "Then talk to Layla."

It rained hard that day after Don went home. Wet cloth and paper washed down the paths and mixed with mud and grass. Everyone in the architecture building crowded into the cafeteria to play cards and talk; they all agreed that the job of cleaning up after Hallowe'en night could wait until tomorrow. The air was musty with the smell of water on masks and old clothes. The rain let up toward evening, and Mary put on her coat and went outside.

All the crazies seemed to be out. She wondered, not for the first time, how they survived. Some of them worked in the fields when they could, and some panhandled on the streets of Berkeley, but Brian had told her that there were fewer and fewer of them every year. The asylums, she knew, had turned them out to make room for political prisoners.

One of the crazies started walking back and forth across the path, heading obliquely toward her. She knew that he would try to block her way and she sidestepped him neatly. Another danced in a small circle, talking to herself. Two or three of them wore masks.

She stopped in front of the anthropology building. Did she dare to go in? Someone screamed behind her and she turned around, her heart pounding loudly. When she turned back Layla was coming out the front door, limping a little. Mary moved back into the shadows.

Could she talk to her? All it took was one step forward, one step to show herself to Layla. Don wanted her to do it, and so did Brian. But she couldn't. After a long inner struggle she had achieved balance, a stability she never thought would be hers, and she knew that if she talked to Layla she would be thrown off-center again. Layla would try to draw her back into the strange world of masks and animals and trances, and that part of her life was over. Could she trust herself not to get angry at Layla if she brought up the masks? She didn't want to start an argument. Layla didn't argue like normal people. And did Layla really think she didn't have a soul?

Layla stopped and looked back. Greg came out the door, hurrying to catch up with her. She put her arm around Greg and leaned on him a little, and they continued walking. She said something and Greg bent his head toward hers to hear her better.

Mary waited until they were out of sight. Then she hit the building as hard as she could with her fist. She barely felt the pain. Goddamnit, she thought, feeling miserable. He was her apprentice now.

She sat against the building, her head against her knees and her arms wrapped around her legs. Come on, she thought, trying to still her unhappiness. You didn't want to be her apprentice. And he did. But then she thought of them having the same talks she and Layla had had and her misery returned. She thought of all the things she had loved about Layla—her humor, her rebellious nature, her talent—and she thought, Well, you've lost her now.

If only Don were right. If only you could choose the people you were going to like. Then she wouldn't have this awful ache in her stomach, wouldn't feel that she had somehow proved unworthy of Layla, that Layla had chosen someone better. It wasn't fair. Layla was probably sleeping with him, too. And there was nothing she could offer Layla, nothing except her friendship and a fierce desire to protect her against all dangers. But Layla didn't want that, apparently, not if she was busy turning everyone against her. Layla wanted this idiot, wanted someone who would believe every crazy thing she said about maskmaking and the land of animals, someone who would give her the pleasures of sex. There was no room in her life for someone who was just a friend.

The rain had started again. Mary stood heavily and pulled her coat around her. None of the crazies bothered her as she made her way back to the architecture building. She went up to her room and tried to sleep.

Jennie Andrade lifted the crow's mask out of the box and shook it free of the shredded newspaper it had nestled in. Now who would send such a beautiful thing to the central police department? Wait, there was a report here too, buried under layers of newspaper. She glanced at the report and sighed. Escape from a rehab center, that meant her report had to be made out at least in triplicate, one for her department, one for the Special Problems branch, one for the head of prison security so he could decide what to do and make out a report that she would have to sign and copy in triplicate, and then a copy would have to be sent back to the rehab center in California. . . .

But in the meantime she could hang the mask opposite her desk in the little cubicle where she worked. She knew that the masks were popular outside Washington, but she had never seen one and had not imagined that they could be so haunting, so charged with meaning. The mask filled a hunger she'd never even known she had. What had happened to art? There were the boring dramas on the variety channel, and the boring dance group, and that was about it. For the first time in a long time she remembered the passionate discussions in college when she'd stayed up until three in the morning arguing about art's place in society. That had to have been at least twenty years ago. Maybe art couldn't survive if it was sponsored by the government. Maybe art always had to be subversive, underground like this woman who had made the mask and then escaped from the rehab center. What did the report say her name was? Layla MacKenzie. She would like to meet her, to ask her how she had made the mask, what had given her the idea to become a maskmaker.

But no, what was she thinking? This woman was obviously dangerous, an enemy of the state. And anyway she couldn't afford thoughts like that. Her position with the police department was the best-paying job she'd ever had. It even allowed her to put her mother on the government health plan, and her mother couldn't have gotten the insulin she needed any other way except the black market, which was expensive and dangerous.

Still, the mask was beautiful no matter who made it. Andrade put it on the wall next to the photograph of the General. There was something right about putting the two of them together, though the mask looked nothing like the General. But hadn't the report said that the woman—MacKenna, no, MacKenzie—had made the mask for the General? Weird. No doubt about it, the woman was definitely strange.

Andrade sat down at her desk and put Anderson's report on the pile of things she had to do. As she opened the next letter in the stack of mail that had come that day she had the feeling the mask was watching her.

11

LAYLA SAT ON THE BED AND
stared straight in front of her. They had given her one of the best rooms in the building, a room on the first floor with a bed, and she didn't have to do anything for it. She didn't even have to make them masks, though everyone was hoping that she would.

Sometimes she knew that they wanted her to make masks, knew who Greg was, knew that she was in the anthropology building. But most of the time she was unsure. Was she on film and was this a memory of her last time on campus? If it was she didn't remember it. And the colors were all perfectly normal, not bright as though a light shone through them from inside. But if she wasn't on film how did she get here? And why did her calf hurt and throb sometimes, especially at night?

Yesterday she thought she had seen Mary. But Greg hadn't seen anything, only shadows, he'd said. She had never lived with Mary on campus. Was the drug taking her memories and running them together, blending them like colors so that she would forget all her history? Or—worse, much worse—was Mary dead and now only to be seen in trances?

But if Mary were dead then her head would have been a sea-otter's head. Nothing was right, nothing followed the rules she had learned so long ago from Archangel. Sometimes Greg would talk to her, would tell her about a place she'd been, called a rehab center, and about their escape. "Come on, Layla," he would say. "Sure you remember it." Then he would go away, fade into the mists that always seemed to surround her, and she would forget about him.

Seeing Mary had reminded her of something. A while ago—a week, a month—someone had told her about a group of people who were planning a raid on a police station, and she had come out of her fog long enough to speak against them. People who lived on the same level as the General would lose their tribal souls, she'd said. Greg had repeated her words and interpreted them, as he was doing so often lately. But it seemed to her that Mary had been involved somehow in the plan. She couldn't see how that could be. Mary was her apprentice. Maybe the drug had been playing with her memories again.

What would she do if Mary achieved her initiation? Would she be well enough by then to teach Mary, to guide her through the next stage of her learning? If only she could get back to the land of animals, or see Archangel once more. If only she could get to her small canister of film—but she couldn't find the place she had left it, or Archangel had made her throw it away. If only she could remember where she was, figure out what had happened.

Maybe she should have talked to Mary. Mary was powerful. The spirit of the maskmaker was in her; Layla had known that long before she had seen the power catch her up and throw her to the floor and ride her. Time was reversing itself: She had been on campus once a long time ago and now she was on campus again. Maybe now the apprentices would teach the masters, Mary would tell her how to get back to the clear heights of the land of animals.

But maybe that would hinder Mary's own initiation. She wished she knew what to do. She wished she could talk to Archangel. The other maskmakers in the building respected her too much to realize that she was drifting, was lost. She moaned a little, shifted on the bed. The same questions chased themselves inside her head. She was cold and her calf hurt. She lay down on the cot—no, it was a mattress, soft and yielding—and tried to sleep. Maybe Archangel would visit her dreams.

■ ■ ■

The next day she was a little better. Greg brought her some bread and juice, and she sat up and ate. She couldn't remember the last time she'd eaten. But she knew who Greg was, knew that she was on campus, and she remembered that she wanted to talk to Mary. She got up, ran her fingers through her knotted hair and went outside.

She wandered aimlessly for several hours. Once she joined a group of people dancing to the intricately patterned beats of two drums. Then it rained and she went inside, walked up and down the white halls of an unfamiliar building, running her fingers along the walls and talking a little to herself. Her calf throbbed. No one paid her any attention; people were used to crazies coming in from outside. The rain let up and she went back out.

Groups of people were coming back from the fields. Greg was probably back now and wondering where she was. She looked at the people closely as they passed her; if Mary was on campus she might be working with them. Several people turned away from her close scrutiny. Then she saw her, waving good-bye, separating herself from the knot of people, turning toward a large concrete building. Layla ran after her.

Mary turned before she could call out. She saw Mary shrink away from her and she said quickly, "Mary? Wait." For the first time in a long time she wondered what she looked like, what she must look like to Mary.

Mary stood still, as though bracing against something. "Listen, I want to—"

"Layla?" Mary said finally. "Are you—how are you?"

"Not too good," Layla said. She tried to smile, but her face trembled, threatened to collapse on itself. "It's all gone away, gone wrong. Archangel's gone. The land of animals . . ." She started to cry, tears running silently down her face. Mary took a step toward her, stopped. She looked horrified. "I can't get to the land of animals anymore. So I thought—I thought you could show me the way. Since time's reversed itself. You could be my teacher, you could—help me." The last two words sounded like a plea.

"Listen, Layla," Mary said gently. "I'd help you if I could, you know that. But I don't know what you're talking about. I can't get to the land of animals. I can't show you the way there—"

"Yes you can," Layla said. "The power is in you, I saw it. You're a born maskmaker."

Mary was shaking her head. "Maybe I do have the power," she said slowly. "But I don't want it—I don't want to use it. I think we both made mistakes. My mistake was that I asked you to teach me maskmaking. But your mistake was that you wouldn't admit you were wrong, that you picked the wrong person to be your apprentice. You're so used to being right, to having people listen to your every word. Everyone looks up to you. You can't admit you were wrong."

Layla said nothing. Mary was not supposed to be saying these things. Mary was supposed to help her, to show her the way to the land of animals. If she had been wrong about Mary then she was wrong about everything, about the tribes, the trances, the land of animals. She had been that sure about Mary. For the first time since she'd met Archangel the foundation of her belief shook, began to crack. She looked around wildly for something to catch hold of, something to steady her.

Mary was speaking again. ". . . got to stop talking to people about this raid," she said. "You don't understand—we're going on the raid to help you, among other people. Once we get your file, your fingerprints and your retinal scan, you'll be free to go anywhere you want. But we can't do that without your help. People listen to you. You've got to start telling them the raid's okay—that there's nothing wrong with it. Okay? Do you understand?"

Layla stepped back. What was Mary talking about? The raid had nothing to do with her. All she wanted was to get back to the land of animals. Why was Mary talking about fingerprints and retinal scans?

"Do you understand, Layla?" Mary said. "We need your help. We can't do this without you."

"I can't help anybody anymore," Layla said. "I can't even help myself." She backed farther away from Mary. Her last hope, and it was gone. She had been stupid to think that Mary could help her, she had been so desperate that she would believe anything.

"I'm not talking about the tribes," Mary said impatiently. "I don't care about the tribes anymore. All I want is for you to stop talking about the raid. Tell people it's okay and then stop talking about it, all right?"

Layla turned and ran. "Layla!" Mary said, calling after her. "Wait! Are you okay? Do you have enough to eat?"

Layla ran to the anthropology building, went inside and ran to her room. I don't care about the tribes anymore, Mary had said. Layla slammed the door to her room and sat hunched against the wall. The words would not go away. I don't care about the tribes. How could Mary have stepped so far off the path? She wished she had film, had any drug at all, anything to take her mind off the present.

Other words came back to her. You were wrong, Mary said. We were both wrong. You made a mistake. She put her hands over her ears to stop the voices but she heard them anyway. Everyone looks up to you. You can't admit that you were wrong.

Archangel shone white and silver against the wall in front of her. *It's true*, the owl's beak said. *You were always stubborn, Layla. You could never admit that you were wrong.*

Archangel! she said. She looked up. Hope filled her. *Tell me what to do. I'm so confused. She doesn't want to complete her initiation.*

Then maybe she shouldn't, Archangel said. *Maybe it's time to admit you were wrong about your choice of apprentice. Time to let her go.*

But, Layla said, *but you told me, you said that once you step on the path you can never step off. Isn't that what you said?*

I said that, yes, Archangel said. *But in this case it is clear that she will never become a maskmaker, that she should not have started on the path in the first place. You must let her go, let her follow her own path. You must admit that you were wrong.*

He was starting to fade. *Archangel!* she said. *Wait! How do I get back to the land of animals?*

You are there, said the owl's beak. And the walls began to suffuse with green, she smelled the healing air of the heights, and she ran forward to play with the animals.

Mary walked slowly back to the architecture building. That had been weird, meeting Layla like that. She wished she had gotten a chance to ask Layla the important questions, was she feeling all right, did she get cold at night? She wished she didn't get into an argument every time she saw Layla, that she had had time to explain about the police raid and what they were trying to do. Probably Layla hadn't understood a word she'd said.

But her heart eased a little as she thought about the meeting. She had been glad to see that Layla looked better, that she was no longer limping. And Layla didn't hate her after all, if she would stop and speak to her. Maybe someday they could be friends again. Maybe next time they could talk more, she could find out what it was that was making Layla so unhappy. Mary sighed. She was still trying to protect Layla against the world. You really can't choose the people you're going to like.

Mary went inside the architecture building. Layla didn't hate her. And she hadn't said anything one way or the other about the raid. Maybe next time she saw Layla she could get Layla's approval, explain to her what they were trying to do. After all, Layla would be helped by the raid too. And then they could start making plans. But it had to be done soon, Mary thought as she went up the narrow stairs to the third floor. The General would get the computers in three weeks.

Layla came back from the land of animals calm and rested. It was late—the room was filled with shadows. She remembered everything immediately, where she was, how she had gotten there. She remembered Archangel's words to her: Mary should not have been on the path in the first place. You must let her go, let her follow her own path.

Had that been her problem all these months? Had she been afraid to admit that she was wrong? Had all her concern for Mary's initiation really been a concern for herself, a way of hiding her mistake?

She shook her head and tried to laugh. All her craziness over the past few months, all her attempts to find the land of animals, and the answer had been so close all along. It was true, she didn't want to admit she had been wrong. Even now the thought of going up into the hills and confessing her mistake to the other maskmakers made her burn with misery and embarrassment. But it had to be done. She had to tell them what to do next, how they could help Mary.

Mary, she thought. It hadn't mattered to Mary that she had led her to the rehab center, that she had wanted something from Mary that Mary hadn't been able to give. Mary had cared for her there just the same. Not even Mark would have done that for her, not even Ayako. It had been a long time since someone had helped her that selflessly, with no hope of gain, since before the General. . . . She could not follow the thought, anything to do with politics was opaque to her. But when the General had come to power it was as if people's hearts had cooled, even her own. As if people had turned to stone, had hidden behind masks and at the same time only allowed their emotions out in paint and fur and feathers. And now someone had warmed her, woken her after a nine-year winter. It was very strange.

Greg came into the room, carrying dinner. "Are you all right?" he asked. "You looked like you were in a trance."

"I was," she said, amazed that she could sound so matter-of-fact about it. "What day is it today?"

"Today?" Greg said, sounding surprised. "It's Wednesday."

"What date?"

"I don't know," Greg said. "Let's see. The third, I think. The third of November. That's right, because Hallowe'en was three days ago. You don't remember?"

"No," she said. But she remembered something, a vast crowd of masked figures in the meeting hall, on the paths and in the main plaza, all carrying candles. . . . She concentrated, trying to remember when the last meeting of the maskmakers had been, when they would be meeting again. Every five weeks on Thursday, she thought. She had definitely missed one. But the next one might be tomorrow. Let's see, if tomorrow was the fourth . . . She needed a calendar. The hell with it. She would just go up in the hills and see if they were there.

"Thanks," she said, taking the plate Greg held out to her. It looked like some kind of meat, and she thanked the animal-spirit under her breath. Then she ate it all. Greg's eyes went round with happiness.

On Thursday Layla got up early, bathed and washed her hair in the women's part of the stream and left the campus. She had lost long ago the coat that Greg had given her, but someone—she didn't remember who—had given her another one, and she wrapped it around her. The day was cold but clear.

She was halfway down Telegraph Avenue when she remembered that the police would be looking for her. The wind blew past her, carrying leaves and old newspapers, and she huddled farther into the coat. Her walk slowed, became an old lady's walk, bent and arthritic. She was good at deception, when she remembered to be.

She remembered Ayako's suggestion—that she change her appearance by changing her mask—and she laughed a little. It was funny how many people didn't understand that the masks were meant to reveal, not to conceal.

She turned left on Ashby and started walking toward the hills. She was going to have to stop being so intolerant of other people's mistakes. Even she had been wrong about something and she was one of the best maskmakers in Berkeley, one of the Five. What would the others say when she told them? Great deeds were remembered and celebrated long among them, but their memories were just as long for errors and deeds gone wrong. She almost hoped that they wouldn't be there, that she had come on the wrong day. Not even when Archangel had corrected her sternly in the first awkward stages of her apprenticeship had she felt so uncertain about anything.

You can't turn back now, she thought, and began to climb into the hills. She felt Archangel's presence around her, Archangel who had never made it into the hills while he was alive.

The leaves on the trees had turned brown and orange. Out in the bay the ocean was the flat gray color of old machinery. She heard no sounds except that of her feet on the cracked asphalt road and the occasional chirping of birds. What would the others say? Susan would be the worst, probably, but the rest would not be kind. You can't turn back now.

As always she forgot the exact spot of the meeting. Each time she rounded a bend and saw no one she was sure she had come on the wrong day. Part of her wanted to give up, turn around, go home. She was starting to breathe heavily now. Just one more turn, she told herself. She walked around another bend in the road and saw the four of them sitting at the old picnic table.

Bone rose when he saw her. "Layla!" he said. "You keep coming back from the dead."

The others stopped talking and turned toward her. Layla said nothing. She knew that it was important to make this moment last as long as possible, to impress the others with her mystery and natural authority. It would make what she had to do later much easier. She walked toward them slowly, her back erect, and sat at the table.

"Well," Rose said. She had stuck a blue feather through one of her braids. "Aren't you going to tell us about it? Did you give the mask to the General?"

"I gave the mask to the police, and I have no doubt that it will eventually make its way to the General," Layla said, picking her words carefully. "It came with us to the rehab center, and it inspired one of the guards there to leave the army and join the tribes. It caused a great deal of uneasiness."

Bone and Willie grinned like wolves. "I'll bet," Willie said. "But how did you get out?"

"My task was done and I left," Layla said. "But there is something more urgent that needs to be done now, and I need your help to do it." She looked around at each of them, saw that they were watching her closely. She had them, for the moment. As she had made herself small and insignificant on the streets of Berkeley, now she drew herself up so they could not look away if they wanted to.

"I've been living on campus," she said. "I lived there before, when I was an apprentice to Archangel, and the time has come for me to live there again." They all knew about her apprenticeship, of course, but she wanted to remind them. It would do her no harm for them to remember that she had been initiated by the man who was probably the first maskmaker. "A movement has started on campus to raid a police station, to recover some files before everything is transferred to computers. To recover my file, among others. I am going to go on this raid. And so should all of you."

There was silence when she had finished. Finally Susan said, "Why? The General's politics aren't our business. Why should we meddle in things that don't concern us?" Layla noticed that she had sewn another small plastic doll to the front of her coat.

"Because if this raid is not successful I will have to stay on campus for the rest of my life," Layla said. "And so will other people. And because I think it's a good idea. Archangel told me to do it."

There was a slight stir at this. Archangel's name was still potent. And it was not really a lie to say that he had wanted her to go on the raid. He hadn't said anything one way or the other, but sometimes she sensed his approval.

"I guess I don't really understand," Rose said. "Even if you have to stay on campus, so what? A maskmaker can work anywhere. And you don't really have to stay on campus if you don't want to. Look at you—here you are. I agree with Susan. We make masks. What the General does isn't our business."

"You thought it was our business when I made him the mask," Layla said.

"That was something else," Rose said. "You were trying to bring him up to our level, to give him a soul. But now you're going down to his level, becoming concerned with police files and computers."

"Whose idea was this, anyway?" Willie asked.

"Some people on campus," Layla said, hoping he wouldn't press her. She wanted their support before she told them about Mary.

Willie looked hard at her. "But who?"

"Mary," Layla said.

"Mary?" Susan said quickly. "Isn't she your apprentice? What kind of thing is this for an apprentice to be doing anyway, going into police stations? Is this supposed to be part of her initiation?" She laughed harshly.

"She's not my apprentice anymore," Layla said, trying to keep her gaze level. Their attention was coming unraveled. She was losing them.

"Not your . . ." Willie said. "But how could that happen?"

"She has the power of a maskmaker," Layla said. "I was not wrong about that. But she did not have the desire. She did not want to walk the path to the end. So I released her from her apprenticeship."

"I never heard of anything like that," Willie said. "What happens when you don't walk the path to the end? Are you stuck in one spot for the rest of your life?"

"Archangel told me to do it," Layla said, but this time Archangel's name held no special magic.

"So you're saying you made a mistake in choosing your apprentice," Susan said. Her left eye bulged behind her glasses. "You made a mistake but you want us to trust you, to follow you, to do something that will probably turn out to be another mistake. Is that it?"

"I made a mistake, yes," Layla said. "I admit it. Everyone makes mistakes, and I made one. But I don't think this other thing is a mistake. I think it's something that we should do."

"I'm sorry, Layla," Willie said. "I'd like to help you out, but I don't really think I can. Anyone else can do what they want, of course, but I'd rather not do it." He looked around the table. Both Rose and Susan were shaking their heads.

"What about you, Bone?" Layla said. "You haven't said anything this whole time. I bet you want to do it."

"I'd like to," Bone said slowly. "Part of me wants to go into that police station and burn it to the ground. I can see just what it would look like. It's a very attractive idea. But I have to agree with the others. I don't think the General's business is something we should get mixed up in."

"You're the one who wanted to kill a cop!" Layla said. "Don't you think that's getting mixed up in the General's business?"

"No," Bone said. "That was a personal grudge. He was out to get me."

Layla sat up as straight as she could. The wind blew her hair into her eyes and she brushed it away. She knew she had lost face in front of the maskmakers and that she would probably never get it back. "All right," she said, trying not to show her dismay. "It doesn't really matter if you want to do this or not. There are plenty of people on campus who are with us. I just wanted to give you a chance to do this because—well, because they look up to us. I just thought we should be there."

"That's just why we shouldn't do it," Willie said. "Because they look up to us. We don't have any kind of responsibility to improve the life they're living under the General. We have a responsibility to set an example, to show them that there are other ways of life besides the General's. That there are other paths. That, finally, the General's rule doesn't matter. We could be living before the Collapse and we'd still be living exactly the same way."

Layla shrugged. She never understood it when people talked about responsibility. There was no response she could think of to make to him.

"Well, let's do the exchange," Bone said. "Did you bring anything, Layla?"

Layla shook her head. She watched as the others took out bones, fur, feathers, leather and paint and heaped them in a bright pile in the middle of the table. They took what they wanted and the pile diminished, disappeared. No one asked her if she wanted anything.

When the pile was gone they started to walk down the hill. Susan talked about a young maskmaker who had become her lover and might become her apprentice. Bone described a skull he had found that he had made into a Hallowe'en mask. Layla said nothing. They waved good-bye at the bottom of the hill. "See you at the next meeting, Layla," someone called back to her.

"Sure," Layla said.

The harvest was over. Some of the people in the architecture building were busy repairing the roof or painting the cafeteria but Mary had a free week until she had to start work again. On Monday morning she left her building and started down the path without any clear destination in mind.

"Mary?" someone said, coming toward her from the anthropology building. It was Greg.

"Hi," Mary said.

"Can I talk to you for a minute?" he said.

She hesitated a minute and then said, "Sure."

"It's about Layla," Greg said. "Just when I thought she was getting better . . . I haven't seen her for a few days. I think she's going off campus."

"Off campus?" Mary said. "Why?"

"I don't know," Greg said. "She went somewhere Thursday morning, and she came back that afternoon looking kind of upset. Then she left again Friday. I haven't seen her since."

"Well, I haven't seen her since last week," Mary said. She felt annoyed to hear Greg say the same things she had said when she was responsible for Layla, and her jealousy returned. Her old worry for Layla surfaced and would not go away. "Why do you think she's gone off campus?"

"Some things she said on Thursday," Greg said. "She's changed her mind about the raid on the police station. She says she wants you to do it—"

"She does?" Mary said, surprised.

"Yeah," Greg said. He looked disgusted. "She says it's your path, or something like that. I think she's wrong on this one. I even told her—I said that she'd told me that an apprentice can never step off the path. Hell, if I was her apprentice—"

"I thought you were," Mary said.

"Someday," Greg said. "Someday I'll be her apprentice, I know it. But she hasn't asked me yet. How could you give something like that up? To study under Layla . . ."

"It's a long story," Mary said. "What about the raid?"

"She said she was going to help you out," Greg said. "That she owed it to you, because of all she'd put you through when you were her apprentice, that she'd made a mistake about you. And that she was going to get some people to help you out."

Mary thought quickly. How did Layla think she could help them? Would she and her friends do something crazy like walk into the police station and ask for her files back? Layla's help might be more trouble than it was worth. But if Layla approved that meant they could go ahead with the raid. With her on their side they might make it. "I wish she'd talked to me about this before she left," Mary said. "The best help she could give us now would be to convince Luisa and those people to help us out. No one wants to talk to us since she said not to."

"So you don't know where she could be?" Greg asked.

"No," Mary said. "Wait a minute. Why don't you just tell people that she said the raid was okay? People listen to you the same way they listen to her—I've seen them. Then we can get Luisa and the others back. We can get started."

"I'm not going to have any part of this," Greg said. "Layla told me once that the raid on the police station was wrong and nothing that's happened since then has changed my mind. She might feel guilty about something, feel bad enough to compromise her principles, but I'm not going to compromise mine. In fact, as long as she's gone I'm telling people she's still against the raid. She'll realize she was wrong on this one. She'll thank me for this someday."

"You've been telling . . ." Mary said. "Thanks. Thanks a lot. Shit. You mean it's because of you that we're going to go in there with three people and probably get ourselves killed?" Her voice rose wildly. She had known from the first she couldn't trust him. But another part of her mind, listening calmly to what she had just said, was startled to realize that she had decided to go on the raid no matter what, even if Layla didn't come back to help them, even if they had to do it with three people. Layla would give them luck.

"I'm not going to compromise my—"

"You've already compromised your principles, you idiot!" Mary said furiously. "You lied—you lied in Layla's name. You think she's going to take you on as an apprentice after that? You'll never be a maskmaker now. You might as well go back to the General's army— that's the only place that'll have you."

"What do you know?" Greg said, unperturbed. "You're a failed maskmaker, maybe the only failed maskmaker ever. Layla's told me about you. What do you know about who she takes on as an apprentice?"

"I'll tell her about you," Mary said. All her hatred and jealousy of Greg flashed through her, leaving her trembling. "When she comes back. I'll tell her how you lied. We'll see if you become an apprentice after that. Maybe if you're lucky she'll still talk to you. If you're lucky."

"I've said all I had to say," Greg said. "I stand by what I've done, and I'll stand by it when Layla gets back. In the meantime I probably shouldn't be talking to you. You've lost your tribal soul by attacking the General. That's what Layla said." He turned and walked away, down the path.

"You're crazy!" Mary said, shouting after him. "I may have lost my soul, but you're nuts! You'll end up back at the rehab center, but as a prisoner, not as a guard. Aliens! Aliens on the moon!"

Greg kept walking. Mary watched him as he went down the path. After a while she remembered something she had nearly forgotten in her argument with Greg. Layla was missing. They had both acted as though she would return, but what if she didn't? What if she was in trouble? Whatever had given her the idea to go off campus?

Mary sighed. As if she didn't have enough to worry about. Organizing a raid on a police station with only three people, and that idiot Greg, and the seizures. She hoped Layla was all right. She hoped Layla wasn't doing anything crazy.

■ ■ ■

Norman Blair, the General's aide, came into Jennie Andrade's cubicle without knocking. "The General's making a tour of the facility again next week," he said. "Now remember, just dazzle him with statistics. Don't tell him about—where the hell did you get that?"

"What?" Jennie asked. She was in the middle of typing a report and hadn't looked up as Norman had come in.

"That," Norman said. He looked as though he'd swallowed something that tasted bad. "That mask."

"It came with a report from a rehab center in California," Jennie said. "Some woman there made it. Then she and a couple of other people escaped. Apparently a guard helped them."

"Now that's exactly the kind of thing I don't want you telling the General," Norman said. "Tell him how many people are in the rehab centers, not how many get away. And anyway, why didn't you send it down to Evidence?"

"I will," Jennie said. "Just as soon as I get caught up here and copy the report."

"You could be in lots of trouble for keeping that mask," Norman said. "Don't you know the General's outlawed them?"

"Of course I know," Jennie said. The truth was that she'd forgotten about the law as soon as she'd opened the box and seen the mask, even though Anderson had mentioned it in his report. How could you be so stupid? she thought, furious with herself. Did Norman have the power to fire her? She had never been clear on what his job really was. At the very least he could talk to her supervisor. "I'm sorry. I'll send it down to Evidence right away."

"No, don't do that," Norman said. "I think I'll take it and give it to the General myself. He's been acting strange lately, starting to think that he shouldn't have outlawed masks. He thinks the police are spending too much time on this law and ignoring some of the others. But see, he doesn't know what the masks are like. This'll probably be the first one he's ever seen. Then he'll understand that they have to be outlawed, because—"

"Because art has to be sponsored by the government," Jennie said quickly. Maybe he wouldn't fire her after all. "Because otherwise people can do and say anything they want. Unpatriotic things."

Norman looked at her in surprise. "That's right," he said. "That's exactly right. And besides that, it's so ugly. Doesn't it bother you, having something like that on the wall?"

"It is disturbing," Jennie said. A few times she had been sure that the mask was watching her while she worked. She wouldn't be sorry to see it go.

"Well, all right then," Norman said, taking the mask off the wall and tucking it casually under his arm. "And remember what I told you about the General. Statistics!"

He left. Jennie sat still at her desk for ten minutes after he'd gone, feeling relief pour through her. Don't ever do that again, she thought. Don't ever stick your neck out for a piece of art. Only then did she remember that the woman who'd made the mask had wanted to give it to the General.

12

DON AND MARK SAT WITH Mary at a table in the cafeteria. It was a few hours before dinner and the cafeteria was deserted except for an old man who sat near the wall, reading the mimeographed campus news sheet.

"Here's what I thought," Mark said. "We'll sleep over at my place next Saturday night—it's fairly close to the police station. We should start out at about three in the morning. I'll get an ID card for Mary, so if we're caught on the way all they can charge us with is violating curfew. Unless they recognize Mary, of course, and check her file, but that's a risk we have to take. Right?"

Mary nodded, her mouth dry. How did she get herself into this? When she'd thought Luisa and her friends were going along it had seemed easy, a lark. Now she thought it was crazy. She probably wouldn't even get off campus safely. And where was Layla? If she really wanted to help them, now was the time.

"I'll check out the station this weekend," Mark was saying. "See what kind of guards they have at three in the morning. If I'm caught I can always show them my ID from the road crew."

"Do you think they'll buy that?" Don said.

"They might," Mark said. "I've been out with the crew that early before."

"Yeah, but this time it's just you," Don said. "Don't you think they'll ask you where you lost the rest of the crew?"

"I'll play it by ear," Mark said. "But I won't get caught. They're not really expecting people at that time of night. They wouldn't have seen Mary if Layla hadn't given herself up, or whatever she did."

Mary tried to think of something to say. The raid had been her idea, but Mark and Don seemed to have taken it over completely. In a way she was glad. She wasn't sure if she could plan and carry out something that dangerous. It made her feel safer to leave the details to Mark.

"What about the Purple Press?" Mark asked.

"They don't want to do it," Don said. "Of course. The person I talked to, and this is someone I'd always thought was my friend, said that he'd been approached hundreds of times with ideas like mine, and that nothing had ever come of any of them. He said if we had something more solid to show him then maybe he'd consider it."

"Well, we'll just have to show them something more solid," Mark said. "We'll just have to pull this off."

"It's really time for an underground movement," Don said. "These goddamn sheep get more complacent every year. I'm not saying things were great before the Collapse, but it seems like people don't even remember what life was like back then. I feel like an exile, like someone from another country."

"Yeah, I know what you mean," Mark said. "An exile. That's exactly how I feel." Now Mary could see what Don and Mark would be like when no one else was around, Mark's admiration for the way Don spoke and wrote, Don's willingness to be admired.

"Remember Marvin, that computer they thought was intelligent?" Don said. "And how they would close the news broadcasts with a quote from him? He even had his own theme song—how did it go?" He whistled a few notes tentatively.

"Remember President Warwick?" Mark said. "And how his eyes were always popping out, and everyone was sure they'd land in his lap someday?"

"Remember that computer game—what was it called?—the one you could play with kids all over the country. All over the world. You'd draw your own character and animate it—"

"Yeah," Mark said, excited. "I used to play that for hours. What was it called?"

"All right," Mary said impatiently. She hated it when people talked about the time before the Collapse; she was too young to remember most of it and what few memories she had were specific and concrete, like her family's visit to Chinatown. She always felt left out, as though she had missed something vital. "Has anyone heard from Layla?"

"No," Mark said. "She still hasn't come back?"

Mary shook her head. "I've tried telling people that she really supports the raid, but they don't believe me," she said. "They believe that idiot Greg. If she came back it would be a lot easier for us. And I'm worried about her."

"Don't worry," Don said. "She can take care of herself."

"Last time you said that she got sent to a rehab center," Mary said. "And this time if they arrest her they'll probably send her someplace worse. I keep remembering the last time I talked to her—she seemed confused, like she didn't really know where she was. I just hope she's okay."

Don shrugged. "There's nothing we can do for her now," he said. "We'll let you know if she turns up at the house."

The kitchen workers were starting to come into the cafeteria. Luisa passed Mary's table and turned away from her, calling to someone going through the door to the kitchen. Mary sighed. She was getting used to being an outsider, first at the rehab center and now on campus, but it would never be easy. If only Layla were here to set everyone straight.

The stocky guard came in and took her usual place by the door, looking suspiciously at Mark and Don. "All right," Mark said. "So we agree that the raid will be the weekend after next. I'll scout out the police station and get back to you, and we'll plan some more next week. Does that sound okay?"

Mary nodded. Mark stood up and Don stood with him. Mary had hoped Don would stay, but she couldn't bring herself to ask him with Mark there. Probably he was going to Mark's house for dinner. It was unfair, she thought. Just because she couldn't give him dinner he was leaving her. She'd thought their relationship was more important than that. What did he expect—that she go without a meal so he could have one?

"See you later," Don said, winking at her. She noticed that he couldn't wink very well, that both his eyes closed, one more than the other, when he tried. Still, she felt cheered that he'd paid some attention to her.

"Bye," she said. "See you later."

A week and a half later Mary lay on Mark's floor, trying to sleep. They had taken the unpaved roads to Mark's house but Mary had been sure that a policeman waited around every turn. She had stiffened at every noise. Now her eyes were open, staring into darkness, and she tried to remember what her doctors had said about tension and fear. Some of them had thought that stress brought on seizures and some of them hadn't, but she couldn't remember how the argument had ended. All she needed was a seizure at the police station.

She turned over and wrapped herself in Mark's torn blanket, trying to get comfortable. A year ago in Stockton she could have asked her father or her doctor, but here in Berkeley there was no one to ask. Don might talk about being in exile from the past, but Don was a writer and writers probably dramatized their lives like that all the time. She was really in exile, living neither in Berkeley nor in the rehab center but in the tiny circumscribed space of the campus, a ghost in both worlds. But before the night was over she would be back in one or the other.

Don slept soundly on the floor next to her. She heard his deep even breathing and she thought how strange it was that this was the first time they had actually slept together. Maybe before the night was over— before the week was over, certainly—she would find out how he felt about her. He seemed to admire her for her daring, a daring she didn't think she possessed, but whenever she asked him for anything more he would slip away, tossing words like firecrackers to cover his escape.

And Layla still hadn't returned. Mary wasn't sure how she felt about Don, but she knew she cared about Layla and always would, no matter what happened. She hoped Layla was all right, that she wasn't hurt or in a rehab center. But if something had happened to Layla she would probably never know.

It seemed as if she had closed her eyes for only a second or two when she felt someone gently shake her shoulder. "Wake up," Mark was saying. "It's time." Don stood some distance off. She thought he was watching her, but in the darkness of the room it was hard to tell.

She sat up and yawned, trying to come awake. She felt chilled, colder than the temperature of the room, and she was hungry. "Is it three o'clock already?"

Mark nodded, but she could barely see him. "Here," he said, and tossed her a small shapeless bundle. It landed in her lap and came apart. Gloves. She would never have thought of gloves. She put them on.

"Let's go," Mark said. She stood up. Mark opened the door to the hallway and then the outer door. He looked outside for a long time, then stepped through the door and motioned to them to follow him.

Mary felt as though she were walking in a dream. Most of the streetlights were out and she could barely see Don and Mark in front of her. She had been here before, following Layla to the police station, and she could not shake the feeling that this night would have the same ending, arrest and a trip to the rehab center for all of them. But she felt no fear, only the chill and a vast tiredness. If only she had had more time to sleep.

Mark had said that there were fewer guards at the station on the weekend. Mary hoped he was right. He hadn't been able to watch the station that often during the week, and only once on Saturday. Maybe one of the guards had been sick that day. She found she almost didn't care. She had survived a rehab center once and could do it again if she had to. Maybe she had outgrown her fear.

Up ahead Mark raised his hand and they moved as quietly as they could between two houses. Nothing happened for a long time. Mark stepped out and went back to the road, and they followed. Mary hoped no one in the houses had seen them.

Why were they doing this for her? Neither one of them had a police file; they could just as easily have stayed home and let her live the rest of her life on campus. For adventure, for glory, maybe. For Mark it was another act of rebellion, the same as owning an illegal radio. And they both hated the government and the General, more so than most people. She felt warmed that they were doing this for her, and wished that she could have offered them more people.

Light shone up ahead, and she saw that they were coming close to Ashby. The fear she thought she had banished returned. It was not too late to go back. Mark and Don walked on and turned behind a row of houses. If they were willing to do this for her then she could not let them see her fear. She followed.

There was a lighted parking lot at the back of the station, surrounded by a fence topped with barbed wire. Mark took out wire clippers from his pocket and, awkward in his gloves, cut a strand of wire. He waited, listening, but no alarms went off. Quickly he cut a hole large enough for them to duck through and went inside.

A jagged wire caught on Mary's coat and she desperately worked it loose. Don and Mark were already halfway down the side of the parking lot. Harsh lights caught them pitilessly from all sides, and three or four shadows walked with them. She hurried to catch up with them.

Mark paused a little at the rear of the station. Then he took a rock from his pocket and threw it with all his might against a blacked-out window. The crack of glass breaking sounded sharp and loud to their ears, and they heard the sound they had been dreading, the wail of sirens. Mark reached inside the hole he had made and snapped a wire in half and the sound stopped.

He drew his coat sleeve over his hand and smashed out most of the windowpane. "Hurry," he whispered, and lifted himself over the window. Don went next. Without stopping to think Mary pulled herself up, and then she was inside the police station.

They fled wildly down the hallway, their only thought to get away from the broken window and the place where the siren had come from. Doors with numbers on them passed by on either side. Mary wondered where they were, how close they were to the jail she had stayed in overnight. She wondered how Mark would ever find the room where the records were kept. A staircase came up on their right and Mark went down it two steps at a time. Did he know where the records were kept or was he just guessing?

The basement was dusty and dimly lit. Mark walked a little slower now, checking the doors carefully. "Men," one said, then two blank ones, then one that said "Payroll." They turned a corner, and the first door on their right said "Records."

"Yeah," Mary said. Her voice sounded loud in the empty corridor and she wished she hadn't said anything. Mark turned the knob. It was locked.

Mark took a long thin wire from his coat pocket and tried the lock. They heard heavy footsteps overhead, and a loud squeak from the ceiling. After a long time Mary heard a small click from the lock, and it opened.

Mark switched on the light near the door. Nothing happened. "Damn," he whispered, and looked over his shoulder. Mary understood. They were going to have to keep the door open for the light from the corridor.

Don stood by the door while Mark and Mary went into the room. There was a long wooden counter in front of them, and behind it heavy metal shelves came at right angles into the room, making small alcoves. They climbed over the counter, too much in a hurry to look for the way around it. Mark went to one end of the room and Mary to the other. The files were jammed close together, some very thick, some thin, with numbers written on tabs on the side facing outward. After a while Mark whispered, "It's by dates. What date was it?"

For a long time—too long—Mary could not figure out what he meant. Then she said quickly, "End of August. The twenty-ninth or thirtieth."

"That's on your side," Mark said, coming to join her. "Let's see—twenty-eighth, twenty-ninth, here it is. Mary Owens, August twenty-ninth."

"And Layla?" Mary said. "Where's she?"

"Here," Mark said. She pulled out the two files. Mark turned to go.

"Wait a minute," Mary said. "Brian. I promised. He was a few weeks before us, but I don't remember—"

They heard the footsteps again. Mark turned back impatiently. "What's his last name?" he said.

"I don't know," Mary said. "Look! Here it is! Let's go."

They hurried over the counter and out the door, then ran around the corner. Two men in uniforms were coming down the stairs toward them. They stopped. Mary moved closer to the wall.

"Hold it right there," one of the policemen said.

Don started back for the corner. "I said hold it," the policeman said.

He was carrying a gun, pointed at them. The two policemen moved closer.

Mary looked at Mark. This was the end. This was it. Mark had nothing in his pockets to get them out of this one. She had known they were not going to make it, she should never have tried it with only three people . . .

A noise came from the stairs, a muted sound like a broken piano key being pressed down. The policeman half-turned, still holding the gun on the three of them. Bright silver flashed overhead, a spark or a shooting star. Mary looked up, and at the same moment the man with the gun fell forward heavily, a knife in his side. Everyone else stood still, actors in a play that would start at any moment.

A woman moved gracefully down the stairs into the dim light of the corridor. Half a dozen braids fell around her shoulders. As the other policeman started to move she reached for the gun on the floor, picked it up and held it in both hands. Just as Mary began to react, to think, Who is she? She can't be with the police, the woman pointed the gun at the other policeman and said, "Don't move."

A short black man, his hair tied back with a scarf, came down the stairs carrying a coil of rope. "What do you say we tie them together?" he said. "The live one and this other guy?"

"You won't get away with this," the policeman said.

"I don't see why not," the black man said. "Sit down. Next to him." He nodded at the man sprawled on the floor. Blood was pulsing around the knife in his side. The policeman sat.

An impossibly tall man, his eyes and forehead darker than the rest of his face, walked down the stairs and stood over the dying man. Then with a sudden deft movement he pulled the knife from the man's side. The man grunted softly.

Mary shivered once and looked up at the tall man's face. Some kind of mask covered his eyes and forehead. Who are these people? she thought. Where do they come from? How many of them are there? But another dim shape was running lightly down the stairs, someone very familiar . . . "Hello, Mary," Layla said. She sounded almost shy. "I brought you some maskmakers to help you out."

"Layla!" Mary said. "How did you—why—"

"Later," Mark said. "Let's hurry."

"You won't get away with this," the policeman said again. "I know what you look like."

The tall man reached for the gun. He and the woman struggled for a few seconds and then the gun was in the man's hand. "No—" the woman in braids said. The man aimed the gun carefully and shot the policeman in the chest. The policeman jerked and fell back, a red star raying out on his white uniform, a stupid surprised look on his face. The noise from the gun echoed loudly in the corridor.

"You moron," the woman said. "What did you—"

"You heard him," the man said. "He knew what we look like. He could have identified us."

"Shit," the woman said.

"Let's go," Mark said. "They've got to have heard that shot."

They ran up the stairs and back toward the broken window. Another alarm sounded somewhere in the building. Mark stayed back, watching as everyone climbed over the sill and dropped into the parking lot. Mary waited impatiently for her turn. She thought she heard the sound of heavy footsteps echoing in a corridor somewhere. "Okay, Mary," Mark said, helping her through the window. She jumped to the pavement below.

A loud shot came from behind her, more footsteps, and the sound of a body dropping to the floor. Horrified, Mary looked back through the window. Mark lay on his side, his legs bent at different angles. "Oh no," Mary said. "Oh no."

"Run!" someone called from the gap in the fence. "Run, you little idiot!" Mary looked up. For a half-second she saw a gun pointed straight at her, a vague impression of a policeman coming toward her, and then without thinking she turned and began to run.

She followed the others as they ran down darkened side streets, every nerve alert for the sound of gunfire behind her. She ran as she had never run before in her life, untiring, only hoping that her strength would last until she got to a safe place. Ahead of her she saw Layla turning at Mark's street.

"Not there, you idiot!" Don said. He gasped for breath. "That's the—first place they'll look. Campus!"

They continued running. Mary noticed with surprise that she was still holding the files. That's good, she thought. That means Mark won't have died for nothing. Mark. Dead. She ran, trying not to think, trying only to feel the slap of her shoes against the dirt road.

They seemed to have run the entire night, though dawn was still as far away as ever, when they finally came to the dark buildings of the campus. She led them to the architecture building and up the two flights of stairs before she realized that they couldn't possibly all fit into her tiny room. Against the rules of the building they lay down in the narrow hallway, huddling against the walls. Brian woke when she came in. "How did it go?" he said.

"Later," she said curtly. She went to her side of the room, lay down and fell asleep almost immediately.

She was still holding the files when she woke late next day. She remembered making sure of them whenever she woke up, between dreams of an endless procession of people walking down a stairway and then stopping as if under a spotlight. Because if the files were lost then Mark . . . She sat up. Mark was dead. She hadn't dreamed it.

Voices sounded in the hallway and she went outside. Layla sat leaning against a wall, facing a wide semicircle of people who were listening to her so intently they barely noticed Mary come out. As Mary listened Layla told them about the armed policemen, the wild ambush of the maskmakers, their narrow escape and Mark's death. The story grew as Layla told it; she embellished it and added animal-spirits and maskmakers long dead; she called everyone by the name of his or her tribal animal. Mary tried to interrupt her a few times, to explain things or correct something Layla had said, but she soon gave up. Layla's story, though not always accurate, was far more interesting than the truth. The group around them listened entranced until the end. Then they looked at Mary, as though trying to connect this sleepy girl with her tangled hair to the bold daring woman of Layla's story.

"Are those the files?" someone asked. Mary noticed the three maskmakers in the crowd, noticed too that Luisa stood at the back, a puzzled look on her face. No one else seemed to want to ask Layla why she had joined the raid after all. Mary couldn't see Greg anywhere.

"What?" Mary said. "Yeah, they are."

"What are you going to do with them?" someone else asked, one of Luisa's friends.

"I don't know," Mary said. There was nothing to do with the files;

Mark had wanted her to have them and now she had them. She couldn't think beyond that. "Burn them, I guess."

"Good idea," Luisa's friend said. "Anyone got a match?"

For a while it looked as if no one did. Matches were still on the UC list. Then the tall thin man put his hand in his pocket and took out a book of matches. He had taken off his mask of the night before but his hands, Mary saw with distaste, were covered in the same supple black leather. He took the files from Mary and set them on the floor. A few people cheered as the fire caught, peeling back the corner of the file and turning it black. The fire blazed for a long moment and then died.

"Well, hey," someone said. "We've got to celebrate."

"Celebrate?" Mary said. "Mark's dead . . ."

"We'll get revenge for that later," someone else said. "Let's go." Three or four people left to get the bottles of wine locked in the basement.

Revenge? Mary wanted to shrink back into her room, to close the door on their proud and gloating faces. Who said anything about revenge? Everything had gone wrong. Mark was dead and so were the two policemen, and all for a few pieces of paper. She looked around for Don but she didn't see him anywhere in the crowd.

The party lasted long into the night. It moved from building to building, ending at last in the meeting hall, where they threw out two groups of people who were shouting insults back and forth and arguing about water rights. Layla repeated the story of the raid until her voice grew hoarse, and Mary told her version wearily half a dozen times. At the meeting hall Mary finally ran into Don and he introduced her to three of his friends from the Purple Press, two thin men and one fat one, all with the same glasses and the same intense expression. A man from the campus news sheet came up to her and asked to interview her, promising that no names or descriptions would be used in his article.

At last, around midnight, she managed to get near Layla. "Who were those people with you?" she asked. "Those maskmakers?"

"Oh," Layla said. "I thought you knew. Bone, and Willie, and Rose. Everyone except Susan."

"How did you know to be there just at the right time?" Mary asked. "How'd you know what day we planned the raid for?"

"Everyone in your building knew what day the raid was," Layla said. "So we just had to follow you. We waited outside Mark's house until we saw you leave."

"But why . . ." Mary said. "Why the hell didn't you just tell people on campus you supported the raid? That way we could have gotten a lot more people to go along with us, and Mark—and Mark— You just did it that way because it was more dramatic, didn't you? Risked our lives, and, and . . ."

"No I didn't," Layla said, looking hurt. "No one on campus would listen to me. They all listened to Greg. And I only had a certain amount of time to convince them."

The noise around them grew louder. "Hey Layla!" someone called. Both of them looked up. It was the tall man—Bone—calling to Layla. She moved away. "Gotta go," she said.

"Wait—" Mary said, but she was gone.

Mary stood still a minute, watching them go, and remembered the policeman falling back, surprised, bright red marbling his white uniform. That man is a murderer, she thought, feeling a chilly uneasiness. No. I'm a murderer. If it hadn't been for me those two men would still be alive. And Mark. Was it worth it? Standing there, watching the crowd flow around her like water around a stone, she didn't think so.

It was one or two o'clock when the party finally came to an end. Mary waited impatiently until the last group of people congratulated her and went off on dark roads to their buildings. She had wanted to talk to Don all evening. If she could walk into a police station and come back out alive she should be able to summon the courage to ask Don how he felt about her.

She and Don sat down at two old chairs with desks attached that had been used since the time of the students. Layla had gone off somewhere with Bone and some other people. Mary smiled at Don, feeling very tired.

"Well," Don said. "What's next?"

"What do you mean?" she said.

"I mean what are you going to do next?" he said. "Now's the time, while you've still got all these people supporting you. Even the Purple Press is willing to help."

"I don't—I'm not going to do anything like this again," she said.

"It was horrible. You want to start some kind of underground movement, you do it."

"I can't do it," he said. "You're the obvious choice to lead this thing. You're the one everyone respects. Well, really Layla is, but she's too flaky to do anything. If we do manage to get rid of the General God only knows what kind of government she'd want us to have. Political leaders chosen by dream, probably. Someone to represent each tribe in Congress."

"Yeah, well, I'm not going to do anything," she said. "I'd make a terrible leader. Nothing went the way I planned it."

"You mean Mark's death," he said. "I agree with you. I wish that hadn't happened. Mark was a good friend to me. But now we've got a martyr to the cause. You heard them—they're all eager to avenge his death. I know, I know—that sounds callous. But I know that's what Mark would have wanted us to do. He wouldn't have wanted us to give up now."

"I wish he was here now," she said. "I wish he could have seen this."

"Yeah, me too," he said. "But you know, you're being very naïve if you thought we could have done this without someone getting killed. The General's got army and police all over the place. There's a reason he's been in power for nine years."

"Why not?" she said. "Why couldn't we have done it without getting anyone killed? Without killing anyone?"

"Oh, a pacifist," he said, laughing a little.

She frowned. Why did he always have to have a word for everything? It was still a good idea, even if it wasn't original, even if someone had thought of it before and given it a name. "I bet we could fight the General without killing anyone. I bet there's a way."

He laughed again. "I don't think so," he said. "Like I said, the General's too powerful. If we go up against him someone is going to die."

"Well, who?" she said angrily. "You? You want to die like Mark? Me? Layla? It's easy to say, just as long as you don't have to do it. I bet we could do it my way. I just have to think about it for a while."

"So you're going to start a movement," he said, looking satisfied. "I thought you would."

"Not right now," she said. "All I can think about now is Mark. He was the first person to invite me to his house in Berkeley."

"I think you should start as soon as you can," he said. "Everyone loves you now."

She barely heard him. She was thinking that she had heard him use the word love for the first time, and how strange it had sounded coming from him. "And you," she said. "How do you feel about me?"

"What—what do you mean?" he said.

"Everyone loves me, you said. How do you feel about me? Do you love me too?"

He looked down at his hands resting on the desk. "Well," he said. "Well, that's—well, of course I like you. I like you very much, and I admire you for everything you've done. If you do start a movement I'd definitely want to be part of it." He looked up suddenly and she knew that he was going to give her one of his set speeches, knew that she had lost him. "Love just isn't possible the way things are now. The General manages to pollute everything, even the way two people feel about each other. Everyone spies on each other, everyone's out to turn the other person in. There's just no way two people can trust each other long enough to fall in love. I've never been in love, ever, never let myself get close to anyone. That's just the way it's got to be in this society, at least until things get better. I know I can probably trust you, but I've been this way for too long now. I'm too old. It's too late for me to learn to let my guard down."

"Bullshit," she said.

He looked at her from under his eyebrows, the same mocking look he had given her when they first met.

"Plenty of people love each other," she said. "Even in this society. Look at Nick and Jayne."

"Oh, sure, look at a police informer," he said. "That's a great example. What do you want to bet Jayne is watching him carefully, wondering how long it's going to be until he turns her in? Or turns the kid in? What do you want to bet someone's going to kill him soon, make it look like an accident, someone at the station who's tired of having him stick his nose in where he isn't wanted?"

"Well, not just them," she said. "Other people too. Me and Layla, for example. I love Layla."

"That's different," he said.

"How is it different?" she asked.

"Oh, come on—"

"You mean because we don't sleep together," she said, interrupting him, absorbed in following the thought. Love: That was the word to describe the bond between her and Layla. Why had she thought the word for it didn't exist? "But that doesn't matter. First I loved her because she was Layla the maskmaker, this person I'd only heard about in Stockton. Then I found out she wasn't like that at all, that she was a real person, funny and interesting and talented, someone unlike anyone I'd ever met, someone who made mistakes and got into trouble. . . . And I loved her for that. I knew there was something between us, almost from the beginning." She remembered the dream, Layla coming to her as she stood naked in her room, and she wondered if that had been the dream's simple way of telling her about love. And when Layla had said, "You won't need clothes where you're going," had she meant the land of animals? Or the soundless journey to the pit of her epilepsy? Layla was right: dreams were more important than she ever would have guessed.

"Yeah, but does she love you?" he said. "She's so weird you can't tell what she's thinking half the time."

"Of course she does," Mary said, but she wondered. Had Layla gone on the raid because she felt she owed it to her, as Greg said? Or had she done it out of something stronger, friendship or love? But she couldn't let Don know her doubts.

"All right, all right," Don said. "You and Layla love each other. That's wonderful, if it's true, which I can't really believe." Mary started to say something but Don held up his hand to stop her. "But even if it's true, even if you could find dozens, hundreds of people who are genuinely in love, that still doesn't change the way I feel. I just can't get close to anyone. I mean, look at Mark. I might have gotten close to him and then look what would have happened. I would have lost him. No, it's better to keep your distance from people. That's the way the government teaches you to get by in this society. You know that if you ever get close to anyone you're going to lose them."

"Bullshit," she said again. "You made yourself the way you are. You can't blame this one on the government."

"Okay," he said. "Have it your way."

"And if you did it to yourself you can change," she said. "Don't you see? You can get close to people again. You can be happier, less cynical about things."

"I can't change," he said. "I've tried. I've tried lots of times. You're not the first person to point these things out to me." He said nothing for a while, and Mary wondered who else had argued with him the way she was doing. Ayako, maybe? "Well," he said, "do you still want to see me, now that you know?"

"No," she said, before she could change her mind.

Don stood. "All right," he said. "That's what I thought you'd say, actually."

Sit down, she wanted to say. She watched him walk away, out into the dark night. Where would he go? Would the police be at Mark's house already? She wanted to follow him. Come back, she wanted to say, I don't care what you're like, take me back to my room and make me feel better. She felt her face had been turned to stone. Then she laid her head on the desk and cried for a long time.

Layla found her there near dawn. "What's the matter?" Layla said. "Are you still thinking about Mark?"

Mary took a long breath. "I just talked to Don," she said.

"Oh," Layla said. She sat next to Mary, at the desk Don had used. "Don's an idiot. You shouldn't listen to him."

"He said—he said no one in this society can ever love each other," Mary said. "Because the General makes everyone so suspicious of everyone else. That's why he can't love me, he said."

"Listen," Layla said. "Don never did know what he was talking about."

"I don't know," Mary said wearily. "I'm starting to think he was right. Maybe when I'm as old as he is I'll feel the same way."

Layla shook her head. "He's not right," she said, staring straight at Mary, her eyes wide. Mary thought she looked very beautiful in the gray morning light.

Mary exhaled loudly. "How the hell do you know?" she said. "Everyone looks up to you. Everyone respects you. You're Layla, the maskmaker. You don't have to worry about what people think of you."

"Let me tell you something," Layla said. "You know that I was against this raid in the beginning." Mary nodded. "Well, so were all the maskmakers, and for the same reason I was. They thought that we shouldn't get involved in the General's politics, that we shouldn't bring ourselves down to his level." She laughed. "Don said something last night about me joining the underground and fighting the General. I can't think of anything I'd hate more. *You'll* do it, though, and you'll be good at it." She said this last sentence with great assurance, as though she had seen the future. Maybe she has, Mary thought. "But I've already fought him in my way, by giving him the mask. And maybe that'll be what brings him down in the end. But anyway, do you know how I got the maskmakers to go along with me?"

Mary shook her head.

"I argued with them for two solid weeks," Layla said. "I wouldn't leave them alone. They refused to let me in their houses. But nothing I said could change their minds. Finally I asked them to do it because of our friendship. To do it for love. They couldn't believe what they were hearing. Like Don says, no one ever mentions love. And especially maskmakers. We're tough, and mean, and people are afraid of us. We all have reputations to protect. Except me—I'd lost my reputation already. So I could show them that they loved each other, that they all loved me. And you know, they believed it. And they agreed to come along. All of them except Susan, anyway."

"Why did you lose your reputation?" Mary asked. "Because you wanted to go on the raid?"

"No," Layla said. She smiled her thin, sad smile. "It was before that. Because I still don't have an apprentice. Because I made a mistake in choosing an apprentice."

"Oh," Mary said. "I'm sorry. Look, you can tell them I'll be your apprentice again, if it'll help. I'm sorry. I didn't realize—"

"No, it's okay," Layla said. "I made a mistake. It took me a long time to realize it, but I finally did. Of course, you'd been telling me almost from the very beginning."

"Well, what about—what about Greg?" Mary said. "He wants to do it—he told me so. And he's crazy enough."

"I thought of him," Layla said slowly. "I wanted to. But then he lied to people about what I'd said. I don't want an apprentice who lies."

"I think you should talk to him," Mary said. "He really wants to do it. Maybe you can convince him that he was wrong."

"Maybe," Layla said. "But I never finished my story. Do you know why I changed my mind about the raid?"

"Yeah," Mary said. "Greg told me. He said you felt guilty for putting me through everything, just so I'd be a maskmaker, when I really wasn't supposed to be one at all. He said you were trying to make it up to me."

"Then Greg didn't know," Layla said. "I did feel guilty, and I did feel bad for you because it took me so long to realize my mistake, but that wasn't why I did it. I did it out of love." Mary blinked, startled to hear her argument to Don repeated by someone else a few hours later. "I'd forgotten about love, until I met you. So you see," Layla said, "Don was wrong."

General Otis Gleason felt the acid eating away at his stomach and took another sip of his medicine. Chalk, he thought. It tasted like chalk. What if his doctors were actually feeding him chalk? Then someone would find out and someone else would die. But what if they didn't find out?

He paced up and down his office and tried to pay attention to the job in front of him, the Japanese computers. He had to decide who would get one, and who would have access to what files. The job seemed endless, but he couldn't trust anyone else with it. Three computers to the Gleason Information Institute, where people had been trained for years to be able to look at a computer and reproduce it. There had been a disturbing rumor coming out of the Institute, a student reporting something unpatriotic a teacher of Information Theory had said, but Gleason couldn't remember any more than that. He'd have to check into it, see that the teacher had been sent to a rehab center, before he could trust the Institute with any of the computers.

And then there was the business with the mask. Why had Blair brought him the damn thing, anyway? It was disturbing. It seemed to suck up all the light in the room. He looked again at the black mask on his solid oak desk, all flat planes and sharp angles, and told himself angrily to forget about it, to call Blair and have it taken away. He had a job to do.

He paced in front of the desk. If only the Japanese had told him how many computers they were going to send. Maybe they wouldn't send any at all. Maybe they had been lying all the time. His stomach twisted at the thought and he took another sip of the medicine. Well, we still have the nuclear weapons, he thought. Only trouble is, so do they. Would we be able to wipe them out before they can retaliate? They probably have bases all over the world by now.

His pacing had brought him in front of the mask again. Damn Blair! He moved as if to pick up the mask, stopped himself and ran his fingers over the smooth black paint. There was something about the mask, something compelling. He wanted to—to do what? He picked it up. Blair had been wrong; the mask wasn't ugly. It was beautiful, hard and cold like a warrior, like he had been before the weight of all his responsibilities, before he'd gotten old. He wanted to put it on. Hesitantly, he lifted the mask to his face.